The Crowns

Vengeance

Andrew Clawson

Cover design and illustration by Books Covered

ISBN: 978-1481856454

Get Andrew Clawson's Starter Library FOR FREE

Sign up for the no-spam newsletter and get two novels for free.

Details can be found at the end of this book.

Epigraph

Nothing is so secure as that money will not defeat it

~ ~ ~

Philip Dormer Stanhope, 4th Earl of Chesterfield

Prologue

Footsteps echoed off towering stone walls as a solitary figure strode through the cavernous hall. Ahead, framed by a roaring fire, a portly man sat at an enormous desk, chin held heavily in the palm of one hand. White curls draped across a wrinkled skull to cover each ear, the powdered wig a brilliant white in the flickering light cast by dozens of candles.

None of this assembled warmth penetrated the gloom that hung heavily around the rotund figure. In the midst of an unprecedented crisis, he longed for a ray of hope to brighten his perilous situation.

"I bring news from the latest ship."

The seated man stared downward as a deep sigh escaped his lips.

"Our messengers bear distressing reports, my liege. Cornwallis has surrendered."

Time stood still as the diminutive man rose. Though short in stature, his presence exploded throughout the room.

"That is not possible." Spittle flew through the air. "These, these *commoners* could not have defeated us. There must be some mistake."

"Alas, sire, it is true. Cornwallis capitulated to the rebels only days ago. His entire army is lost."

George III, King of Great Britain and Ireland, stood in silence, words having failed him. From behind the thick walls of Buckingham Palace, George III had little notion of his armies' precarious foothold in America. Unaccustomed to American ferocity, the proud English desire to fight for king and country had steadily eroded, until the most recent defeat.

Eight thousand of England's finest men had laid down their arms and surrendered.

The notion was unthinkable.

However, Lord Ramsey Fawkes, Third Earl of Wroxton, did not dwell on the defeat. As one of the king's closest advisors, he had long practiced the fine art of diplomacy with his liege lord, carefully crafting his statements to manipulate the sovereign, though the foolhardy little man was quite incapable of recognizing this skillful deceit.

"Your majesty, there is yet a chance for us to secure victory."

King George focused on the earl, his eyes pleading.

Fawkes felt nothing but disgust. Resplendent in his citrine cloak cut from the finest silk, an imposing ceremonial sword on his hip, the divine leader of the most powerful nation on earth was helpless. Exactly as Fawkes had known he would be.

"There is little to be done with the colonies, Your Majesty. In your great wisdom, you will no doubt see fit to forgo our direct assaults on those wretched lands in favor of a more subtle approach."

"Such as?"

Lord Fawkes glanced around. They were alone in the king's massive study, free from any prying ears.

He leaned in and described his plan to King George, whose eyes first clouded with confusion, before the light of understanding dawned.

After a brief pause, King George voiced his approval.

"We shall bring those colonists to their knees. Prepare your man to depart at once. The necessary funds are at your disposal."

"As you command, Your Majesty."

Fawkes bowed deeply before turning on his heel.

Now that his ridiculous excuse for a king had agreed to fund the operation, it was only a matter of time before the glory of England was restored, the rebellious colonists crushed beneath the fearsome weight of St. George's Cross.

Chapter 1

A never-ending line of motorcars crawled down the street, headlights shining rheumily in the evening gloom. Soot-stained clouds overhead stopped any sunlight from reaching the dry street, dusty and dirty beneath a yellowish haze cast by omnipresent streetlamps. Should a fog have rolled in, one wouldn't have been remiss to expect a horse-drawn carriage to appear from within the golden glow. All in all, it was a typical London evening, pedestrians and commuters alike moving slowly through the humid summer air.

Inside his office at No. 11 Downing Street, The Right Honorable Roland Francis Sutton leaned back in his desk chair and stretched his palms skyward. An entire day's worth of tension tingled past his elbows, dozens of bureaucratic nightmares evaporating like the morning dew.

As chancellor of the exchequer, one had to know how to relax in order to survive. Tasked with overseeing the world's sixth largest economy, Sir Roland directly affected the finances of nearly sixty-three million citizens.

Unsurprisingly, some of these people didn't like him.

He'd spent the day in meetings with his junior ministers, offering advice when necessary, allowing them to chart their own course more often. Regardless of what decisions he made, what policies were passed or which taxes were lowered, there was nothing to be done about the constant vitriolic displeasure to which he was routinely subjected.

Today had been no exception, and it was with great enthusiasm that Her Majesty's faithful servant traitorously poured two fingers of Mr. Jack Daniels's finest Single Barrel whiskey into a crystal tumbler, the velvety smooth amber liquid clinging to its vessel, aromatic waves of charred oak and flowery vanilla warming his senses.

After allowing a moment for the blend to settle, he savored one sip. *Ahhh.*

A marvelous slow burn rolled down his throat. A dinner appointment with his wife was on the books tonight, and he relished the idea of spending several carefree hours in her company.

Sir Roland had assumed his position less than a year ago, a promotion that surprised him more than anyone. After the retirement of his predecessor, Roland had assumed, like most of the world, that another junior minister, Colin Moore, would be chosen as successor. The prime minister's call had come as a complete and total shock. His wife and family had been ecstatic, as had he, initially.

Looking back, he'd never quite shaken the image of the previous minister leaving office on his last day. He'd walked out, carrying a single photo of his family, and never looked happier.

Right now, Roland knew why.

He was honored, of course, to serve queen and country, though in private, he felt this to be the most thankless job on earth. Just as in physics, there were laws in the world of economics. The most basic was that when one person profited, another person did not. Every day men, businesses, lobbyists, and other sovereign governments cursed his name, only to praise his policies the next. He had little to do with any of it, being as beholden to the whims of a free market as any man. Certainly he could influence events in small ways, but as for pulling the strings like a puppeteer, that just wasn't possible.

But enough of this. He had a dinner to enjoy.

A million-dollar view jumped through the tinted office windows. St. James Park Lake to his rear, the Thames in front. A cornucopia of English pride surrounded him.

As Roland threw back his glass and drained the delicious American whiskey, a flash of red blinked into existence, sparkling rays distorted across the crystal tumbler. It came from straight across Downing Street, on the roof of the Foreign and Commonwealth Office.

His eyes narrowed. No one should be up there.

The last sound Sir Roland ever heard was the soft tinkle of breaking glass as a sniper's bullet ripped through the window in front of him.

Chapter 2

All around, drunken students shouted, a semester's worth of tension and angst lifted from their shoulders. It was the end of finals week, and the young men and women at the University of Pennsylvania were letting their hair down.

Summer was nearly upon University City, home to Benjamin Franklin's famed institution, bright sunlight warming all who partied beneath a cloudless blue sky. Shapely legs demurely covered by low-cut sundresses offered teasing glimpses of the feminine mystique, a welcome respite from the winter wardrobes still fresh in each young scholar's mind. Fraternity men worked the crowd, full of liquid courage and youthful bravado.

Erika Carr strode confidently through campus, fully aware of the attention her tall, lithe frame demanded as she passed. Effortlessly beautiful, she too had taken advantage of the breezy summer weather and dressed accordingly. College men stood helpless in her wake.

A rush of cool air sent tingling goose bumps across Erika's flesh when she entered the history department's main office building.

Situated in the middle of Penn's campus, just across the Schuylkill River from downtown Philadelphia, the ancient mysteries of civilization thrummed with a vibrant intensity in College Hall. This building may have been over a hundred years old, but it was populated by scholars with an intense thirst for knowledge, of whom Erika was a proud member.

Overhead lights flashed on when she entered her office, the cool leather of her desk chair crackling as she sat down.

Eyes wide with anticipation, Erika opened the metallic suitcase on her desk. Inside was the artifact she had been waiting for all week. As the recipient of a federal grant to document recently unearthed personal effects of Alexander Hamilton, Erika's mind raced with anticipation as she finally laid eyes on the documents.

The sharp trill of her desk phone intruded.

"Erika Carr."

"Hey."

One word, and Erika's heart fluttered.

On the line was Parker Chase, the man with whom she had recently reunited after a year of separation. Prior to that, they had spent nearly eight years together. Parker was calling from his office in Pittsburgh, where he plied his trade as a financial advisor.

"How are you?" she asked.

"Up to my eyeballs in work. You wouldn't believe how demanding rich people can be."

Sarcasm oozed through the phone. His job invited stress on a daily basis.

"Who would have thought? Not to change the subject, but guess what? I just received the Hamilton artifacts."

"That's wonderful. Are you working with anyone else on the project?"

"No, this one's my baby. I'm going to start my study immediately, try to have a preliminary report drawn up within two weeks."

"Think you can spare a few hours this weekend? You only have me for three days, so don't waste them."

He was coming into town for the weekend and staying with her before a meeting on Monday.

"I'll see what I can do. Be careful driving."

Before hanging up, Parker promised to call her that night. As she clicked off, Erika couldn't wipe the smile from her lips, anticipation already building for their weekend. After the events of the past few months, she'd realized how badly she missed him and was determined to treasure every day they spent together.

On her desk were two framed pictures. One was of her and Parker standing on the football field after his last collegiate game. White jersey covered in dirt, beads of sweat running through his eye black, they stood arm in arm, faces shining.

The second photograph was of Parker's recently deceased uncle, who had also been her colleague until his murder.

Joseph Chase had been a star in Penn's history department, internationally renowned for his work on America's battle for independence. Brilliant and personable, Joe had been there for her whenever she needed anything. Less than a year ago he had been shot to death, murdered by a group of men intent on protecting a centuries-old secret. She and Parker had become embroiled in the conspiracy, forced to run for their lives.

The shiny metal suitcase on her desk opened to reveal a wooden box, worn and warped from the passage of time. Originally a soft shade of chestnut brown, years of exposure to the elements had darkened the container until it was nearly black. However, in a testament to the eroding standards of modern craftsmanship, this two-hundred-year-old box had protected the paper documents contained inside from any type of water damage whatsoever.

Erika leaned over the box, now brightly illuminated under a powerful observation lamp attached to her desk. Teeth clenched, she forced the rusted metal hinges open to reveal an astonishing piece of history.

Several months ago, an estate sale had been planned in the suburbs of New York City, and during a routine inventory of the items, a wooden chest had been found. Inside was the box she now held, donated for study by the deceased homeowner's estate.

While the wooden contraption alone wasn't extraordinary, what made this box special was the cache of paperwork inside.

This little gem contained a collection of Alexander Hamilton's personal correspondence, hidden for centuries inside an innocuous book.

A rush of excitement flooded Erika's system as the first letter flipped open, thick paper crackling softly under her touch. Perfect lines of elegant script covered the page, a product of Hamilton's university education, while the small letters which utilized every available space hinted at his humble upbringing in which waste was not tolerated and resources were scarce.

Erika ran a practiced eye over the artifact, scribbling notes as she went. The sun fell from its lofty perch as she worked until shadows crept up the walls and her stomach rumbled in protest. A dozen letters were spread out on a table to her rear, each one summarized in her notes. Every piece was unique and insightful in its own way, offering a previously unseen glimpse into the mind of America's first Treasury secretary. The majority of the artifacts were personal correspondence, relative mainly to Hamilton's personal life. However, her heart had skipped a beat when she unfolded an official letter from Thomas Jefferson, written on Jefferson's personal stationary. Mundane contents aside, it was still an amazing treasure.

The constant stream of people walking by her open office door had dwindled to a trickle, most of the department personnel now gone for the night. Classes were over, and it was a dedicated professor who spent much leisure time in his or her office. Erika cast an eye to the rapidly diminishing sunlight, thoughts of catching the day's final warming rays gaining momentum.

One artifact remained in the box. Gloved fingers gently gripped the surprisingly sturdy paper as she unfolded this last letter.

What Erika saw took the breath from her chest.

Chapter 3

Pittsburgh, Pennsylvania

A forearm wrapped across his throat. Parker struggled for air, spots flashing in front of his eyes as his brain shouted for oxygen.

Suddenly the pressure vanished. He gasped, his head light, chest on fire.

"That's how quickly you'll be out if your air supply is cut off."

Behind him, the instructor stood, arms gesturing to the mat on which Parker sat.

"Chase is a strong guy, tougher than most. Look how quickly he went down without air. If you can't breathe, you're done."

As he spoke, the black-belt-clad Krav Maga instructor put out a hand, which Parker used to haul himself off the mat. All around, students young and old soaked in the knowledge, aware that one day it could save their lives.

Inside this brand new gymnasium, martial arts instruction was dispensed daily to practitioners of all levels. Two sparring areas with padded floors and walls flanked a full-sized boxing ring, the centerpiece of a vast training area replete with heavy and speed bags, weight benches and squat racks. Farther away a climbing wall was visible, along with an aerobics studio and even a lap pool. A red sun cast its final rays through floor-to-ceiling glass windows that fronted the complex.

Parker shook his head to clear the cobwebs. He'd been coming here for several years now, fully hooked on the adrenaline rush this art form provided, as well as the subtle movements it demanded. Originally developed by Israeli Special Forces, Krav Maga was not only an intense workout, it could be a lifesaver.

Years of lifting weights had grown tedious, but Parker had no alternative outlet into which he could channel his competitive spirit. His entire life had

9

been spent on a playing field, and it was on the gridiron that he'd found the most success. Football had paid his way through school, his athletic prowess earning him a full-ride Division I scholarship. After hanging up his cleats, he'd found that Krav Maga relieved the stress of his pressure-packed job, so every jab Parker threw contained a fury born from a disdain for his more difficult clients.

"All right, everyone pair off and practice a chokehold escape. Chase, you're with me."

Parker had picked up the martial art rapidly. Recognizing this, the instructor had taken Parker under his wing, challenging him daily to better his skills, never letting him leave without dishing out a reminder that as good as he was, a long road lay ahead.

An hour later, Parker was bruised, battered, and thoroughly pleased. Sweat dripped into his eyes as he headed to the locker room.

Darkness had fallen by the time he'd showered and made it home, a pile of letters greeting him on the front doorstep. Parker scanned his investment account statements, most doing surprisingly well. The past few months had been kind to him. Not enough to retire, but he couldn't complain.

Before he could even grab a beer, his phone vibrated.

Work never really stopped. It only took a lunch break.

"Parker Chase."

A familiar voice taunted him. "How's the slowest safety to ever step on the field doing?"

"Still faster than you."

The caller chuckled. "How are you, old buddy?"

Parker had met Ben Flood in college, and they'd remained close friends ever since. Both studied finance, and they'd quickly bonded over a shared love of sports, beer, and pretty women. Ben had taken a job in Boston after graduation, a position similar to the wealth management that Parker now practiced.

"Just fine. Getting older, though. How are you?" Parker asked.

"Same here. You know the drill. Anyway, I wanted to see if you're still going to be up here next week?"

Parker's office had dealings with Ben's firm, so Parker jumped at any chance to travel to Beantown for work. It didn't hurt that Flood's employer was one of the largest financial service providers in the city and always provided great seats to a game, free of charge.

"Wouldn't miss it. I hope that famous Aldrich Securities expense account hasn't run dry."

"It took some work, but I secured two seats in the company box at Fenway."

Fenway Park was where the Boston Red Sox played, an iconic baseball stadium that was on every fan's bucket list.

"You're the man. Can't wait."

They chatted for a few minutes before hanging up. Parker was excited to see a game at Fenway and spend some time with Ben. With a beer in hand and some leftover pizza on the table, he flicked on the television.

A scene of terror filled the screen.

Beneath a hollow-eyed reporter speaking into the camera, a rolling text bar flashed the same words over and over.

British Chancellor of the Exchequer Assassinated.

Parker's beer stopped halfway to his mouth, forgotten. The somber voice of the reporter broke through.

"Less than an hour ago, Sir Roland Francis Sutton was found in his office with a single bullet wound to the head. He was rushed to the hospital, only to be pronounced dead on arrival. As you can see from the chaos behind me at number eleven"-she turned and indicated a building Parker assumed was on Downing Street-"authorities are only just beginning their investigation."

Who would want to kill the Treasurer of Great Britain?

"Sir Roland was appointed to the chancellor's post only ten months ago. He was somewhat of a surprise choice, tapped for the post ahead of the presumptive nominee, junior minister Colin Moore."

Parker vaguely recalled hearing about the minor controversy.

"We don't have much information at this point, but we're being told the chancellor was shot while standing in front of the broken third-story window to my rear. As you can see behind me, Scotland Yard's forensics teams are currently inspecting the building's exterior. Across from us"-the cameraman swiveled around to a structure across the street-"we can see a team of investigators on the rooftop of a second building, situated across the way from Number Eleven Downing Street. From what we know right now, this particular office is utilized by the Ministry of Finance, though details are scant as to its purpose."

The frazzled reporter came back into view.

"The prime minister is set to make a statement within the hour."

As she repeated the same details over and over, Parker set his beer down. Why would anyone want to kill the British treasurer? Parker, better than most, knew that few things upset people more than money, but this Roland guy would have had little impact on the day-to-day finances of the average citizen. It didn't make sense for an angry person to come after the head of the country's finances. That would be like shooting Bill Gates because your computer kept crashing.

And weren't government ministers well protected? You'd think that anyone who worked on Downing Street, which he knew was also home to England's prime minister, would be well protected. Snipers on rooftops, cameras everywhere, basically an army of security working round-the-clock.

Apparently the only sniper around had been one of the bad guys.

Parker stared at the screen as he ate, trying to figure out all the angles. Who would want to do this?

And not only who, but why?

Chapter 4

Next door to the murder scene, the prime minister of the United Kingdom stepped into his office. The media horde standing outside had been avoided, leaving him to deal with the only slightly less numerous gathering within Number Ten Downing.

Over a dozen people lined the hallway outside his door, each of them waiting for a moment of his time. Thirty minutes ago he'd been on the golf course, happily launching drives into the woods, when his security detail had received word of the assassination. Within minutes a helicopter settled onto the pristine fairway to whisk him into the heart of London.

"I will speak with everyone in five minutes. Please wait out here."

His deeply stained walnut door slid noiselessly shut, finally affording a sense of privacy. As he massaged his eyes with the flat of his palms, the Right Honorable Donald Duncan, prime minister of the United Kingdom, First Lord of the Treasury, and Minister for the Civil Service, wondered what the hell was going on.

His good friend was dead, shot in one of the most secure places in the country. The area was literally crawling with security personnel at all hours, so the thought that a lone sniper could access a nearby rooftop, shoot a government minister and vanish had everyone on edge.

Duncan gave an inadvertent glance at his office windows. Despite the manufacturer's claims they were bullet-resistant, this apparently didn't extend to armor-piercing rounds. He'd seen a photo of poor Roland's corpse, head shattered like a dropped pumpkin. However, now was not the time for grief. A country was in disarray, desperate for answers. It was his job to find them.

The prime minister set his angular, clean-shaven jaw. Weakness was not an option.

"Secretary White, please come inside."

The Right Honorable Bradley White, secretary of state for defense, hurried through the door. Clasped in both hands was a depressingly thin file that contained everything they knew about the murder so far.

"Bradley, please have a seat."

The tall, slender man sat down across from Duncan, his erect posture giving him the appearance of a worried stork.

"What do we know?"

The harried secretary laid the folder on Duncan's desk and removed a single sheet.

"Approximately one hour ago, Sir Roland was shot while standing in front of a closed office window facing south. A single bullet was fired through the window, entering Roland's skull just below his right eye. The round was a .338 cartridge, fired at a range of less than one hundred meters. From such a close distance, the round is capable of piercing the bullet-resistant glass installed in Sir Roland's office. He was killed instantly."

"Do we have any idea who shot him?" the Prime Minister asked.

"To be frank, sir, we haven't the foggiest. The man must be a damn ghost. Surveillance footage doesn't show anyone traversing the courtyard around the building from which the shot was fired. The first time we see anything is when the shot is fired."

Duncan's face burned.

"Are you telling me this man is invisible?"

"Not exactly, sir, but we don't have any idea what he looks like."

Secretary White slipped the glasses from his pointed nose.

"Right now, our best guess is the shooter fired from a ventilation duct on the roof across from Sir Roland's office. It's hard to tell, but several cameras captured what we believe to be a muzzle flash coming from the duct."

"How could he have accessed that duct? Bloody hell, that's a treasury building. You can't just walk in and out, much less without being caught on camera."

Minister White's eyes remained downcast as he spoke.

"That's just it, sir. We reviewed all the footage from the past hour, and not a single person is seen heading toward either the roof or entering any maintenance rooms, the only places from which one could access said ducts." His shoulders rose slightly. "I know it doesn't make sense, sir, but it's simply the truth."

There was no need to berate Bradley. He was a good man, intelligent and hardworking. If he said there was no footage of the shooter, there wasn't.

Duncan ran one weathered hand through his salt and pepper hair.

"This is a tough spot we're in, no? All right, talk to your security teams and get an update. I have to make a statement before the rumor mill runs amok. I want an update in thirty minutes. And send Mr. Moore in, please."

White hurried from the room. Before the door clicked shut, Colin Moore stepped inside. As chief secretary to the Treasury, Colin Moore was third in the Treasury Department's hierarchy, after the prime minister and the recently deceased chancellor of the exchequer. He was what some people would refer to as a "proper Brit." With his meticulously coiffed hair, perfectly tailored suit and bespoke leather shoes, he oozed gentility and class. Educated at Eton, he was part of the good old boys network that ran through English politics-and had been the presumed heir to the chancellor's position.

When Donald had elevated Roland Sutton to chancellor of the exchequer less than a year ago, it had registered as a mild surprise in financial circles. A few eyebrows were raised, but for the most part, the matter was soon forgotten. Donald worried, however, that Colin Moore may have a chip on his shoulder. In light of today's events, Duncan felt it best to keep Moore on board with all developments, as he was the logical choice to replace the murdered Sutton.

"Colin, please have a seat."

"Thank you, sir."

Colin inclined his head in appreciation. If he harbored a grudge, it was well hidden behind a curtain of platitudes.

"We have a sticky situation here. Bradley just informed me the assassin evaded our security cameras and is nowhere to be found. They have no idea who this fellow is or where he went."

Moore's gray eyes met his, concern evident in their icy reflection. The man's stark features betrayed no angst, high cheekbones framing a thin nose that Duncan always felt was raised ever so slightly.

"That is terrible, sir. We must find the bastard and make him pay."

Duncan ran a second hand through his hair, which seemed to grow sparser with each passing day. He had little doubt this job would rob him of every last strand.

"Though it feels coarse, we must look to the future. I'm to make a statement in a few minutes, and one of the issues I'd like to address is Sir Roland's office."

Try as he may, Duncan failed to note even a glimpse of reaction. Colin Moore would have been one hell of a poker player.

"I can only imagine the panic people are feeling right now. We need to stop that, and to do so we must restore order. The government is larger than one man, and the last thing I'm going to do is let these bastards win. If we give in to our fear, then they have succeeded."

Moore inclined his head ever so slightly.

"I'm going to announce that you are replacing Sir Roland as chancellor of the exchequer, effective immediately. I trust you will accept this post?"

Moore sat frozen, unblinking. After a few moments silence, he answered.

"My heart is heavy with grief, but you are correct as always, sir. We must show the citizens that we will not cower in the face of evil. I will accept this honor. For queen and country."

"That's the spirit. Now, if you'll excuse me, I've a speech to cobble together."

Colin Moore rose, shook Duncan's extended hand. As he walked from the room, back ramrod straight, Duncan couldn't help but wonder what went through the man's head.

He said all the right things, was unfailingly polite, but the fact was he always came across as acting slightly above everyone around him, Donald Duncan included. Duncan was familiar with the aristocratic set, having come from a family blessed with both title and money, but he never considered himself to be better than anyone.

Hard work and diligent preparation were the currency of success in his mind, and despite having no evidence to support the notion, Duncan always felt Colin Moore didn't share those beliefs.

His gaze fell to the blank computer monitor on his desk, and the prime minister focused on the task of calming an embattled nation.

Chapter 5

French Riviera
Saint-Tropez, France

A gentle breeze drifted over light blue water to send soft ripples across the glassy surface. Afternoon sunlight sparkled on the Mediterranean as seagulls floated toward the white sandy beach on which sun-worshipping tourists sipped from crystal glasses.

Anchored at an adjacent marina was a veritable armada of luxury yachts. In a town known the world over as a destination for the rich and famous, there was no such thing as a modest boat.

Fully half the anchored yachts measured one hundred feet in length, with many approaching twice that. Full-time crews bustled about on deck, cleaning, stocking, shining and serving. In addition to the beautiful crafts berthed dockside, several of the floating castles were at sea, anchored just off shore, their wealthy owners enjoying the trappings of moneyed life. However, even among this treasure trove of seafaring toys, one stood out.

Two hundred fifty feet from stem to stern, this shining vessel was painted a deep black, protected by a coat of reflective sealant. She had four decks above water, one below, and boasted a helicopter pad in addition to an array of smaller watercraft that included jet skis, landing boats, and a two-man mini-submarine.

These were only the visible accoutrements, however, as the black-painted hull covered armor plating and a guided missile defense system, custom built in Germany. Intruder detection devices covered the entire craft and surrounding water, and bulletproof windows and doors were standard should any invader manage to board the ship.

Below the waterline, the engine room housed twin Rolls-Royce diesel behemoths capable of propelling the boat at over twenty-five knots.

Even at anchor, the magnificent craft outshined each surrounding vessel with its uncompromising size and elegant construction. Every pair of eyes on the beach and water had stolen a glance, envy in all, and not just for the status it brought. There were other things of beauty than just the boat to take in.

Two extremely gorgeous and completely nude fashion models lay on the sun deck. It would get cold at night, and they took advantage of the early afternoon heat to bronze their flawless skin.

Just below the sun deck's overhang, shaded from the heat, a man sat alone, eyes hidden behind a pair of sunglasses. Dressed in linen pants, creamy white shirt halfway unbuttoned, he enjoyed this privileged view of Saint Tropez's famed shoreline. At his side sat a cell phone, precariously close to the tumbler of room-temperature Guinness beer that had just been delivered by one of the dozen servants on board.

A sultry voice drifted from overhead.

"Nigel, come join us."

It was one of those idiotic models begging for attention.

"I'll be up in a moment. I've an important call to make."

Halfhearted moans of displeasure followed, though he couldn't have cared less. There was one reason those two were on board, and it wasn't for the conversation. A soft chuckle escaped his lips, for he understood they, too, were in his company for one simple reason. If Nigel Stirling's net worth weren't measured in the billions, those anorexic girls would disappear in an instant.

As if on cue, the phone rattled. Though he appeared to all the world a man at ease, Stirling's muscles tensed, his throat suddenly dry.

"Yes?"

"I suggest you turn on the news, sir."

Nigel clicked off. The mission had been a success.

"Turn on the television."

At his words, a servant appeared from around the corner, remote control in hand. Behind the wet bar to his right, a massive LED screen, barely two inches thick, flashed to life.

Stirling was greeted with a picture of chaos. He watched just long enough to confirm it. The chancellor was dead. Scotland Yard had no leads.

Perfect.

"Mute it."

The harried reporter went silent. Nigel again picked up the phone and

18

dialed a ten-digit number, beginning with a one, the international code for the United States.

"Sir?"

The man sounded slightly out of breath, almost excited.

"It is done," Nigel said. "The position should be filled today."

"That is excellent news. I trust we are to proceed as planned?"

"After I speak with our friends from the Emirates. I'll be in touch."

Stirling clicked off, the anxiety in his system slowly giving way to a sense of anticipation. He considered the white beach in front of him, aware that despite the centuries that had passed since his organization was born from a single goal, those beaches had remained the same. A testament to the patience required for success.

Soon, his vision would come to fruition, vindicating all the men whose vision and sacrifice had led to this moment.

The cool breeze ruffled his unbuttoned shirt, whistled past his ears. Nigel felt like celebrating.

"Girls, I do hope you've saved room for one more up there."

Chapter 6

Boston, Massachusetts

It was appropriate that storm clouds hovered over Boston's Financial District. Inside each sleek, towering building employees sat riveted to a television as news of the British treasurer's assassination dominated the airwaves. Leveraged buyouts and equity securities took a backseat to the dramatic murder investigation playing out in real-time, the normally oppressive din reduced to quiet murmurs and hushed conversation.

On the top floor of one such building, Spencer Drake was also glued to his television, albeit for a different reason.

President and CEO of Aldrich Securities, Drake's office oozed power. As Aldrich controlled over half a trillion dollars in total assets, his was a lofty perch. An original Jackson Pollock hung behind his desk, overlooking an office large enough to play basketball in. Plush carpet covered the floor and supported several authentic Persian rugs. Mahogany covered three of the room's walls, while a fourth consisted solely of floor-to-ceiling windows equipped with automatic dimming and retractable blinds. Seated at a conference table designed for twenty, Drake leaned back in his Herman Miller Aeron chair and waited, his mind far away.

Approaching his sixtieth birthday, Drake considered that this could be the moment he'd been groomed for, the time when two hundred years of effort came to fruition. A manicured hand ran through his light brown hair, professionally styled every two weeks for a mere five hundred dollars. One had to keep up appearances.

Normally quite relaxed, Spencer flicked a tiny speck of dirt from his charcoal gray pinstriped suit. Like every one he owned, it was sewn by his personal tailor at Gieves & Hawkes, the finest in London.

A shrill ring cut through the still office air.

Caught off guard, he glanced at the number. It had been less than an hour since the news had broken.

"Sir?"

"Spencer, do you have a moment?"

The pleasantry was quite unlike Nigel Stirling's usual brusque tone. Spencer snapped to attention.

"Of course, sir."

"Excellent. I have on the line my dear friend Khalifa bin Khan, President of the United Arab Emirates."

Spencer straightened in his chair. This was unexpected.

"Mr. President, it is a pleasure."

"The pleasure is mine, Mr. Drake. I trust you are well?"

Silky smooth, the soft voice of the emir of Abu Dhabi drifted over the phone like a desert breeze. As hereditary leader of seven of the most oil-rich nations on the planet, bin Khan was one of the most powerful men in the world.

Bin Khan was the man who controlled the flow of oil.

"I am, Mr. President," Drake replied. "I hope you are as well."

A quiet wheeze that might have been a laugh filtered through.

"As well as a man can be with four wives. There is no end to their constant chattering."

"May they bless you with a hundred sons, Mr. President," Nigel offered.

"Spencer," Nigel continued, "the president has called regarding some recent news I am happy to share. I thought you would like to hear this as well."

Whatever was going on, it was big. Men such as Nigel Stirling and Khalifa bin Khan didn't waste time.

"I was just informed that Prime Minister Duncan has appointed the replacement for the recently deceased Chancellor Sutton."

Suddenly it all made sense. Drake's breath caught in his throat. This was what they'd been waiting for.

"The prime minister has chosen your former classmate, Colin Moore."

Khalid bin Khan's soft baritone filled the room. "It seems as though all of the English are connected in one way or another."

"Colin and I were Oppidans together at Keate House during our time at Eton. We had quite the experience during our five years."

"Nigel, would you arrange a time when I may congratulate Mr. Moore on his elevation? This is certainly a proud moment for his family."

"I will, President bin Khan. He will greatly appreciate your call."

"Thank you. You must excuse me, gentlemen, for I have a prior engagement. I bid you good day."

The oil magnate clicked off.

Nigel Stirling was all business now. "Spencer, I don't have to tell you what this means. As soon as bin Khan is on board, we can move forward."

Drake stood and stretched his arms overhead, filled with newfound energy.

"That is excellent news, sir. I await your instructions."

"Don't go far. I have to speak with Colin first, but things appear to be back on track."

After Nigel hung up, Spencer allowed his mind to wander. He had no idea what kind of a man Khalifa bin Khan was, nor what his political leanings were. Based on this conversation, it appeared Mr. bin Khan was a believer in what drove them all.

Profits.

As long as bin Khan agreed to join them, and Spencer didn't doubt for a second that he would, Nigel was correct. Their wait would be over, and a new era would be upon them.

Satisfied with the progress, Spencer poured two fingers of single malt into a crystal glass, and the smoky scent of peat filled the air. As he savored the aged Scotch, an e-mail from Nigel Stirling popped up on his phone. Spencer read through twice and then immediately shouted toward the door.

"Liz, get in here."

His secretary scurried through the door, bronzed legs generously on display between a high-cut skirt and blood red Manolo Blahnik's.

"Get my broker up here immediately."

Liz's flowing black hair bobbed once in acknowledgement before she vanished out the door. Nigel Stirling had given him a task to complete, one that was critical to their success.

Spencer needed to purchase oil futures. Millions of barrels worth of them.

Chapter 7

Philadelphia, PA

Tires screeched as the yellow taxi shuddered to a halt. In back, a wide-eyed Parker Chase breathed a sigh of relief, once again amazed at the breakneck driving style of Philadelphia hacks.

On the sidewalk in front of Erika's apartment, a warm breeze blew through fresh leaves, though the slender saplings' aesthetic effect on their urban environment was somewhat spoiled by pieces of trash that swirled around his feet. At least it was sunny, blue skies overhead free of clouds.

The sidewalks were filled with pedestrians enjoying the beautiful weekend weather. As Parker hefted a carry-on suitcase up her steps, his thoughts flashed back to the strange phone call he'd received yesterday evening.

Erika had recently received a grant to study some of Alexander Hamilton's personal effects, a proud moment for both Dr. Carr and the university. However, when they'd spoken late last night, she'd seemed out of sorts about the assignment. Though he couldn't put his finger on why he felt that way, he'd known something was up even before Erika ended the conversation by telling him he needed to see the artifacts.

Despite his pleas, she said nothing further, promising to explain herself when he arrived in Philadelphia.

Erika stood inside the open front door when he made it to her floor, and his train of thought derailed with crashing finality. No matter how many times he saw her, Erika Carr never failed to impress.

Just under six feet tall, her athletic frame as toned as the day they'd met, she was a knockout. Her flowing blonde hair carried a floral scent as he wrapped his arms around her waist, returning the welcome embrace.

"How was your flight?"

She turned on her heel and led him inside, where a small plate of pastries lay on the kitchen table.

"Early." To prove the point, a wide yawn escaped his lips. "You better appreciate all the sleep I lost getting here at this ungodly hour."

"Stop complaining. It's not my fault you don't have any friends in Pittsburgh. You're lucky I'm letting you hang out with me."

Freshly cut prosciutto on the table distracted him. Mouth full, he looked up to find Erika gazing at him, the excitement from moments ago vanished.

"What's up? Everything all right?"

Her soft blue eyes held his for a moment longer, before she abruptly stood and disappeared into her bedroom, re-emerging moments later with a single sheet of paper.

"This is what I wanted to show you."

His eyes locked onto the page. It was a photocopy, completely covered in numbers.

11 26 7 14 11 24 8 7 20 3 4 23 22 7 18 4 3 19 6 3 24 8 19 13 23 17 15 7 26
26 10 17 18 3 6 7 11 20 18 4 3 19 25 3 19 19 3 16 7 19 4 11 26 26 10 20 7
11 1 11 24 13 19 17 9 4 19 7 20 7 24 3 18 13 13 23 17 22 23 19 19 7 19 19
11 19 13 23 17 15 7 26 26 1 24 23 15 8 17 20 3 24 5 25 13 18 3 25 7 4 7 20
7 3 24 26 23 24 8 23 24 3 4 11 16 7 9 17 26 18 3 16 11 18 7 8 11 5 20 23 17
22 23 6 26 23 13 11 26 3 24 6 23 20 25 11 24 18 19 15 4 23 4 11 16 7 11 9 9
7 19 19 18 23 1 3 24 5 5 7 23 20 5 7 19 3 24 24 7 20 9 3 20 9 26 7 3 24 18 4
7 22 11 19 18 18 4 7 3 20 3 24 6 23 20 25 11 18 3 23 24 4 11 19 22 20 23 16
7 24 10 7 13 23 24 8 20 7 22 20 23 11 9 4 20 7 9 7 24 18 26 13 23 24 7 19
17 9 4 16 11 26 17 7 8 22 11 18 20 3 23 18 3 24 6 23 20 25 7 8 25 7 23 6 11
8 11 19 18 11 20 8 26 13 22 26 23 18 10 7 3 24 5 6 23 20 25 17 26 11 18 7 8
11 18 18 4 7 4 3 5 4 7 19 18 26 7 16 7 26 19 23 6 18 4 7 25 23 24 11 20 9 4
13 3 10 7 26 3 7 16 7 18 4 11 18 19 7 16 7 20 11 26 25 7 25 10 7 20 19 23 6
18 4 7 1 3 24 5 19 18 20 7 11 19 17 20 13 4 11 16 7 24 23 18 13 7 18 11 9 9
7 22 18 7 8 18 4 7 3 20 20 7 9 7 24 18 8 7 6 7 11 18 23 24 7 23 6 23 17 20
19 22 3 7 19 20 7 9 7 24 18 26 13 17 24 9 23 16 7 20 7 8 11 22 26 11 24 18
23 3 24 6 3 26 18 20 11 18 7 23 17 20 24 7 15 5 23 16 7 20 24 25 7 24 18 3
15 3 26 26 6 17 20 18 4 7 20 22 17 20 19 17 7 18 4 3 19 26 3 24 7 23 6 3 24
21 17 3 20 13 3 25 25 7 8 3 11 18 7 26 13 11 19 22 26 11 24 24 7 8 25 13 24
7 14 18 20 7 22 23 20 18 15 3 26 26 10 7 8 7 26 3 16 7 20 7 8 15 3 18 4 3 24
11 19 4 3 22 25 7 24 18 18 23 20 11 9 4 7 26 18 15 23 23 22 22 23 19 3 24 5
11 20 20 23 15 19 11 8 23 20 24 7 8 10 13 25 13 18 23 17 9 4 6 3 20 7 8 18

24

23 5 7 18 4 7 20 15 3 26 26 20 7 16 7 11 26 18 4 7 18 20 17 18 4 22 20 7 16 7 20 7

"What is this?"

Her expression had him worried.

"I found it two days ago. In the box of Alexander Hamilton's correspondence."

It took a few seconds, but the expectant, earnest look she gave him finally made sense.

His jaw dropped.

"You think it's a code. A Caesar cipher."

"I don't think it is. I know it."

Several months ago, following Joseph Chase's death, Parker and Erika had discovered a coded message at Independence Hall which had ultimately led them to Joe's killers. With Erika's help, Parker had cracked the code, written several hundred years ago by one of America's greatest patriots.

A Caesar cipher was a type of substitution code, in which a number or series of numbers represented a letter. Originally developed by Julius Caesar, the particular cipher he and Erika had uncovered was decoded when they discovered that the number seven corresponded with the letter "e" and went *backwards* from there.

Parker's mind flashed back several months. "It's the same type of sequence from the Hall."

"It not only looks the same." As Erika spoke, a second paper materialized from behind her back. "It was the same code. And read what it says."

For the second time that year, Parker found himself on the receiving end of a centuries-old hidden passage.

Alexander,

I hope this finds you well, but I fear this missive shall break any such serenity you possess.

As you well know, during my time here in London I have cultivated a group of loyal informants who have access to King George's inner circle. In the past, their information has proven beyond reproach. Recently, one such valued patriot informed me of a dastardly plot being formulated at the highest levels of the monarchy.

I believe that several members of the king's treasury have not yet accepted their recent defeat. One of my spies has uncovered a plan to infiltrate our new American government. I will further pursue this line of inquiry immediately.

As planned, my next report will be delivered within a shipment to Rachel. Two opposing arrows adorned by my touch, fired together, will reveal the truth.

Yr. Faithful Servant,
P. Revere

"Paul Revere? As in the midnight ride Paul Revere?"

Erika nodded.

"Paul Revere was a spy? I thought he was a silversmith."

Her face was alight.

"According to the history books, that's all he was. I've never seen anything suggesting Revere was involved with espionage in any way."

A sudden rush of memories ripped through Parker's mind as he considered her find. Most of them were filled with bullets whizzing past his head, and in one case, taking a piece of his shoulder with it.

"What kind of papers were you studying when you found this?"

The suspicion must have been evident in his voice.

"Parker, I swear I was told they were documents from a container found during preparations for an estate sale. The owner went to a museum after she found the letters, and the entire batch was identified as personal correspondence from Alexander Hamilton. I had no idea this was inside."

As improbable as it seemed, he realized there was no way she could have known.

"I'm simply surprised you'd find a letter written in the exact same code."

Erika immediately switched into professor mode.

"If you think about, it's not that strange. The first coded letter, the one we found at Independence Hall, was written in the years immediately following the Revolution, in the late eighteenth century. It makes perfect sense that this code"-she held up the photocopied page-"would have been in use ten years earlier, immediately following the war, when Revere would have served as a spy. In case you forgot, he was involved with the struggle for Independence from the very beginning."

Parker was familiar with the legend of Revere's midnight ride to warn Colonial troops of a British invasion.

"Was there anything else unusual in the papers you studied?"

"Nothing." Her head shook emphatically. "They were just as I was told, letters Hamilton wrote to a variety of people."

"You tested the papers?"

"Of course. This type of paper is correct for the period, as is the ink and style of prose. If it's a fake, it's a damn good one."

"But how would anyone know to fake this with the same cipher we found? That coded letter had been hidden for two hundred years."

"I agree. Also, why would someone go to the trouble of forging a coded message? Even if anybody knew what we found at Independence Hall, there's no way they would have known I would be studying this find. I was only told about it a week ago."

Despite the type of reservations you can only get from a near-death experience, Parker couldn't help but consider the message.

"If we assume this is true, what the hell is Revere talking about?"

"I thought you'd never ask."

She grabbed the decoded message from his hands and laid it on the kitchen table.

"The first thing that jumped out at me was the time frame. Revere references both King George and the king's recent defeat. Combined with the words 'new American government,' I think it's clear this letter was written soon after America's successful Revolution."

"I'm surprised the English would let Revere, or any other American, for that matter, get so close to King George right after the war."

She favored him with a sly grin.

"Come on, Mr. Finance. You of all people should know that a little bad blood can't get in the way of making money. After the war, Britain found itself in a crisis of sorts, with their shipping lines disrupted by the French coupled with loads of debt taken on to finance the war. To pay all these bills, and to maintain their enormous military, one of the first orders of business was re-establishing relations with their former colonists."

Parker understood. "And if you want to do business, you need to have businessmen from each side."

"Exactly." Her finger stabbed the air for emphasis. "And who are the businessmen between nations? Diplomats."

With that, she pointed to the decoded message.

"This letter alludes to some amount of time spent in London, which is where a diplomat would be. Revere also notes that he'll be sending additional reports at a later date. When you put it all together, I can't help but think Revere must have served as an American envoy in some capacity."

Images of Hillary Clinton surrounded by Secret Service and personal assistants flashed across his mind.

"I'd bet diplomats had an entourage, even back then."

"They did."

"So it wouldn't have been difficult to bring a few spies along for the party."

Erika patted his head in mock admiration.

"I agree. At the time, Revere was not well known outside of Boston. His midnight ride didn't become famous until Henry Wadsworth Longfellow wrote a poem about it sixty years later. After the war, Revere would have easily blended in with a diplomat's support group."

Parker thought back to his history classes in college.

"Alexander Hamilton was the architect of America's financial system, if I'm not mistaken. Why would he be involved with espionage?"

Erika slid onto a stool across the table, hands moving rapidly as she lectured.

"It wasn't uncommon for government figures to wear multiple hats in those days. Kind of like a small business, there were only a few men who were intimately involved with each aspect of our nation's development. Hamilton was the go-to guy for financial matters, but there's no reason he couldn't also have worked in espionage, especially if it involved money or financial policy in any way."

"A renaissance man of sorts."

"Correct. Look at Benjamin Franklin. He was a diplomat who founded the US Postal Service. There's no reason Hamilton couldn't multi-task."

Viability established, Parker focused on the next big question.

"Assuming Hamilton and Revere worked together as spies, we still have no idea what Revere is talking about. Any idea about what kind of infiltration he discovered?"

"I'm glad you asked," Erika responded.

Without explanation, she jumped up and went back into her bedroom, bare feet moving silently across the bamboo floors, only to re-emerge with her laptop.

"I haven't done a thing over the past twenty-four hours but analyze this letter."

Her fingers flew over the keyboard as she spoke.

"Regarding your question, I don't know what kind of plan Revere is talking about. There's nothing out there, at least anything substantiated, that refers to or discusses a British spy infiltrating America's government immediately following the Revolution. Now, is that because the British never tried, or because they were never caught? I don't know."

With a flourish, she flipped her screen around for him to see.

"What I did find, however, is going to blow your mind."

On the screen was a snapshot of the interior of a room with wooden floors and walls. A brick fireplace sat in one corner, near a small table surrounded by four wooden chairs. Against the far wall sat a bureau, stained to a deep shade of brown.

"This is a receiving room inside of Paul Revere's house. The structure still stands and contains quite a few pieces that date from when Revere lived there. It's a museum now."

"Why am I looking at Paul Revere's living room?"

His question was met with a mischievous grin.

"The answer's in front of your face."

If that was how she wanted to play it, fine. He scoured the room's contents for any clues. Every piece of furniture appeared to be hand-hewn, worn, but crafted to last.

He recalled a phrase from Revere's letter. "All right, clearly I need to find two arrows that can be shot at each other."

The reference contained in Revere's report wasn't even hidden. Unfortunately, no bows or winged munitions presented themselves.

"Am I missing his hunting gear?"

"It's not that simple, but you're on the right track."

Of course it wouldn't be. He began to search methodically, dividing the photo into quadrants and combing through each one before moving on. As he searched, Erika watched him intently, but he didn't give her the satisfaction of displaying any frustration. On the last quadrant, his eyes narrowed.

"What about this?"

He enlarged the picture, focused on the single bureau. Six drawers filled the container's center area, each decorated with several triangle-like designs turned on their side, which left each apex pointing to the drawer's center.

"These triangles that are pointing at each other kind of look like arrows."

One glance at her face was all it took. He'd found it.

Erika hopped up from her chair and darted around the table.

"These designs"-her fingers traced the page-"look exactly like arrows. And if you imagine they're the points of an arrow, look what happens when you fire them."

Her two fingers crashed into each other, directly where the drawer's knob sat. "I worried I was twisting the facts to fit my theory, but it's the only thing that makes sense."

Parker wasn't buying it yet. This was all well and good, but her idea had one major flaw.

"So we may have found the arrows, but how do we know this dresser is involved? Some museum curator might have added it a hundred years after Revere died."

"That particular piece was crafted in England, and I located the page in Revere's household records that lists each item he had delivered to his foundry from England," Erika said. "This bureau was described in detail. On the invoice was a note that specifically stated it was to be given to his wife. Care to guess her name?"

"Rachel."

"Right again."

"So you're saying this desk is still in the museum, on display, waiting for us?"

Erika nodded her head in the affirmative.

"You know what happened the last time we went to a museum."

Parker absentmindedly touched the gunshot scar on his shoulder, a stark reminder of their harrowing experience.

For a minute, neither of them spoke. Parker looked out of her living room windows, down on the rapidly filling sidewalks. Couples walked past, arm in arm, some with dogs on leashes. Mothers sat on porches with their children, gossiping with the other women. A peaceful scene, typical of people everywhere enjoying their weekends and the short break from their normal, uncomplicated lives.

The type of life Parker now envied.

"Honestly, how long have you had this?"

The fact that he was currently in Philadelphia on business and would be traveling to Boston next week was too convenient.

Both her hands shot up, palms out.

"Two days, that's it. I had no idea the letter existed until this week. I know what you're thinking." Fire flashed across her features. "I didn't use your trip to Boston as an excuse to spring this on you."

He'd known her for nearly a decade. Parker could tell when Erika was lying. Right now, she wasn't.

A sigh of resignation escaped his lips. "Are you going to take a week of vacation?"

"I knew you'd agree," Erika replied. "Yes, I'll take a week of personal time. I thought you might want to take a few days as well, spend some time together after your meetings are finished."

"I'm supposed to spend three days with Ben working on foreign accounts, so I suppose I could extend the trip."

His pleasant look fell away, replaced with a deathly serious stare.

"I know you're excited, but you remember what happened last time. We almost died."

She frowned at his tone.

"Yes, but no need to be a buzz kill. This will be fun."

"I hope we don't find a damn thing in that dresser. In fact, I hope they don't let us anywhere near it. All we do is look at it, maybe poke around a bit, and then we leave. I have no interest in getting involved in another one of your awful conspiracy hunts."

"Excuse me, but let's not forget who started the last fiasco. I loved Joe, but he was your uncle, and he sent that letter to you."

She was right, of course. His murdered uncle had mailed him a letter the day he died, which ultimately set them on a path that had nearly killed them both.

"Okay, you're right about that. However, that doesn't mean we can't learn from our mistakes. I'll go along with you, but in no way are we going to get involved in anything illegal."

"Deal."

She slid across the floor and embraced him, her hands kneading his shoulders.

"Thank you. I promise we won't get in any trouble this time."

Chapter 8

Rich Patton slapped Parker on the back. "Come on, let's grab a drink. I know a great spot for happy hour."

As Parker walked down JFK Boulevard in Center City after another marathon session of meetings, the words were music to his ears. For the past three days he'd been working fifteen hours at a time, hammering out a deal with a competing firm. After two days of arguments, compromises, and a few outright threats, they'd finally reached an accord this afternoon that should make everyone a tidy profit.

"Lead the way, my friend. But just one. Our flight leaves early tomorrow morning."

Erika was at home, packing her bags for a long weekend with him in Boston. Parker had to meet with his old classmate Ben Flood tomorrow when they landed, but after that, he and Erika would be free to enjoy the city. First stop on their itinerary, the Paul Revere House.

Parker followed his host down the sidewalk, which was jam-packed with people. Businessmen in suits, college kids on skateboards, and bums with trash bags mixed together, some more fragrant than others in the amber sunlight. Parker soon found himself inside a bustling Irish pub, surrounded by dozens of people enjoying a few pints.

"You're a real bastard, Chase. Why do you have to bust my chops so hard on our service fees? My boss is going to kill me when he gets a look at those numbers."

Rich Patton put his glass out for a cheers.

Parker tipped his pint. "You got a good deal and you know it." Each man felt the strain of the past few days. Parker had worked with Rich quite a bit over the past few years, reaching a point in their relationship where they could curse each other out during the day but put those feelings aside and enjoy a drink together at night. It was a solid, profitable relationship.

"I don't mean to talk shop after hours, but have you seen all the activity with oil futures?"

As Parker sipped the blessedly cold beer, he recalled a barrage of e-mails he'd read that morning. "Did some dictator blow a gasket and threaten to shut off the pipeline?"

He couldn't remember any volatile news coming out of the Middle East, supplier of a vast majority of the world's crude. Parker knew that oil futures, which were financial instruments purchased by traders predicting the cost of oil at some point in the future, could fluctuate for any number of reasons. If a war started, or if an oil-rich nation threatened to reduce their production, the cost of oil would likely rise. Should investors get wind of such an event, they could try to profit by immediately purchasing oil futures before they rose in price.

If a trader could buy an oil future today for one dollar, when news broke that oil might become scarce in the future, the value of that financial instrument, or future, would rise, earning the trader a profit. However, should the expected not occur, and the market value of the oil future remained stagnant or dropped, the trader would lose money.

Parker knew more than a few speculators who had lost fortunes betting incorrectly on the futures market. It seemed like an easy way to profit until you realized the market could be a fickle mistress.

"No, and that's the strange part. There's been nothing to suggest that so many futures would be snapped up."

Patton had been in the business for over a decade. He wasn't easily spooked.

"How much activity are we talking about here?"

Rich's hands spread out wide, beer spilling onto the floor as he spoke.

"Ten million contracts, give or take a few hundred thousand. That's five times the normal amount. Of course, all these trades are sending the price of crude up as well."

Which only made sense. As the volume of futures purchased rose, so did their price. "Damn, that's a lot of oil. Any idea why people are snapping it up so quickly?"

"That's the thing. It doesn't make sense. Nothing is pointing to the cost of oil rising. I mean, it could go up or down a little, but nothing unusual."

"So what idiots are buying? Do they know something we don't?"

"If they do, they're not telling. And as to who, that's actually quite interesting." Rich leaned closer to him, his voice low. "I have no idea who's doing the buying."

That grabbed Parker's attention. Having previously worked for a firm in New York, Patton was intimately connected to the financial scene. He knew everyone.

"How is that possible? I thought you knew everybody."

Rich's shoulders went skyward. "So did I. Apparently most of these futures are being purchased by a half dozen companies no one's ever heard of. My buddy did some digging on one of them, and the only thing he found was their incorporation date."

Parker waited. Rich was a showman.

"It was created three days ago."

"So? People start companies all the time. Anyone can do it."

"But how many people have a hundred million to throw around? That's the big question."

Rich had a point, but Parker just couldn't get himself fired up about oil futures. He dealt with personal wealth management, so unless Rich was offering a surefire moneymaker involving oil speculation, Parker wasn't interested.

"It could be a front for some place like Goldman Sachs or Morgan Stanley. Maybe some trader has an in with the Saudi royal family and knows something we don't."

A frown spread across Rich's face before he took a long swallow of his beer. He clearly had high hopes for a conspiracy of enormous proportions.

"Maybe, but if that's the case, what do they know?"

"Then what are you waiting for?" Parker teased. "Liquidate all your assets and get as many futures contracts on your balance sheet as possible. You can invite me to your new ski house in Vail after you make a few hundred million for the advice."

"I'll buy an island and invite everyone but you, smart ass."

Parker chuckled and glanced at his watch.

"On that note," he said, finishing his beer, "I have to get going. Erika won't be happy if I stay out too late. Let me know if you hear anything else about this conspiracy of yours. I'll keep my ears open for you up north."

Rich narrowed his eyes, alternating between Parker and his empty glass.

"I'm serious," Rich told him. "If I'm right, we could make a killing if we get in early."

"The only oil speculating I'd do is filling my tank before gas gets more expensive, because right now all these new companies are doing is driving up the price of oil. As if the sheiks needed any more money."

"I'll drink to that. Have a safe trip and stay in touch."

Parker shook Rich's outstretched hand before weaving his way through the crowded bar, carefully avoiding the more intoxicated revelers. Outside, the sun had fallen considerably, leaving the air pleasantly warm. Parker slid into a cab, all thoughts of oil and half-cocked conspiracy theories melting away as he considered the three day vacation he and Erika had in store.

Chapter 9

Boston, Massachusetts

A colorful stream of expletives filled the air inside Spencer Drake's office. At her desk outside his door, his secretary nearly smeared bright red lipstick all over her face.

In the office behind her, Drake sat glued to his massive television, damning the Liverpool soccer club with every fiber in his being.

"You no good sons of whores. That was a bloody pile of shit."

On the screen, several men in black jerseys celebrated the goal they'd just scored to put them ahead of Everton two to nil.

Spencer was a lifelong Everton fan, and the only thing he hated more than losing money was when his beloved Blues lost to Liverpool. The two clubs were intense rivals, each passionate in their hatred for the other.

"The hell with this."

He flicked the game off. Nigel was supposed to contact him shortly about a personnel issue of some kind, whatever the hell that meant.

On cue, a soft tone came from his desk. With the push of a button, his desktop slid open to reveal a hidden compartment underneath. A single monitor rose from the interior, Spencer Drake's private connection to a select few others located across the Atlantic. Custom-installed SSL/TLS video connections powered by on-site servers ensured that no uninvited parties would ever eavesdrop on a conversation.

The system was more secure than standard Aldrich Securities office connections, though Drake would never admit it to his employees, some of whom swept this specific line for bugs daily as part of the CEO's security plan. What he discussed on here was far more volatile than any mere financial transaction. These conversations were the product of a plan set in motion hundreds of years ago, when the seeds of Aldrich Securities were planted.

As far as the investing public was concerned, Spencer Drake was the chairman of a respected financial institution, one of the largest investment banking and securities firms in the world. Though the current incarnation of his organization had only been established within the last thirty years, the company had been founded over two centuries ago.

Less than a half dozen living men knew the true story of the financial giant's birth.

On the monitor, Nigel Stirling's gaunt visage materialized.

"Good afternoon, Spencer."

"Sir. To what do I owe the pleasure of this call?"

Nigel had been reticent about the purpose of this conversation. Typical of the wily old codger.

"What is the status of your purchase program?"

Several days ago Stirling had instructed Drake to establish a set of shell corporations in the Bahamas, none of which could be traced back to Aldrich Securities. The sole purpose of these entities was to purchase oil futures in massive quantities.

This was not the first time he had established offshore corporations. Normally these companies were used as fronts through which to funnel illicit earnings from the stock market, monies that stemmed from a mutually beneficial and highly improper relationship he had cultivated with a member of the Food and Drug Administration.

In exchange for a monthly bribe, the FDA official informed Drake when any new drugs would be approved for use by the general public. All he had to do was purchase said company's stock, and a few days later, when the price inevitably rose, he was that much richer.

"Seven new entities were incorporated in the Bahamas on Monday, as per your instructions. Each company purchased one hundred fifty million barrels of futures contracts with the expectation that the price of crude will soon rise and continue to do so indefinitely."

Stirling's icy gray eyes betrayed no reaction.

"Has your activity garnered attention?"

Both Drake and Stirling were so far removed from the day-to-day financial world that most of the normal market chatter never reached their ears.

"One of my associates reported the uptick in oil speculation has been noted, though no one seems to know what it means."

"Which is to be expected, given the lack of a clear reason for such activity. Excellent work, Spencer. Continue purchasing the commodity through this week."

Stirling's digital face glanced down as he opened a folder on his desk, though he remained silent for several beats.

"Spencer, I need you to transfer one million dollars to this account number."

Drake hurriedly copied down the numbers written on a piece of paper that Nigel held to the camera.

"May I ask what this money is for?"

"Once the deposit is completed," he continued, ignoring Drake's question, "you will be contacted by a man with whom we have contracted a service. He will provide you with a time frame and instructions for where to deposit an additional million dollars after our agreement is consummated."

Spencer was lost. "Forgive my asking, sir, but time frame for what?"

Stirling leaned toward the camera, tiny red veins on his eyes visible on-screen. "We have contracted to have the next impediment to our operation removed."

"That is excellent news, sir. I'll initiate the transfer immediately."

Nigel leaned back in his chair, one hand manipulating a keyboard rapidly. "As to the next phase of this operation, President bin Khan is waiting for our call."

Seconds later the monitor went to split screen, and a snowy white beard flashed into view, a drastic contrast to bin Khan's deeply tanned face. A few mumbled words in Arabic came from off-screen, and the presidents eyes filled with recognition.

"Hello, my friends. It is good to see you again."

"It's our pleasure, President bin Khan. Thank you for taking the time to speak with us today."

The soft-spoken Arab dismissed Nigel's comments with a wave of his hand. "I believe that we are men with similar interests. So please, what is it you wish to discuss?"

Drake's heart sped up. Their entire operation rode on this call.

"Spencer, would you kindly bring President bin Khan up to date regarding our recent acquisitions?"

Drake briefly summarized his activities over the past few days, relating the incorporations and oil futures purchases he'd coordinated.

"I appreciate your activity, Mr. Drake. A rise in the price of crude bodes well for my pocketbook."

President bin Khan may have been an old man, but beneath the wizened exterior was a ruthless businessman, dispassionate as a shark. Spencer appreciated such qualities in a man.

"However, as you gentleman can likely surmise, my finances are quite healthy at the moment. Why have you orchestrated these transactions?"

Drake and Stirling locked eyes, aware that everything hinged on bin Khan's reaction.

"President bin Khan, what are your thoughts on America?"

The president seemed to freeze for an instant. Just as quickly, his eyes softened, though the anger that flashed across his features had been unmistakable.

"The answer is complicated."

Even if Stirling and Drake didn't already know about bin Khan's past, there was no mistaking his tone. The man hated America with a passion, and Drake didn't blame him. In 1948, bin Khan had been a child living in Iraq. His mother and father, both members of the Iraqi military, were deployed to fight the newly formed state of Israel. Their only son Khalifa had stayed at home while his parents went to war.

They never came back.

Five-year-old Khalifa bin Khan would later learn of the United States involvement in the creation of a Zionist state in Palestine, a precursor to the 1948 war that killed his parents and sent eight hundred thousand Palestinians into exile, forever altering the dynamic of the Middle East.

As he grew, bin Khan laid blame for his parents' death at the feet of the United States, his hatred for their western culture and meddlesome politics growing with each passing year. Time and again, America prevented the heathen Israelites from being overrun by the righteous Muslims whose land had been stolen from underneath their feet.

After his adoption by an influential cleric, bin Khan had quickly risen to prominence in his new home country of Dubai, aided by his adoptive father's paternal relationship to the ruling family. Within a decade, bin Khan was so beloved within Dubai that he was appointed to the Federal National Council, the supreme federal legislative body for the United Arab Emirates.

Ten years later, he was elevated to the presidency.

Now in control of one hundred billion barrels of crude oil reserves,

Khalifa bin Khan was the perfect man to bring Stirling and Drake's plan to fruition.

"I understand that the loss of your family can be directly attributed to the American government's support of Israel."

President bin Khan remained still.

"You have done your homework, Mr. Stirling."

Spencer Drake cut to the chase.

"President bin Khan, we have a proposal for you. First of all, I must admit my near total ignorance as to how your country's oil production facilities operate. Your secrecy is legendary. That being said, if you, as the president, decided it was in the best interests of your nation to reduce the supply of oil coming onto the market each day, would it be within your authority to make that a reality?"

For several seconds, bin Khan was frozen, not so much as twitching a muscle. Finally, he responded. "Gentlemen, as president of my country, my authority is without question. In my capacity as leader of the UAE, it is the same. If I decide that our crude output should be reduced, it will be done."

"That is excellent news. Here is what we propose."

As Drake spoke, bin Khan's features became chilling in their ferocity. Thirty minutes later, it was settled.

"Gentlemen, thank you for including me in your plans. I cannot express the joy you have delivered to my soul."

Drake leaned back in his chair, his thoughts already beyond the aged president on screen.

"President bin Khan, it is we who owe you a debt of gratitude," Nigel Stirling replied. "Rest assured you will not be disappointed."

"I look forward to speaking with you soon."

The president's face faded from view, Stirling's parchment-like skin once again filling the monitor.

"I think that went fairly well, old boy."

A dry laugh escaped Stirling's throat at his own joke. "Once you are contacted by our asset, apprise me of his proposed timeline."

Spencer nodded once, and then the monitor faded to black. Drake did not move for some time, contemplating what was to happen. Soon, a second tragedy would rock the financial world, further solidifying their hold on certain markets. As gratifying as this would be, it was but a prelude to the true purpose of this operation, the reason their group had toiled in anonymity for two centuries.

Finally, the colonists would be put in their place, left to flounder as England reclaimed her rightful position as a world power.

A sharp ringing filled the air. An unknown phone number flashed across his personal phone line. With the care one would expect while handling a live grenade, Spencer lifted the phone from his desk. His throat was unnaturally dry.

Chapter 10

Boston, Massachusetts

A jet engine had fired to life inside the hotel room.

Parker lay still, the overpowering roar assaulting his senses. After a moment, it all came clear. The noise wasn't an engine-it was Erika's hair dryer, blowing incessantly several feet from his head. For some reason she had chosen to use the infernal device while sitting on the bed.

One eye cracked open and was immediately attacked by sunlight streaming through a window.

"Wake up, sleepyhead. You're missing half the day."

"What time is it?" Parker's voice was muffled, head buried under the covers.

"Nearly nine. We have to get moving."

What was wrong with her? They'd been out last night, had a few glasses of wine with dinner, then a few more. His head ached and all he wanted to do was sleep. Erika, on the other hand, was full of energy.

"Go away."

His wish was not granted, and Erika ripped the covers from the bed.

"Not today, party animal. Get up and take a shower. We only have two days here, and I'm not wasting them sitting in this room waiting for you to wake up."

Parker had finished his meetings, a long three days spent in the company of his old classmate Ben, who now worked for a securities firm in Boston. In the financial world, as in life, it was often who you knew as opposed to what you knew. Through his personal relationship with Ben, Parker had delivered consistent profits on a regular basis, one perk of which was the expense account with which he'd booked this lavish hotel room.

"I am not getting up. Leave me alone."

42

For a few moments, nothing. This made Parker nervous. When he rolled over, it was just in time to catch a face full of cold water, the shock of which sent him hurtling from the bed.

"What's the matter with you? That's freezing cold."

Erika stood, one hand on a hip, head cocked.

"Oh, you decided to get up? Now go take another shower. There's a city to explore."

Parker knew he wouldn't win this battle, and twenty minutes later they walked outside onto Atlantic Avenue, blue skies overhead. A warm breeze blew through Parker's wet hair. The headache was gone, replaced by a rumbling in his stomach. The sidewalks were busy, small groups of people out enjoying the summer air. A short walk along the waterfront brought them to a coffee shop filled with tourists and locals alike.

Outside in the sunshine, Erika studied a map on her phone as he devoured his breakfast.

"While you were getting your beauty sleep, I laid out a plan of action. First, we're going to the Revere House."

Parker grunted his agreement. May as well get this over with and enjoy the rest of the weekend.

"I called the house, and a tour guide said the big crowds don't usually come until the weekend. The place should be fairly empty until tomorrow."

"And exactly what do you propose we do? I have no interest in breaking any laws."

"All we're going to do is look," Erika answered. "If we don't find anything, we'll leave. I promise."

"Why do I not believe you?"

Her lack of response did nothing to ease his mind.

They hopped in a cab, and five minutes later they found themselves outside a two-story, gray, wooden house, notable mainly for its diminutive stature in comparison to surrounding buildings. A single sign above the front door was all that identified the historical landmark.

"Are you sure this place is open? When I told Ben we were coming here he thought it might not open until later in the day."

Parker didn't see anyone outside the building. Trees had been planted along the roadway, and warm air rustled the green leaves, bringing with it the promise of a beautiful day.

"Yes, I'm sure. In fact, I think this is ideal."

He leaned in close, his voice low. "And why is this so ideal?"

"I would prefer to have some privacy inside."

"You remember when I said I wouldn't break any laws? I wasn't kidding."

"All you're doing is keeping an eye out for anyone who walks into the room. I'm a history professor with a keen interest in some of the artifacts. We're two perfectly normal, law-abiding tourists."

As much as he didn't want to, Parker couldn't help but wonder what they might find. If the message Erika had uncovered was correct, the bureau inside might contain a clue regarding Revere's alleged conspiracy.

"What exactly are you planning to do?"

A glance around ensured no one was listening.

"I think that Revere's directions are straightforward. The decorative designs, which are shaped like arrows, point to each other. My guess is they're the triggers for a locking mechanism of some kind, and if we push them closer together, something interesting might happen."

"You do realize this piece of furniture was built over two centuries ago, don't you? I doubt any moving pieces will still work. Even if there is a hidden area, it's probably rusted shut."

"We'll cross that bridge when we have to."

With that, Erika turned on a heel and headed toward the museum, her sandals slapping over the red brick sidewalk. She first stopped at a circular kiosk that sold entrance passes. Two stubs in hand, she marched to the diminutive front door. Trailing behind, Parker saw the doorknob turn in her grasp, and the gray boards opened into the museum. When he walked inside, creaking footsteps filled the air.

Directly in front of him was an ancient brick fireplace, inside of which sat a large bronze cauldron, the golden color tinged with a deep green patina. Several hand-carved pieces of wooden furniture surrounded the hearth, each stained a deep brown. A tiny crib sat across from a rocking chair, underneath a row of enormous cast iron pots and pans.

"Everything looks so small."

"Why are you whispering? We're the only ones here."

She was right, but the room carried a sense of history, a weight that was impossible to ignore.

"According to this map, the sitting room is just ahead," she said, and was off.

Each step echoed like a gunshot in the still room, the boards protesting his weight as he passed. The museum was designed to control their movements, with each room flowing to the next, a single path forward. Through a low-hanging archway that nearly clipped his head, Parker saw a dining table set for two. Placards on the tablecloth informed visitors that each piece had actually been used by the Revere family, handcrafted by the patriarch.

"There it is."

He followed Erika's outstretched finger, aimed at the purpose of their visit. A gorgeous bureau constructed of reddish-brown mahogany sat against the far wall. Six drawers comprised the lower half, atop which sat a single cupboard framed by open shelves on both sides. Each of the drawers was adorned with two V-shaped designs on either end, the tips of which pointed to a handle midway between them. The lines that composed each triangular piece were accented with silver.

Parker glanced behind them, though he'd have to be deaf to miss any footsteps on these cacophonous floors. When he looked back, Erika was already halfway to the bureau.

"Hold on a second. What exactly is your plan?"

Erika didn't turn around as she spoke.

"To solve the riddle and find whatever Revere left behind. Stop wasting time and get over here."

Her hands ran over the polished drawers. Perched atop the piece was a typed card that informed Parker the desk had indeed been made in England as a gift for Revere's wife.

"I can't move these at all."

Erika's arms shook with effort as she attempted to force the triangular designs closer together.

"Don't do that." Parker grabbed her hands. "If you break this thing, we're going to have some explaining to do."

"I didn't come all this way just to look at it."

She ripped her hands free and studied the drawers, nose inches from the wood.

"Two opposing arrows adorned by my touch, fired together, will reveal the truth."

Erika ran a finger over the woodwork. "That's the key. These designs look like arrows, right?"

Parker grunted in agreement.

"Each of these designs is accented with silver, which to my untrained eye looks to be the real stuff. As we all know, Paul Revere was a silversmith." Her logic was flawless. "So it stands to reason that these are what Revere was referring to in his encrypted letter to Hamilton."

Parker still wasn't convinced. "If you're right, how do we know which drawer he's talking about? You'll break those off if you try to force them towards each other."

Erika responded by reaching into her back pocket and removing a small white tube.

"That's why I brought this."

His mouth nearly fell open.

"You have to be kidding. You're going to use superglue?"

"It should hold for a few hours, until we can get out of here."

Without waiting for his approval, Erika squatted down and began her search with the top left drawer, shoving the two designs at one another, biceps straining with effort. Parker looked around, expecting a museum attendant to walk through at any moment.

"It won't move."

Erika pulled the drawer out, her fist knocking the wooden piece, one ear in close.

"It doesn't sound hollow. Here, you try and push these together."

Realizing there was no other choice, Parker knelt down and put one hand on each triangular decoration. Despite his best efforts, the two designs wouldn't budge.

"These things aren't going anywhere."

Erika was already on the third drawer, forehead strained with effort.

"Try the other ones. Your muscles must be good for something."

He tried the second drawer with similar results. Whoever had installed the decorations had done a fine job. They didn't move an inch. As Erika was inspecting her fifth drawer, Parker took the fourth one in his hands, which now ached from the exercise. As he struggled to shove the silver-coated triangles together, his hand slipped.

The decoration had torn from the drawer's surface, ripped cleanly off.

"Shit. I need that glue."

Erika took the broken piece in her hands, though her attention was focused on the drawer itself.

"Look, you can see where this was nailed on."

He noted the tiny piece of metal that protruded from the damaged decoration.

"And here, you can see the wood behind this decoration is a single piece," Erika noted. "There's no way these things could move."

Parker didn't respond, a swell of anger growing inside his chest. He was sweaty, pissed off, and slightly hung over. The last thing he needed was to be caught breaking Paul Revere's furniture.

"This is a waste of time. Let's get out of here before an employee calls the cops."

Erika slid the broken drawer back in, the silver triangle attached once again.

"Stop being a baby. We only have two more."

He opened his mouth to protest, but Erika laid a hand on his forearm, her eyes wide, pleading.

"Please?"

"Fine, but after this, we're out of here. This is supposed to be a vacation."

The next to last drawer did not yield either, and Parker began to think they'd be on their way. As he slid the fifth drawer back into the bureau, Erika gasped.

"Parker, this one moved."

He peered at the drawer in her hands.

"Give it to me."

With the drawer now bathed in sunlight, Parker studied the centuries-old piece. Right away, he saw it. The triangular design had shifted. Years of sun and dirt had dulled the drawer's polish, but where the silver arrow had been, the wood was bright where it had been protected from the elements.

Erika's eyes flashed. "Push the triangles together."

For a moment, the designs held fast, stuck like all the others. Parker redoubled his efforts and was rewarded as the two arrow-shaped decorations jerked closer to each other by several inches.

"Damn, this thing is tough to move. The arrows are stuck."

She smacked his arm. "Stop making excuses and push harder."

Her face was alight with anticipation as he squeezed, certain the wood was going to splinter apart in his hands. Just as his arms were about to give out, the arrows shot together with a terrible clatter. The unexpected movement sent the drawer flying from his grasp, and he could only watch as it tumbled to the floor with a tremendous crash.

"We need to get out of here."

"Not before we see what's inside."

There were no visible changes other than the arrows, which now sat inches apart. Erika ran her fingers around the interior, probing the polished wood. "I don't feel any hinges inside. Those arrows had to have done something."

With a gentle touch, she lifted the drawer and turned it upside down. On the bottom, a previously invisible panel had retracted to reveal a slender leather pouch, secured to the underside. Before they could speak, the door behind them creaked open.

Chapter 11

An elderly man walked through the door.

"Is everything all right in here?"

Parker said nothing as the man tottered their way, a kind look on his wizened features.

"I'm glad you're here, sir." Erika pushed Parker aside, holding the drawer in front of her like a peace offering. "When we came in here, this drawer was sitting on the ground. I almost tripped over it."

The frail old man ran one hand through a thick shock of snowy white hair atop his wrinkled forehead.

"Where, uh, where did you say you found it?"

"Right here." She gestured emphatically at the ground. "We were walking through, and oh my, it was just sitting there. I don't know what to do." Before the old man could respond, she said, "Oh my goodness, would you look at that. I found where it goes."

Just as the bespectacled man reached for it, Erika turned around and slid the drawer back into its proper slot.

"It must have fallen out. You can't be too careful."

"Yes, I suppose you can't."

Bewildered, the old man nodded slowly as he spoke.

"Do you work here?"

Erika flashed a megawatt smile his way. She grabbed Parker's arm and slid closer to the poor guy, so close they nearly touched the nametag on his chest.

"Yes, I'm the curator."

"This is just the loveliest place." Erika didn't give him a chance to think. "Would you tell us about the house? Is there anything here that Paul Revere actually used?"

Parker nodded as she pinched his arm, an absurd grin plastered across his face. For a few moments, the old guy scratched his head, completely overwhelmed.

"Actually used? Why, yes, there are many items here that date from Revere's time."

With one final glance at the bureau, the curator launched into a lengthy description of the home's contents, pointing out period furnishings and original construction. Nearly an hour later, the trio emerged from the small structure, Parker and Erika waving good-bye to their impromptu tour guide. As soon as the door closed behind them, Parker grabbed Erika's arm.

"What were you thinking? Now there's no way we can get back inside the drawer. That guard is going to go back and find the hidden compartment."

A playful light flashed in her eyes.

"No he won't, because there's nothing to find."

"What do you mean, nothing to find? There was a leather pouch hidden inside the drawer. We both saw it."

"Do you mean this leather pouch?"

With a flourish, one hand slid down her shirt and removed the container in question. He couldn't believe it. As he reached for it, she pulled the artifact away.

"Not here, dummy. Let's get away from this museum before that old guy comes looking for us. If he does go look at the drawer, he's going to find the hidden compartment."

Erika turned on her heel, leaving Parker flat-footed, mouth hanging open. He couldn't believe what she'd done. Not until she was halfway to the street did he start moving, adrenaline speeding his pursuit to learn what had been secreted away in Revere's hidden drawer.

Chapter 12

Spencer Drake stared at the phone in his hand.

It had begun.

A twinge of fear knifed through him. The man who had called was perhaps the most unsettling individual he'd ever spoken with. Their conversation had lasted less than ten minutes, and Drake had said very little. For one of the few times in his life, decisions were completely out of his control. Simply put, Drake had just contracted for a service to be performed. Nothing more.

If that was the case, then why did it feel as though he had freed a caged lion? Pushing the thought from his mind, Drake called Nigel Stirling.

"Yes?"

"It will happen within a week's time. The operative couldn't be more specific than that."

"Under what circumstances?" Stirling asked.

This was what had left Drake with a sense of unease.

"He declined to specify. The only issue is access, which is why we have such an open-ended time frame."

Music was audible in the background, what sounded like a string quartet.

"Hold for a moment, please. This dreadful charity function has absolutely no privacy." The music soon faded. "That's better. As much as I abhor these soirees, one must attend when Her Majesty is the host. As you were saying, we must wait for a week?"

"At the most. If he is able, the assignment will be completed more quickly. He also declined to provide me with any updates until it is finished."

"Frustrating, but understandable. In that case, I shall keep an eye on the evening news."

After Stirling hung up, Drake flicked on his television. If their man completed his mission, every person in the country would learn of it immediately. A soft knock came from his office door, and he looked up just as Liz strutted around the corner, her flowing hair pulled into a loose bun supported by only a pencil. The glasses she wore paired nicely with the tartan skirt that hugged her slender hips.

"There's a message for you, Mr. Drake. From one of your personal numbers."

He shot out of his chair and snatched the paper from between her manicured fingernails.

"Thank you, Liz. That will be all."

To better facilitate the private operations Drake participated in with Nigel Stirling, Spencer maintained several open lines of communication with an eclectic collection of individuals the world over. These lines were specified for use by one person only, each with unique instructions for when the individual was to contact Spencer. Infrequently used at best, no one besides Drake and Stirling knew of their true purpose. Drake punched in the return number. Nearly a dozen rings later, it was answered.

"Hello?"

The voice could have belonged to his grandfather.

"What happened?"

"Well, sir, I'm not sure if you're even interested in this."

This particular line was assigned to a museum employee with whom Drake had a unique financial arrangement, one that had existed in one form or another for over a century, ever since the museum had opened its doors.

"I'll be the judge of that. Tell me everything."

The initial arrangement had been made with this man's great-grandfather, the first curator. Ever since, once a year, a suitcase filled with cash had been delivered to the current museum curator's home. In exchange, the curator agreed to call this number any time there was an unusual occurrence at their workplace. The instructions were intentionally vague, and the curator had no idea who was on the other end of the call.

"We had a strange thing happen today here in the Revere House."

Chapter 13

Drake listened silently to the elderly curator's tale.

"Did you find anything in the drawer?"

"Well, sir, it was the darndest thing. When I went back inside, I thought that maybe I should take a look at the drawer, make sure it wasn't damaged or anything. When I pulled it out, everything looked just fine, until I flipped it over. On the bottom, there was some kind of opening, sort of like a hidden panel."

Drake's knuckles went white.

"What was inside?"

"That's the thing. It was empty. Just two little straps dangling there, holding nothing at all."

"I need you to think very carefully. Is it possible there was something inside the drawer those two visitors could have removed?"

Silence for a beat. "You know, it might be possible," the curator replied. "I don't move like I used to, so when I first heard the racket going on, it took me a little bit to get over there. Those kids might have taken something with them, but I'll be damned if I saw anything."

All those cash deliveries had finally paid off.

"Do you know who the two people are?"

"I thought you might ask, so I pulled out the guestbook. Lucky for you, they actually signed it. Most people walk on by without bothering, but these two, they took the time—"

He cut off the old man's rambling. "What are their names?"

"That would be a Ms. Erika Carr and a Mr. Parker Chase."

Drake scribbled the names down.

"Does your museum have a surveillance system?"

"We do, but the cameras are only outside."

How convenient. "I need copies of the tapes from this morning, anything that shows the two suspects."

"Sure, my grandson can do that. I'll tell him we need a copy for the security company."

"Fine, just make sure you send it to this address today." Drake gave him a post office box he kept in Boston, registered under yet another shell corporation. "If for some reason those two come back, call this number immediately."

"Yes, sir. If you don't mind, what makes you believe there was anything in the drawer, and what is-"

"I do mind."

Drake disconnected before the old man could respond. One finger punched the intercom button.

"Liz, get in here."

She scurried through his office door, lipstick in hand.

"Put that damn makeup away and get someone from IT on the phone."

"Yes, sir."

As a multi-national securities firm with a half-trillion in total assets, Aldrich Securities employed some of the finest technical minds in the country. Information was the backbone of their business, and every second they spent waiting for it was not only time wasted, but also money lost. Moments later, the phone rang.

"Drake."

"Mr. Drake, this is Luke Atwater, Senior Technician with IT."

"Luke, I was told you're the best guy we have, and I need your help. Security recently uncovered the identity of two people who we suspect are orchestrating a money laundering operation and plan to involve Aldrich Securities. However, at this point we're not positive of their intentions, and as such, cannot involve the authorities."

"I take it you require background information on the pair?"

"You're correct. I need to know anything and everything about them."

"Can you tell me anything to help narrow down the search field?"

"Only that they are currently in Boston."

"And you would want this to be quiet, I assume? Everything kept in-house?"

"Correct again."

He sensed the tech's hesitation, but Drake still had a few cards up his sleeve.

"Of course, you would be compensated for your efforts. I believe a one-time bonus of fifty thousand would be in order."

Drake heard Luke Atwater gasp. Fifty grand represented half his yearly salary.

"When would you require the information, sir?"

"Yesterday. I'll have my secretary deliver what we know about the pair so far to you immediately."

"I'll get right on it, sir."

Drake had long ago learned that the best way to get things done was with a smile on your face-and a large amount of money in your hands.

"Liz, get this down to Luke Atwater in IT right now."

Once Drake learned something about these two, he would make a report to Stirling. It was hard to believe, but a two-hundred-year-old piece of information, gained in the torture chambers beneath the Tower of London, may have just saved their plans.

One hour later, Drake had his answer.

"Here is the report on Parker Chase." Atwater handed him a thick manila folder, "And this is for Erika Carr."

"How do you know these are the ones I'm looking for? There must be hundreds of people with those names."

"This pair is currently registered at the Intercontinental Boston hotel."

Drake's eyes lit up.

"Excellent work. I'll arrange for your bonus to be paid immediately. Of course, Mr. Atwater, you understand this assignment was confidential. I value a man with discretion such as yours."

Atwater took the hint. "I understand completely, sir. Thank you for the opportunity."

After his entrepreneurial employee had departed, Drake ripped the files open. Twenty minutes later, he leaned back in his chair, not sure what to make of the pair, and impressed with Atwater's work. The man was extremely thorough.

What troubled him the most was Parker's chosen profession. It may have just been a coincidence, but then again, it could be much more. He needed to bring Stirling up to date. Surprisingly, Nigel answered on the first ring.

"What did you learn?"

"Their names are Parker Chase and Erika Carr. Both in their late twenties. The female is an assistant professor of history at the University of Pennsylvania, hired two years ago. She lives in Philadelphia. The male is in finance with a firm out of Pittsburgh, Pennsylvania. He's worked there for almost a decade, seems to be doing rather well for himself."

"Any idea how they know each other?"

"They attended college together, and each participated in varsity athletics. Mr. Chase was an American football player of some renown. Tax records indicate they shared an apartment in Pittsburgh for some time, though Ms. Carr relocated to Philadelphia when she began her employment with the university."

"So we have a pair of lovebirds on our hands. Interesting."

When Stirling fell silent, Drake shared the other tidbit that had grabbed his eye.

"Not sure what to make of this, sir, but Mr. Chase has recently suffered a series of personal losses. His father was killed in what is described as a hunting accident several years ago, and his uncle was murdered earlier this year. Furthermore, his mother died shortly after giving birth to him. It appears Mr. Chase has no living relatives."

"Murdered, you say? Any motive given?"

"That's the tickler, sir. The police report lists the motive as robbery, though it clearly states that nothing of value was stolen."

"So Mr. Chase has had a string of bad fortune. I hope that doesn't have to continue. What is your take on this incident?"

Drake had meticulously crafted the proper response. If he betrayed his true feelings, that this was no random incident, he had no doubt that Stirling would inject himself into the situation when he was least welcome. For years now, Drake had been in control of their stateside operations. The last thing he wanted was for Stirling to take the reins.

"I don't believe this threatens our plans. I must admit that at first I was worried, but the more I consider everything, the less sinister it appears. All we know is that two kids were found with a drawer in their hands, albeit a drawer with a hidden compartment. We have no idea if anything was ever inside that compartment. Without proof, I would suggest staying the course."

"Even though the two people involved are a history professor and a financial professional? Does that not sound the alarms?"

Drake needed to cut Stirling off before he convinced himself to get involved.

"I don't like this any more than you do, sir, but the fact remains that we have no proof of anything. The only reason we've been paying for information at that museum for the past century is because of a rumor. A *rumor*, sir, and a two-hundred-year-old one at that."

Nigel seemed to take the bait.

"I suppose you may be correct."

"On top of that, now is not the time to get distracted. Now is when we finally remind the world of its rightful leaders."

Drake knew that little shot of patriotism would knock Stirling off course.

"You're right, damn it. We're too close now."

You still have it, Spencer old boy.

"As soon as our operative completes his mission," Nigel said, back on track, "you will initiate a call."

Drake had expected as much.

"Of course, sir. I look forward to updating the membership as to our progress."

"Good man. Stay the course, Spencer. God bless the queen."

"God bless the queen, sir."

After hanging up, Spencer shook his head. Stirling was a bit long in the tooth, but he was no fool. Spencer had gotten lucky. Nigel Stirling could be a meddling old fool when he was of a mind, and that was the last thing Spencer needed right now. His plans back on track, Drake punched his intercom button.

"Liz, I need the head of security in my office immediately."

A minute later, Aldrich Securities head of protection walked into Spencer's office.

Tom Becker was a Marine Corps veteran, who had served two tours of duty in Iraq during Operation Desert Storm. Highly intelligent, he'd served as Aldrich's head of security for the past ten years, and Drake knew that whatever task he was given would be completed successfully and without question.

"Tom, I have a project for you."

"What do you require, sir?"

Even now, the man stood at attention, back ramrod straight, muscular shoulders tapered to a narrow waist. Except for the graying hair at his temples, he could have passed for half his fifty years.

"We have two individuals who I suspect may be plotting to defraud Aldrich Securities. I need you to establish surveillance on them, both physically and electronically."

Becker never questioned the legality of his assignments, which routinely included wiretapping private phone lines. He was extremely well paid for his discretion.

"Understood, sir. What intel do we have on the subjects?"

"Everything you need is in here." Drake passed across the bio sheets for Parker Chase and Erika Carr. "I require daily updates as to their movements, contacts, and conversations. The usual, Mr. Becker."

"Understood, sir."

He saw Becker's arm fight the urge to salute before he twisted on his heels and left. The man was a machine and dependable as hell. With any luck, he would be able to check Mr. Chase and Ms. Carr off Spencer's radar by tomorrow. However, should they happen to be more attuned to his plans than he suspected, Spencer Drake owned a luxurious yacht with which to ferry two unwanted corpses out to sea for an anonymous burial.

Chapter 14

Boston, Massachusetts

The taxi back to their hotel was silent, Erika and Parker both lost in their thoughts. Ten agonizing minutes later, they were safe, secure in their hotel.

At the sight of Erika's white cotton gloves, he muttered to himself. "Of course you have those."

She seemingly never went anywhere without a pair of the anti-moisture gloves used to handle delicate paper-based artifacts. When a historian or archeologist dealt with material of any great age, it was necessary to protect the artifact from the natural oils on their fingers, which could destroy such fragile pieces. Erika was the consummate professional, and Parker knew she wouldn't rush her examination.

"What do we have here, Professor?"

"It's a leather container, about the size of a modern envelope. The material is well made and at least several hundred years old. It appears to have been cared for, which accounts for the limited deterioration." With exaggerated care, Erika turned it over, peered closely at the browned rawhide. "I don't see any markings that would identify ownership. The back flap is secured with a slim length of the same material."

Gloved hands delicately unwound the strip. The string fell away and Erika opened the artifact.

Her mouth fell open.

"Parker, there's something inside."

"That's the general idea with envelopes."

Her eyes were daggers.

"It's a piece of paper, tri-folded. The paper appears to be made from a

59

combination of cotton and linen, which is typical of an eighteenth-century letter, the timeframe during which Revere would have penned any correspondence."

As she continued to study the off-white artifact, Parker's impatience bubbled over. "Erika, I appreciate the historical aspect of this as much as anyone, but could we please get on with it?"

"We have no idea what this is. Well, actually we have a good idea, but that's no reason to hurry. If we're right, this has been inside that bureau for two centuries. Five more minutes isn't going to kill you."

Despite her lecture, she started to unfold the linen artifact. Small, concise script covered the page.

"The handwriting is similar to the first letter we found."

More to the point, Parker could read the letters. It wasn't encoded. Erika laid the unfolded sheet on their room's desk, gently pressing it open on each side.

25 Sept. 1783
Alexander,

I am afraid that I bear distressing news. The associate of whom I spoke has been uncovered. I found him only yesterday, murdered.

We were fortunate, however, that he was able to deliver one final report, though I fear this is what led to his demise. As I mentioned, a plot has been launched to infiltrate our government, and I now know that the focus of this nefarious scheme is our young nation's economy.

Though I cannot confirm my suspicion, I believe that a traitor may be assisting King George's men, possibly within America's borders. Thankfully our murdered comrade was not the only source of information lodged within His Majesty's Court, and I anticipate further knowledge from these loyal patriots within a week's time.

As a fellow American, you must inspect beneath the golden grasshopper from the town of my birth to find enlightenment.

Yr. Faithful Servant,
P. Revere

A small magnifying glass appeared from Erika's suitcase. The paper was inches from her face as she studied the writing.

"The ink and style of writing are appropriate for the time period.

Revere's signature is correct." She finally glanced at him. "This is authentic."

"It looks like you were right," Parker said as he studied the text. "Alexander Hamilton was the first secretary of the Treasury. He would have gone to any length to ensure America's economy wasn't undermined from within."

"I don't believe this was his last message," Erika offered. "Revere clearly says he expects to have more information, so unless he planned to deliver the details in person, there should have been a third letter."

Parker had been thinking the same thing.

Erika's finger hovered over a final few words on the sheet.

"This last line, the part about finding enlightenment. What do you think that is?"

"If I had to guess," Parker answered, "I'd say that's Revere's way of telling Hamilton where his next message will be. One of his spies was just shot, so he'd probably be pretty careful with his next report."

One gloved hand was on her chin, forehead creased with thought.

"If we're right, and that is a clue about where his next message will be, then what in the world is a golden grasshopper?"

"That's your department, Dr. Carr. I have no idea."

Erika's rose-tinted lips moved silently, eyes closed.

"I don't think I've ever heard the phrase before. Pull out your phone and see what you can find."

He knew how much she hated having to resort to using search engines to locate material. Erika was just like him in some ways. She never wanted to admit failure. As he typed the phrase, she continued her interpretation of the letter.

"The date on here tells us something. Do you know what else happened in September of 1783?"

One cocked eyebrow was all he'd give her. She loved to lecture.

"That's the month the Treaty of Paris was signed." His expression remained neutral. "Which," she said, exasperation creeping into her tone, "was the treaty America signed with Britain ending the Revolution. We may have declared our independence seven years earlier, but it wasn't acknowledged by the crown until this treaty was executed."

"And what exactly does that mean to us?"

Erika tucked a strand of silky blonde hair behind an ear. "This period of transition would have given the British government an ideal situation for planting a traitor in America's leadership. Think about it. We were creating an entirely new form of government for a brand-new nation. There were hundreds of posts that needed to be filled, hundreds of jobs for which there was no blueprint. How hard do you think it would have been for England to slip a few loyalists in there? Remember, not every colonist wanted their independence. Many of the wealthy, educated people in America wanted a monarch."

"I doubt there were many people who were loyal to the king."

It was her turn to smirk.

"Some estimates put the number as high as twenty percent of the population. In fact, the state with the highest concentration of Loyalists was New York. Which, I might add, was a major center of commerce. It's not much of a stretch to assume there were a few powerful people in the city who were actually working for England. Again, they were mostly affluent white men."

"I guess if it was working for you, why change?" His phone finally responded to the query. "All right, here's what I found. *The Sign of the Golden Grasshopper* is a biographical novel published in the late nineties, that's no good. Wait a second, look at this." On the screen was an image of a golden grasshopper, hung above a stately wooden door. "This is a statue or sculpture on Lombard Street in London."

Erika grabbed the phone before he could research any further.

"It's the family crest of one Thomas Gresham," she stated.

"That's who the biography was written about, the one I just mentioned. What does Gresham have to do with this?"

"He was an English financier." Her enthusiasm abruptly dimmed as she read on. "He died in 1579. Keep looking."

The next entry demanded his attention.

"Guess what kind of weathervane is above Faneuil Hall, right here in Boston."

The fire in her eyes was back.

Parker read from his phone. "The most famous weathervane in Boston is Faneuil Hall's golden grasshopper. I take it you've heard of the place?"

"Faneuil Hall Marketplace is right down the road. We could walk from here. I know it was originally built in the mid-eighteenth century, and that during the Revolution it was used as a platform to speak out against the British."

"Not bad. It was built in 1742, and both George Washington and

Samuel Adams used it as a spontaneous bully pulpit. Now it's one of four adjacent halls that have stores, restaurants and other touristy stuff."

"And I have to assume the golden grasshopper weathervane is still there?"

"It's been looking out over Boston for two hundred sixty years." As he perused the *"History Of"* section of the Hall's website, one blurb caught his eye. "Listen to this. In 1761 there was a fire at the hall, and the weathervane was damaged. After it was repaired, the blacksmith who fixed the piece put a 'time capsule' of some kind inside. Additional capsules have been added over the past few hundred years."

A frown darkened Erika's face.

"You realize if people have been in and out of that grasshopper for two hundred years, there's a chance that any message inside may be gone?"

He nodded. "Agreed, but there's something else that's bothering me."

"What did Revere mean by *beneath* the grasshopper?"

She had read his mind.

"Considering that people have been looking inside the actual weathervane for years," Parker said, "either the message would be gone, or it could be mixed up with a whole bunch of newspaper articles and children's poems."

"You're right, but we might be missing the point here. Why would Revere go to the trouble of hiding a message inside a weathervane that's a hundred feet in the air? There would be no easy way for Hamilton to retrieve it without attracting attention."

Parker took a step back, recalculating his angle of attack. Sometimes it truly was a case of not seeing the forest for the trees.

"All right, we'll keep it simple. What if Revere's message was literal? As in, directly beneath the golden grasshopper?"

Erika reverently set Revere's second letter on the hotel room desk before grabbing Parker's phone. Seconds later, an enlarged picture of Faneuil Hall Marketplace as it existed today was on the screen.

"Right now, there are three main levels with a small attic area." Her finger dotted the three rows of windows that lined each floor. Above the top row, a triangular half-window marked the attic space. "The cupola that supports the weathervane is on the east side, atop the attic. If you look at this photo from 1776," she said as one appeared on the phone, "the building structure is identical."

"What's your take?"

Erika didn't answer immediately, eyes flipping between the two photos. "You go first, Mr. Chase. I want to hear your opinion."

"Fine. To me, Revere is telling Hamilton that he put a message inside Faneuil Hall, directly beneath the weathervane. That means we need to get on the first and second floors, figure out which is east, and start looking. I wouldn't be surprised if there was a hidden area in the ceiling or the floor, a hollowed out space where Revere could hide a message that wouldn't be too difficult to access. Like you said, it wouldn't make sense to hide it a hundred feet in the air."

"Not bad. That's exactly what I was thinking." His chest swelled just a bit. It felt good to hang with Erika on her own turf. "Since we're in agreement, let's get moving."

The recently recovered letter disappeared into her leather briefcase.

"Hold on a second." Parker held up his hands. "I don't think we need to go right now. We just finished desecrating one historical landmark. We've reached our quota for the day."

"Nonsense. There's still plenty of daylight left, and right now the place will be filled with tourists. No better place to hide than in plain sight."

"What are you talking about?"

The white gloves were in her back pocket as she tied her shoes.

"Unless you plan on breaking into the Marketplace after it closes, we should get moving. With hundreds of tourists around us, no one will notice if we take a casual stroll and look for a sign from Revere. Chances are any guards or tour guides are just like the old man from Revere's house, retired and slow. We'll blend in while we search."

He knew she was purposefully avoiding what came next.

"So let's say no one notices us poking around. What happens if we find what we're looking for? You realize if a message has been hidden for over two centuries, it was hidden very well. It could be in the floorboards or the ceiling, like you said. Unless those tour guides are deaf and blind, they'll notice when we start destroying their building."

She was already on her feet and in front of the door.

"We'll worry about that when we get there. You're good at improvising." Halfway out the open door, her eyes focused on his shoeless feet. "Any day now."

As much as he thought she was crazy, it was what he loved about her.

"If we get arrested, you're paying my bail."

While they walked down the plush hallway, his phone began to vibrate.

It was his old schoolmate with whom he'd had a meeting yesterday.

"It's Ben. We need to figure out where to meet tonight for happy hour. He said there were some great places just down the road." Parker connected the call. "Hey buddy, what's up?"

"Are you near a television?"

Ben sounded shell-shocked, his voice heavy.

"No, I'm leaving the hotel. Why?"

"Find one. You're not going to believe what just happened."

Chapter 15

New York City

There were only a few men on earth who offered the service.

He was an entrepreneur, a man who offered what people required. If there was a demand for something, a provider would soon exist. Such was the nature of the world. As he sat inside a non-descript apartment in Brooklyn, cleaning one of the weapons with which he plied his trade, he felt a slight elation about the recently completed deal, much like any other person would feel before starting a new job.

He was a hit man, and it was only fair that he get to enjoy his work like every other stiff in the country, slaving away for a few dollars.

Well, more than a few dollars in this case. A few million of them, actually.

Over the past twelve years, Michael Brown had killed thirty-nine people. He remembered every single one, though not out of any twisted desire to romanticize his kills. No, he was able to recall the details surrounding each successful operation because he wanted to stay alive. As his old drill sergeant had always said; attention to detail was what kept a man breathing.

He owed quite a bit to that miserable man. The sergeant had taught him how to shoot, how to hunt his prey, stalking them quietly, waiting for the perfect opportunity to finish the job. Michael was nothing if not methodical.

The phone call had been unexpected, a welcome respite from the endless days of walking through the city, taking in the sights and sounds of nine million people living on top of each other. Many days he would go to Central Park and sit on a bench, soaking in the vibrant atmosphere as birds chirped all around him. He loved the simple things in life, and fortunately, he was successful enough to spend most of his time as he wished, admiring the often unappreciated parts of life.

Several of his past assignments had been at the behest of the Englishman. Nigel Stirling wasn't aware of it, but Michael knew quite a lot about the enigmatic Mr. Stirling. He knew that Nigel was a billionaire, owned homes in London, Monaco, and on the French Riviera, and regularly socialized with the queen.

He also knew that Nigel had dumped several bodies in the Atlantic, one a woman who had been pregnant with Nigel's child and unwilling to terminate the fetus. That was the first time Nigel had engaged his services, and the operation had led to three more assignments, each of which paid handsomely.

Michael never asked why he was hired to kill those people. It was not his concern. As long as Stirling never threatened him, never put Michael Brown's carefully crafted existence in danger, he had no issue with working for the wealthy man. He remained on guard, however, with this most recent assignment. Nigel had put him in touch with a friend, and Michael was leery of this new person. The man who called himself Spencer Drake had contracted with Michael to kill a man, so prior to accepting the assignment, Michael had done a bit of research on Mr. Drake.

What he'd found hadn't surprised him. Like most of Michael's employers, Drake was wealthy and arrogant. Rich enough to afford the seven figure price, and arrogant enough to have someone killed. One other quality the man assuredly possessed was intelligence, which Michael liked. A smart man would realize that if Michael could kill someone he'd never met for a fee, he'd gladly kill a man who double-crossed him for nothing.

Satisfied this wasn't a setup, Michael Brown opened a webpage for the United States Department of the Treasury and began researching the man he had been contracted to murder.

Chapter 16

Potomac Falls, Virginia

"Sit, damn you, sit."

On this picturesque late morning there wasn't a cloud in the sky above Trump National Golf Club, situated just outside the nation's capital. Unimpeded sunlight warmed the air, a slight breeze ruffling the flagsticks. Other than scattered birdcalls, the course was quiet, save for the desperate pleas of one golfer who'd just overshot the pin.

"Of course. These damn greens are the stuff of nightmares."

"Bad luck, Mr. Secretary. Still a chance to save par, though."

Gordon Daniels slammed his club into the pristine fairway.

"That was awful, Bill, and you know it. Don't be so kind."

The caddy merely smiled, well aware of Daniels' competitive fire. It was the reason he'd made it so far in life.

Without a word, Gordon Daniels, United States secretary of the Treasury, grabbed his putter and stalked away toward the offending green. His caddy trailed behind, allowing Daniels time to stew in peace.

A scratch golfer, Daniels was coveted as a playing partner among the Washington elite. Not only did it give the Beltway crowd a chance to rub shoulders with a Cabinet member, but also to pick his brain for tips on their own game. A round with Daniels was an education in both political and golfing gamesmanship.

Just past fifty, Gordon was in the prime of his life, having served the past three years as Treasury secretary. Considered one of the finest financial minds in the country, Daniels had been handed a rocking ship, replete with pitfalls, each of which he had navigated successfully and with aplomb, steering the American economy into relative stability while standing as a rock amidst the turbulent economic waters of the past few years.

Despite this, Daniels had been vilified by a small but vocal block of legislators for his policies, skewered by their vitriolic rhetoric. As was to be expected, the inflamed base of public supporters showered him with hate mail, even death threats, which necessitated the black-suited security force that shadowed his every move and had done so for the past year. Today was an exception, however, as Gordon had ordered his handlers to remain in the clubhouse, out of sight for the duration of his round. Amidst the gated privilege that Trump National offered, there was little reason to believe his life would be in danger from anything more aggressive than an angry squirrel.

The hole which Daniels was currently playing featured a small creek that fronted the green, ensuring that any short approach shots would roll into the water and cost a player two strokes. As most golfers couldn't be counted on to jump over a phone book, much less navigate a flowing stream, there was a single bridge that players used to cross the waterway and access the putting green.

The bridge was situated to the left of the green, adjacent to a large group of evergreens. Constructed in a curve, the bridge actually went between some trees as it traversed the creek, out of view from anyone in the fairway.

In the thick cover of the towering evergreens, a man lay on his stomach, mere feet from the bridge on which Gordon Daniels was walking. Clad entirely in green camouflage, he was practically invisible. In one hand was a compact rifle, pointed at the approaching Daniels. His eyes were locked on the secretary, who was muttering under his breath, head down as he walked.

There were no handrails on the bridge, as the water beneath was less than a foot deep. While Daniels walked over the structure, he came within inches of the man lying next to the water. To the rear, massive trees shielded Daniels from view.

A finger tightened on the trigger. The hiss of compressed air, and a tiny dart shot out and struck Daniels in the neck.

The secretary slapped behind his ear, which only served to drive the dart in further. His fingers fumbled with the dart, pulling at it. Before he could react to what he held, Daniels stumbled to his left, landing with a soft thud on the thick grass beside his attacker.

While lodged in his neck, the tiny electrified dart had delivered a controlled burst of electricity to the secretary's nervous system. In a healthy person, such a jolt may cause the heart muscle, which generated a tiny electrical charge for every beat, to contract unexpectedly. The person may have felt a fluttering in their chest, or experienced a rapid heartbeat. A healthy person, subjected to the electric charge that the small dart produced, would likely be fine.

Gordon Daniels was not a healthy person.

By most accounts he was in fabulous shape for a man his age. However, Gordon also had an artificial cardiac pacemaker in his chest, installed several years ago when his heart's natural pacemaker began to malfunction. This device, which mimicked the hearts natural rhythms, was meant to stabilize Gordon's heart should he ever experience a potentially fatal arrhythmia.

Overloaded from the dart's electrical charge, it malfunctioned, the resulting rapid bursts of electrical impulses sending Daniels into immediate cardiac arrest.

His heart had already stopped beating as the dart was plucked from his skin.

The assassin made a quick swipe with a leaf to remove the single droplet of blood from where the Secretary's neck had been pricked by the dart, and then he slithered on his stomach to a nearby fence that lined the prestigious course, keeping any unwelcome visitors away.

With a deft leap, the man climbed the ten-foot high steel bars and vaulted over. He hit the ground running, headed to a nearby motorcycle that would take him far from the course.

The caddy cleaned the secretary's club, ambling slowly over the pristine fairway. When Gordon was upset about a shot, it was best to give him some space.

It took almost two full minutes for the caddy to make his way to the bridge. He glanced around, figuring Daniels had taken advantage of the privacy these trees offered to relieve himself. As he crossed the bridge, the bright red shirt Gordon had been wearing came into view-on the ground beside the bridge.

"Oh my goodness. Mr. Daniels, are you all right?" The bag of clubs clattered on the bridge as he rushed to Daniels's side. "Mr. Daniels, wake up. Come on now, wake up."

Only when he grabbed the man's shoulders and shook him did he realize.

Gordon Daniels wasn't breathing. The caddy's hands shook as he removed a radio from his belt.

"Clubhouse, this is Bill. I need medical assistance on twelve green right now. I think Gordon Daniels is dead."

Chapter 17

The television in Drake's office delivered the news.

"We apologize for the interruption, but we have a developing story. It appears that United States Secretary of the Treasury Gordon Daniels has suffered some type of medical emergency while playing golf today."

A live shot from high above the golf course. Below, another helicopter sat in the middle of the fairway, several white-clothed people appearing from inside a small copse carrying a stretcher. A bright red shirt covered the torso of a body. Roaring wind assaulted the microphone as a reporter shouted.

"Right now, we know that the man being loaded onto the helicopter is Treasury Secretary Gordon Daniels. I'm being told he suffered a medical emergency while playing golf here at the Trump National Club. As you can see, the secretary is not moving, and it appears the paramedics are administering CPR."

Spencer Drake dropped the papers in his hand. They floated to the floor and settled on the deeply stained wood all around him.

"He did it. I can't believe it."

A harsh buzz sounded from Drake's desk before Liz's voice filled the air.

"Mr. Drake, you have a call. Some British guy who won't give his name."

She could be an insufferable wench.

"Put him through immediately."

Two beats later, Nigel Stirling spoke.

"Well, Mr. Drake, I believe we have cause to celebrate. Have you seen the telly?"

"I'm watching it right now. I can't believe he did it on the golf course. The man is a genius."

Stirling's voice turned rock hard.

"It has been some time since our organization last met, and considering where we stand in our operation, I believe that a gathering is in order."

"I agree. When would you like to meet?"

"We will arrive tomorrow evening. I'll have our flight plan sent tonight."

With that, Stirling hung up. Drake leaned back in his chair, the dead secretary momentarily forgotten. If Stirling was coming over, he had much to prepare.

Liz's voice buzzed through as he began to list the necessary preparations for tomorrow night.

"Mr. Drake, Tom Becker from security is out here."

"Send him in." Hopefully Becker's search on the two people from the Revere House had yielded nothing worrisome. "Mr. Becker, please have a seat."

The ex-military man sat stiffly in front of his desk. "The report you requested, sir."

Becker handed him two folders, each labeled with a name. "The first few pages contain basic biographical information. Parker Chase is approaching his thirtieth birthday. He is single, never married, has no children. Attended college on an American football scholarship. Graduated with a degree in finance eight years ago, hired with the firm where he is currently employed, and has worked there ever since. He has personal assets totaling just under one million dollars."

Drake's eyebrow lifted.

"Family money?"

"No, sir. It was all earned through salary and investments, as per his tax returns. He has no family after the deaths of his father and uncle this past year."

"And the woman?"

"Erika Carr is the same age, also single, never married, no children. Attended college with Mr. Chase, graduating with honors. Tuition was fully paid courtesy of a volleyball scholarship. She completed graduate school, and two years ago accepted a position with the University of Pennsylvania as an assistant professor specializing in American history. There are records indicating she and Mr. Chase cohabited after undergraduate school for several years, until she moved to Philadelphia. Mr. Chase still resides in Pittsburgh."

The girl was certainly attractive.

"Assessment of their capabilities?"

"Both appear to be highly intelligent and physically fit. Mr. Chase belongs to a martial arts school and is listed as a brown belt. I would consider him to be more than capable of defending himself. They are each registered owners of several firearms, though Ms. Carr's was only purchased within the past few months."

They may be able to take care of themselves, but they sure as hell weren't trained operatives. Becker was making them out to be a professional hit team.

"I appreciate your input, Mr. Becker. Now, in your opinion, are they in any way involved with an attempt to defraud Aldrich Securities?" Here Becker hesitated, the first hint of uncertainty Drake had seen. "Cat got your tongue, Mr. Becker?"

"In any professional manner, the answer is no. However, last night a call was placed from Mr. Chase's cell phone to the private phone of an Aldrich employee, one Benjamin Flood."

Drake bolted upright in his chair. "What was it about?"

"I wasn't able to ascertain the details, though I did learn that both Mr. Chase and Mr. Flood incurred charges at the same restaurant last evening. I also learned that along with Ms. Carr, they all graduated from the same college together."

"That is interesting."

The more he heard, the more this sounded like a coincidence. They were old college friends, and it wasn't unrealistic to assume Chase and Flood would stay in touch.

"Hopefully I'm overreacting, but just to make sure, I'd like you to tap Mr. Flood's phone and office. Let's listen to what he has to say for a few weeks."

Becker nodded once before marching from the room.

If they didn't learn anything from the taps soon, Drake would put this to bed. A soft chuckle escaped his lips. By that time, it really wouldn't matter what Chase did.

In a few weeks, the world would be a different place.

Chapter 18

Boston, Massachusetts

The day was warm, and late afternoon sunlight streamed through the air. Brilliant green leaves rustled in a breeze blowing off Boston Harbor. Tourists and natives filled the sidewalks as their feet tapped along to the ever-present sound of engines and car horns.

Parker was oblivious to it all in the back of a taxi with Erika that was headed to Faneuil Hall.

"They just confirmed that Gordon Daniels is dead."

"Any idea how it happened?" Erika asked, unconcerned. "He was probably old. Maybe his heart just stopped beating."

"He was barely fifty and in great shape. People like that don't have heart attacks for no reason."

She turned to look out the window, her eyes on the water.

"Well, I don't see what the big deal is. It's terrible, I understand, but why are you so worried? Is this going to affect your business somehow?"

Parker stopped scanning the news article on his phone and stared at her.

"You're telling me you don't find it the least bit suspicious that the financial leaders of the United States and England both died in the same week?"

"I know the English guy was shot. That's different than our treasurer."

For the first time since Ben had called, she finally appeared to pay attention.

"Look, you don't have any idea what happened to Gordon Daniels. You have to admit that the most likely explanation is he died of natural causes. Maybe he had an enlarged heart or an irregular heartbeat. No one knows. One thing you can be sure of is that some news network will scream bloody murder at the first whiff of a scandal. Even if there isn't one, they'll make something up to sell papers."

She had a point.

"I guess you could be right," Parker said. "It's just a little too coincidental, don't you agree?"

Her hand lay softly on his arm.

"We'll see. In the meantime, we have our own conspiracy to worry about."

Outside, he spotted their destination. Beautifully framed between rows of manicured hedges, Faneuil Hall Marketplace was the square's centerpiece, situated between two other open-air markets. A steady stream of visitors flowed in and out of the buildings, every door open to take advantage of the pleasant summer day. Three stories tall, constructed of red brick, the refurbished hall looked much the same as it did when it was built in 1742.

"So would you care to tell me exactly how you plan on doing this when hundreds of people are all around?"

A hint of a smile touched her lips.

"Watch and learn."

Inside the Hall, food vendors lined a central walking path, each one offering a tantalizing aroma. Above them, the second floor was visible, a circular path of tables and other stores set alongside the walls, as the center of the entire floor had been removed to allow an unfettered view straight to the building's cupola far above.

"Not to rain on your parade," he said softly, lips close to her ear, "but what if the message used to be in the middle of the room? That floor's been gone for years."

Erika didn't respond, but he could tell she was worried. Her eyes flicked rapidly about as she studied the building's layout, occasionally glancing outside.

"All right, I think I have it." One finger extended to the far end of the Hall. "That's east. The weathervane should be over there." She took off at a near run, dodging between slow-moving tourists. Parker hurried after her, apologizing to an old woman Erika had knocked aside. Once outside the far door, Erika craned her neck back, looking skyward. "I was right. There it is."

Parker looked up and saw a golden shimmer above them. The weathervane was a magnificent sight, as bright sunlight sparkled off the gilded grasshopper.

"Where do you think it is in relation to the floor?"

He took a few steps further back, tried to gauge the grasshopper's location.

"Probably ten feet back from this edge, and another ten feet in from the side."

They both hurried back inside and looked to their left, expecting to see a table filled with screaming children sitting atop their targeted spot. Instead they saw a rickety wooden door with the word "Private" stenciled across the front. Before he could blink, Erika stood in front of the doorway.

"Wait a second. We can't just barge in there."

"Watch me."

All around them people moved through the building, none giving them a second glance. As Erika placed a tentative hand on the door, Parker prepared for the shriek of a security alarm, immediately followed by the arrival of several guards.

"You do realize there are policemen outside."

Not fifty feet from where he stood, two officers on bikes were watching the crowds behind dark sunglasses.

"No one's looking at us. Don't worry."

With a final glance around, she turned the dingy black doorknob. On squeaky hinges, the door slid open. Inside they found a small storage closet filled with cleaning supplies and other detritus. Brooms, mops, and other assorted implements of sanitation lined the walls. Several rusted chairs were stacked in one corner next to a folding table, and inexplicably, an ancient hand-operated lawn mower.

"Quit staring and get inside." Erika pulled him in and the door flapped shut behind them. Dust filled the air, and Parker unleashed a violent sneeze. "Be quiet and start searching."

Erika was already shifting mops and hanging buckets aside, her face inches from the dusty walls. Windowless, the room's only light filtered in from beneath the closed door.

"It doesn't look like this place has been used in years." He wiped a nearby wall with one hand, which came back gray.

"I'd say that's a good sign for us. If Revere really did put something underneath that bird, and he left it on the first floor, no one may have found it yet. And it's unlikely Revere would have left Alexander Hamilton to stumble around in search of a hiding place. More likely, he would have left a marker behind, something to point Hamilton in the right direction."

She had pulled out her cell phone and turned it into an impromptu flashlight. Parker did the same, the brilliant LCD beams illuminating their dirty surroundings. Dust motes filled the air as they searched the two outside walls which would have existed in Revere's time. Every movement brought a further onslaught of the gray allergen, a light mist of dirt and debris. Ten minutes later, each of them was filthy and hot.

Parker sneezed again. "They need some air-conditioning in here."

Erika rubbed the sweat from her face as she looked around, eyes narrow.

"These other two walls weren't here two hundred years ago, though they look like they're that old. The only other options are the floor or the ceiling."

Parker's light flashed overhead.

"Do you really think he'd hide something in the ceiling? I doubt Hamilton would be able to get in a hidden compartment easily if it's fifteen feet above him."

"Then the floor it is. Help me move some of this junk."

In front of him sat the pile of folded chairs, stacked up to his chest. As he pulled on the top one, it caught. Frustrated and sweaty, Parker tugged the chair roughly. It was stuck.

"The hell with this."

He ripped it backward. Another jerk, and the chair suddenly came loose. Parker tumbled to the floor along with the entire stack of chairs, each one clattering to the ground with a wooden crunch, taking out anything in their path. From beneath the disaster he'd just created, Parker already knew she would be pissed.

"I'm sorry, it was an accident."

Erika's persistent coughing was the only reply.

During the fall, he'd lost his phone. Cursing under his breath, Parker scrambled to his feet, which sent an avalanche of chairs into the space he'd recently vacated on the storeroom floor.

"Well done. Any person within a mile must know we're inside this closet."

In the room's far corner, a glimmer of light poked through the detritus. Faced with the obstacle course he'd created, Parker clambered over several of the cursed chairs, banged his knee on a stray doorknob in the process.

Why in the world was an extra door stored in here?

Finally he reached his phone. Here he was surrounded by brickwork on either side. This corner was where the two original walls met, likely the very bricks set by masons when the building was originally constructed. His phone was lying on the ground, a faint aura of barely visible light. As he bent down to retrieve the device, he was forced to stretch over a tiny bench that lay upside down.

"Got you."

Arm stretched as far as it would go, his fingers scraped the phone's protective cover as he pulled. There were gaps between each board in the floor, which had apparently warped over the course of several hundred years. As his hand closed around the phone, the bright light illuminated where the two walls met. His eyes were drawn to the spot. Parker pushed himself up but stopped short when he focused on the bottom row of bricks.

There was a design etched in one of them. So faint he wasn't sure it was there.

Parker leaned in closer to the wall, literally in the far corner. One hand brushed a thick layer of dust from the brick's surface. As a mermaid shimmers into view through the water, two letters came to life before his eyes.

P R

"Erika, get over here."

"Would you please be quiet?" she hissed. "If you keep shouting, the cops will be here in a second."

"Get over here right now."

Even though he whispered, she must have sensed the urgency in his voice. Fallen chairs clattered as she moved his way.

"What's so important?"

He illuminated the two letters, his fingers tracing them as she watched. Parker looked up just as her mouth dropped open. For once, she was speechless.

"I think I know what these letters stand for."

Her voice finally returned. "That's a perfect clue. If anyone ever saw it, they'd think that was a builder's mark, similar to how an artist will sign his work or a sculptor mark his creation. Revere could have easily made the insignia after the brick was in place." Erika pushed his hands aside as she crouched down, each bare knee settling in front of the decorated brick. "Even if one of the Hall's employees saw these marks, they wouldn't think much of them. No wonder it's remained hidden all these years."

Her fingers ran over the mortar that kept the wall together.

"This material is so old it's impossible to tell when it was laid here."

"What do you mean? We know this place was built in 1742."

"This building was, yes, but this particular brick? I'm betting it was dislodged about fifty years later."

Then it hit him.

"And put back after Revere hid a message behind it."

"Exactly."

As they spoke, the sound of raised voices just outside the storage room became audible.

"What did Bobby do with that window kit? That darn kid couldn't find his ass with a roadmap. If he left it in here I'll wring his neck."

Her dusty hands clenched his arm. "We have to hide."

As the door handle began to turn, Parker did the only thing he could think of. He pushed her to the floor with one hand while dragging a stray chair onto his back with the other. Erika landed on her back, pinned to the ground by his weight. His nose smashed into hers, their sweat intermingling to form tiny rivers of salty dirt that dripped onto the floor, each sending a miniscule cloud of dust into the air.

"Ah, this danged place is one big mess. I'll never find it."

The man was now inside, his muttered words barely audible through the din that followed him through the open door. Parker couldn't see anything except for Erika's forehead, and had no idea if the chair on his back provided any cover.

Afraid to make a sound, he flicked his eyes overhead, silently asking if they were hidden from view. Erika shook her head, the movement so brief he felt rather than saw the motion.

They were out in plain sight.

Random objects scraped across the floor as the intruder searched through the debris.

"I can't see a thing in here."

Suddenly the room became brighter. A flashlight beam darted around. Parker's lungs were on fire as he fought to hold his breath, afraid the slightest movement would reveal them. Fortunately, the man said nothing, his light apparently concentrated on the ground at his feet. Their luck didn't hold, as seconds later Erika's eyes bugged out, their enchanting blue color vividly sparkling under the flashlight's glow.

A second voice filled the room.

"Hey, Jim, I found it. He left it over here."

The light held steady as Parker's lungs burned. For what felt like an eternity they both held rigidly still. When he could hold his breath no longer, the light clicked off.

"That dang kid. We need to make him clean this place up. You can hardly move in here."

Parker exhaled as the door clicked shut to leave them in silence.

"Get off me." Erika pushed his beleaguered chest with both hands, shoving him off her. She gasped in the dusty air. "If he would have even glanced at us, we were done. Your legs were completely uncovered."

"Good thing Jim wasn't too observant."

With the utmost care, Parker cleared an area around the corner brick large enough for them to squat down. Her phone light flashing around, Erika peered among the junk he was moving.

"What is that?" She was pointing at a metal pipe in his hands.

"I don't know, part of a table? I'm just moving this stuff so we can stand here."

"Give it to me." She grabbed the rod, which was a foot long and several inches in diameter. "Shine your light on the brick." Erika held the pipe in both hands, angst covering her face. She whispered to no one, "Sorry about this."

The pipe swung down, crashed into the brick with a heavy thud. Nothing moved but dust in the air.

"Damn. Stand back." She smashed the brick two more times, and again failed to dislodge little more than a few mortar chunks.

"Give that thing to me and get out of the way." Parker handed her the phones in exchange for the pipe. A glance to the door confirmed they were still alone. Two sharp cracks echoed through the room as the brick disintegrated into pieces. Before the dust settled, Erika was on her knees in front of the damage.

"Be careful, I may have just broken down the front door to a rat's house."

If so, Erika wasn't afraid. Her arm disappeared into the hole. "Yuck, there are so many cobwebs in here." She kept digging, her elbow going inside the wall, until her body froze. "I have something."

Her hand emerged from the hole grasping what looked like a cigar box. She held it aloft where he could see it. His hands barely grazed the surface, swiping the accumulated grime onto Erika's legs. She didn't even notice when they saw what was underneath.

P.R. & Sns.

For several seconds, neither moved. Only when a group of voices passed by the door did Parker finally speak. "We need to go."

Erika said nothing, merely tucked the box under one arm and headed to the door.

"We look like coal miners."

She cast a glance up and down their dirty and disheveled clothes. "Follow me and don't stop. If anyone yells, start running."

Without waiting for an answer she twisted the doorknob and walked outside. Left with no choice, he dropped the pipe and hurried out, hoping the police weren't waiting for them.

Chapter 19

Outside Washington, DC

The deep thump of helicopter blades reverberated through normally tranquil air. When the craft itself passed by, every driver on the roadways below looked skyward, entranced by the monstrous bird.

There was one exception. A lone motorcyclist cruised down the DC beltway, his eyes focused squarely on the road ahead. Moments ago a string of police vehicles had careened past him, lights flashing as they descended on Trump National. Eyes shielded behind the smoked glass of a metallic gray racing helmet, the biker hadn't so much as glanced as the cavalry whizzed past.

Less than twenty minutes after Treasury Secretary Gordon Daniels had been shot with the electrified dart, Michael Brown was miles away, headed to Pennsylvania.

The winding route which Michael had laid out for his return trip to New York would take him through eastern Pennsylvania, past a series of remote lakes, one of which would soon be the watery grave of the motorcycle he was currently riding.

The clothes he wore, a racing jacket with camouflage sewn onto the reverse side and matching pair of pants, would be dumped as well, weighted with cement blocks. Afterward, once he returned to his apartment in the city, there would be no way to connect Michael Brown with the lone wolf terrorist who had murdered Gordon Daniels.

The sight of Daniels crumpling to the ground as his heart stopped beating had the same effect on him as watching a baseball game. It was entertaining, almost pleasing, as he'd completed his mission. The job was now stored away, an experience on which to draw from in the future.

Careful to stay just under the speed limit, Michael focused on the asphalt under his tires, and a feeling of contentment settled over him on this beautiful summer day.

Chapter 20

Boston Massachusetts

Their dirty clothes garnered a few stares, but otherwise Parker and Erika moved unmolested through the afternoon crowds. A taxi took them back to the hotel, and once he walked into the blissfully cold room, Parker flopped onto the bed, mentally exhausted.

"Get over here," Erika ordered as she pulled him to his feet. "I need your help opening this box."

Atop the same table on which they had studied Revere's second letter sat the grimy wooden box, emanating a musty odor. It resembled a cigar box, with two rusted metal hinges connecting the lid and body.

"That doesn't smell too nice. If there's paper inside, would it have survived this long?"

The angst on Erika's face belied her answer. "You have to remember that the paper Revere would have used was far more durable than what we have today. Also, many letters during this time period were protected by a leather cover. I'd hope he had the foresight to use one."

Parker watched as Erika grasped the lid. Her mouth contorted into a grimace as she struggled with the rusted hinges. With a skin-crawling shriek, centuries of rust gave way and the lid opened several inches.

"This thing is really stuck. I don't want to break the container if I can avoid it."

"Let me try." Without waiting for permission, Parker grabbed the box and ripped it open. "See, that wasn't so hard."

She didn't respond, her eyes fixed on the interior. A thin leather-bound book lay inside.

"Look at the cover."

Burned into the cracked leather were two familiar letters.

P.R.

"Looks like we're on the right track."

Erika reached for the volume, which nearly filled the box's interior, her white-gloved hands softly flipping the front cover open. The first page was blank.

"This paper appears to be the right age, as does the binding. If you look closely, you can see that there are a variety of colors in the paper, the result of using different colors of materials to make the page."

She had again fallen into lecture mode.

"That's wonderful, but I don't care. Flip the page before I do."

Erika took the hint. On the next page, he saw a familiar script.

"That's Revere's handwriting."

For several minutes neither of them spoke as they read a message composed centuries ago.

Dear Alexander,

My time here is almost at an end, and I have terrible news to report. One of my informants has uncovered a treacherous plot to undermine our entire financial system. George Simpson, an American by all rights, is in league with His Majesty's associates. My confidante personally observed Mr. Simpson directing a shipment of gold to be delivered to America, though to what destination I know not. Simpson was recruited by King George to establish a presence within our borders and wreak havoc on our burgeoning economy.

Several hundred pounds of gold have been shipped to America to fund this enterprise. I fear the worst, as immediately after learning of this plot, my informant disappeared. Whether his true allegiance was discovered or the conspirators sought to bury all traces of their activities, I cannot say.

As such, you must move forward assuming the English know their secrecy is lost. Beware the man who offers advice or funding, as that man may be an agent of King George, bent on destroying America. Before I depart from these shores, I will seek to gain the trust of a new court member from whom I may learn further details.

Should I fail, however, I beg of you to act with the utmost caution, preserving our liberty that was purchased at such a dear price. I trust you will proceed with all haste to uncover the methods behind Mr. Simpson's traitorous plot.

Yr. Faithful Servant,
PR

Parker turned to face her. "If this message was never delivered, then no one had any idea this plot was in motion."

Erika turned back to the first page. In its entirety, the book contained only four pages nestled between the leather cover.

"This could have destroyed the country before we ever had a chance." Erika looked up, confusion clouding her features. "You're the financial guy. What could they have been trying to do?"

Framed by the prism of history, several options presented themselves. "First of all, you have to realize how much money they're talking about. Several hundred pounds of gold would have been an unimaginable fortune to most people, a literal king's ransom. Assuming you didn't want to start an armed insurrection, they could have used the money to purchase the allegiance of any number of politicians. If you control the politicians, you control who they appoint to office. Get enough sympathizers in high places, and you could run America into the ground in no time."

Erika's head tilted to one side. "Not bad, but if that's what they wanted to do, why didn't it happen?"

Parker shrugged. "Beats me. Maybe they tried and failed. Or maybe that money never made it here. You ever think of that? There could be a fortune in gold bricks sitting at the bottom of the Atlantic right now."

"If we assume the shipment was delivered, and I know that's a major assumption given how often ships were lost in those days, what else could it have been used for?"

Not wanting to completely abandon his idea, Parker offered a new take. "The money could have been used to buy votes or the people who governed elections. Democracy was a new experience, so if someone paid off enough of the people who monitored elections, they could stuff the ballot boxes and make sure certain candidates were elected. Now I realize you'll say that didn't happen, but who knows? Maybe some of those handpicked candidates actually were elected, but didn't end up doing what their British supporters thought they would. Politicians aren't the most reliable people."

"You have a point. Maybe this whole plot never came to fruition."

He looked at the problem with a more modern mindset. "You know as well as I do that people have been doing the same stupid things for hundreds of years. Maybe whoever had all that gold told the wrong person, someone they couldn't trust, and was murdered. People get shot for cars, wallets, even shoes. It's not hard to imagine a few people who saw the gold getting together and killing everyone else. For your average criminal, that would have been more money than they could spend in five lifetimes."

An odd look of defeat settled over Erika's face.

"You seem disappointed that maybe this idea never panned out," Parker said. "I didn't think you'd be rooting for England."

"No, it's not that. I don't like the open-endedness of all this." Erika tapped a finger on the desk. "You'd think someone somewhere along the line would have mentioned all that gold or this plot if they knew about it."

"Keeping your mouth shut would be the best way to stay alive, if you ask me. You know what they say about two people keeping a secret."

"It only works if one of them is dead. Thank you, Captain Obvious."

The stress of the past few days was getting to them both. He wrapped his arms around her slender waist, pulling her close. "We've had an action-packed weekend so far. This is amazing, everything we found, but we didn't come here for this. It's supposed to be a vacation, remember?"

Her lithe frame rested on his chest as a great sigh escaped from between her lips. "You're right. I'm sorry, I just get so caught up in this kind of stuff. It really is amazing."

"I agree. However, it's been sitting around for two hundred years. A few more days won't matter."

She shoved him away, a new bounce in her step. "You're right. I'll review everything we've found on Monday, back in my office where I have the proper equipment. No more Revere stuff the rest of the weekend."

As she stepped into the bathroom and the shower turned on, Parker couldn't help but think that regardless of her intentions, Erika had made a promise she couldn't keep.

Chapter 21

Boston, Massachusetts

Nigel Stirling and Spencer Drake sat around a mahogany table, framed by the overstuffed leather club seats Spencer had imported from England. The room was designed like a nineteenth century men's club, a respite from the intense world he inhabited every day. In front of both sat a crystal tumbler of single malt scotch. On the table were two video screens. One displayed the digital image of Chancellor of the Exchequer Colin Moore, and on the other was their group's fourth member. Cigar smoke curled to the ceiling twenty feet overhead.

"Thank you, Liz. That will be all."

Drake's secretary sauntered from the room, Nigel Stirling fixing her with a lecherous gaze.

"Quite a whelp you have there, Drake. Damn fine bit of scenery."

"She serves a purpose."

Seated at the head of the table, Nigel Stirling quickly lost all traces of levity.

"Gentlemen, we are gathered here today to discuss the next phase of our plan. As you are well aware, the operation in Washington was a smashing success." Drake dipped his head in agreement. He hadn't the foggiest clue how the assassin had managed to do it, but after killing the Treasury secretary, the man had vanished without a trace. "As one era ends, so a new one begins. Allow me to be the first to congratulate you on your imminent appointment, Mr. Secretary."

Stirling's comment was directed to the video screen on which was displayed the face of the fourth attendee. From his home in Washington, Deputy Secretary of the Treasury Gerard Webster addressed the room.

89

"Thank you, Nigel, and let me say that my reign will be most memorable. I expect to hear from the president any minute now."

"The time is upon us," Nigel continued. "Two hundred years of hard work and sacrifice will be rewarded in the coming months."

As ridiculous as it sounded, Drake knew that Nigel Stirling was correct. A plan laid out by their forefathers centuries ago was finally coming to fruition.

Spencer Drake knew the story well. In 1781, King George III had funded an operation conceived by Lord Ramsey Fawkes, the sole purpose of which was to undermine the fledgling United States economy in hopes of destroying any chances the country had at successfully establishing itself on the world stage. Lord Fawkes, along with a select few associates, had used the money provided by King George to establish a financial institution in America. That organization had evolved over the ensuing decades, ultimately becoming what today was known as Aldrich Securities.

The initial members had ensured that each successive generation of leaders had not only been educated regarding both their origins and the stated mission, but also embraced the ideas upon which the group had been founded. While not direct descendants of either Lord Fawkes or his comrades, all three men shared one critical component.

They had all been educated at that most British of schools, Eton. Known as "the chief nurse of England's statesman," the independent school brought together some of the most distinguished and recognizable names in the realm. Such an environment was rife with patriotic, impressionable lads, the most intelligent of whom were quickly identified by Nigel Stirling in his role as honorary ambassador.

As the Stirling family was the largest private donor in school history, Nigel, like his father before him, had been appointed an honorary seat on the board for life. This position allowed him nearly unfettered access to Eton's pupils, a privilege he utilized in his constant quest to identify the best and brightest young men. Once targeted, each boy was subjected to a carefully constructed indoctrination period, all the while never suspecting such a process was underway. During the formative teen years spent at Eton, a promising student might find himself to be the beneficiary of an inordinate amount of extra attention and educational opportunity, all of which served to mold the young minds into powerful tools for Stirling's use.

In addition to currying favor with the pupil, Stirling would impart his personal view of American and British relations on the impressionable boy, ultimately convincing him that the United States was not Britain's closest ally, as most of her Majesty's citizens believed. Stirling would convince the young man that the United States was actually responsible for Britain's two-hundred-year decline as a world leader, the main reason England was no longer considered to be a world leader in any true sense of the phrase.

Stirling knew that were it not for the infernal colonists who had fancied themselves to be above their true station in life, England would never have suffered such an unprecedented fall from her perch atop the world order.

Forced to mobilize their armed forces in dealing with the rebellion, Britain had overextended herself, exposing weakness for the first time in centuries. Other power-hungry nations, most notably the damned French, were drawn like sharks to blood and redoubled their efforts to destroy the monarchy. Facing a shortage of capital, an inexorable decline had ensued, culminating with the previously unimaginable period during World War II when Britain had been forced to rely on US intervention to halt the Third Reich's advance. Stirling, and those before him in this crusade for justice, had never forgotten who was responsible for their fall.

A crucial part of utilizing Eton's unparalleled resources was that the school's board of regents, including the Head Master, had no idea of Stirling's true purpose. If a pupil latched on with Stirling, took to his beliefs, he would be considered for indoctrination into the group's fold, all within plain view of the unsuspecting Head Master.

By consensus, the group never numbered more than five active members. Any larger, and they risked not only discovery, but also a dilution of direction. Neither could be risked.

Nigel Stirling leaned to the monitor. "I trust you will ensure the government cannot disrupt our plans this time."

Gerard Webster adjusted his tie as he spoke. "I can promise you that the federal government will take a decidedly hands-off policy in dealing with any future economic crises. The socialist tendencies of my predecessor have been banished to the history books in which they belong. The same history books that will soon contain the account of America's newest financial disaster."

Such words issued by the leader of all monetary policy for the United States, warmed Drake's heart. These men alone knew how close they had come to destroying the American economy over the past two centuries. Each time their efforts had been thwarted.

They would not fail again.

"And I can assure you," Colin Moore chimed in, "that Her Majesty's government will forcefully suggest that any proposal by Secretary Webster be followed to the letter."

"Thank you, Colin. My secretary has just informed me the president will be calling in ten minutes."

Drake said, "Well done, Gerard, well done. Before you go, allow me to update you as to our progress."

Ten minutes later, Gerard Webster had to take the president's call.

"I look forward to our next conversation, gentlemen."

His well-coiffed visage disappeared from view. Before Drake could speak, a soft knock sounded on his office door.

"What is it?"

Liz poked her head into the office.

"Tom Becker from security just gave me a message. Said you had to see it immediately."

Drake jumped from his chair and grabbed the slip of paper. Apparently the tap on Parker Chase's phone had yielded an unexpected result.

"Well, this is interesting. It appears that Parker Chase was just on the phone with an Aldrich employee, one Benjamin Flood."

The further into the report he read, the more Spencer's heart began to race. Stirling must have sensed his reaction.

"What does it say, Drake?"

"This can't be."

"Dammit, man, what are you blabbering about?"

Drake's knuckles were white with tension.

"Parker Chase called my employee today. He and Mr. Flood are old schoolmates, and as we know, Chase was at the Revere House." Both men were well aware of the arrangement their group had with the Revere House management. "During their conversation, Chase told Mr. Flood that he accidentally damaged a wooden artifact and discovered something hidden inside. Nigel, there was something in that drawer on the ground. Chase and his girlfriend found a letter."

Despite his advanced age, Nigel Stirling jumped from his chair.

"What did it say?"

"I don't know. Chase never mentioned anything specific, just generalities."

"We must find out what it said." Stirling was losing control. "This can't be, Spencer, we can't have this. We must recover that letter. Do you realize what could happen if we are discovered?"

Spencer grabbed Stirling by his bony shoulders.

"Get hold of yourself. Listen to the entire report."

Nigel sank back into his chair, his skin the pallor of a ghost. "Please excuse me." He took a deep, ragged breath. "Pray continue."

Spencer cleared his throat. "I understand the shock you must be feeling, but we did suspect that an American agent may have infiltrated the king's circle during the planning stage, may have learned what Lord Fawkes intended to orchestrate. Unfortunately, this bit of skullduggery has chosen a most inopportune moment to reveal itself. We must not be deterred."

Nigel nodded in agreement.

"As I was saying," Spencer continued, "Parker Chase never mentioned exactly what was contained in the letter he located. He did tell Mr. Flood that he located two additional intelligence reports, both prepared by the Midnight Rider, as they call him. Paul Revere."

The reaction was immediate.

"Revere? I thought he was an ignorant craftsman. Fawkes never mentioned him as a possible spy."

Since the inception of their mission, stories had been passed down from generation to generation, many coming from the lips of Lord Fawkes himself. One of the most incendiary regarded the possibility that a spy had infiltrated Fawkes' group, an American confidante who had passed along word of their plans. If this was true, it would explain their repeated failures over the past centuries.

Stirling's gaze was unfocused as he spoke. "I've never heard Revere's name mentioned as the spy. We knew he was there, of course, but no one ever suspected him."

"Nonetheless"-Drake had to keep him on track-"it seems he was the culprit, and even now is back to haunt us."

Stirling came back to the present. "Institute round-the-clock surveillance on Mr. Flood. If he meets with or speaks to this Parker Chase again, we must know."

"Agreed. His phone is already tapped. I'll get a surveillance team on him immediately."

"I would also initiate an attempt to obtain the documents in question," Nigel suggested. "Regardless of what is contained in these reports, if we can suppress their distribution, the issue will be moot. No one will believe mere hearsay from a girl's mouth, even if she is an Ivy League professor. Do you have any men within Aldrich who are capable?"

The thought of putting his white collar espionage team into action warmed Drake's heart. The securities business had grown infinitely more cutthroat over the past decade, an inevitable evolution considering the immense profits at stake. Unwilling to risk falling behind in the revenue race, Drake had quietly begun employing a select team of former criminals adept at obtaining information through illegitimate channels.

These men weren't typical bank robbers. Each of them was highly educated, ruthlessly efficient and morally bankrupt. For the right price, they could obtain any type of information Drake required, either through hacking a rival firm's computer network, or through the more traditional method of breaking and entering. Several times over the past few years an immense, immediate profit by Aldrich Securities could be directly attributed to the work of their specialized skills.

"I have just the team."

"Excellent. I look forward to reviewing Mr. Revere's documents." With surprising grace, Nigel Stirling hopped from his chair and headed to the wet bar. "Moving on. I've arranged a call with Sheik bin Khan to discuss the next phase of our operation. Now that a Treasury secretary who is more suitable to our intentions is in the White House, bin Khan's cooperation is crucial. Thank goodness he hates America, because even we don't have enough money to bribe a sheik."

Ice cubes clinked on crystal as Stirling swirled his replenished drink in one hand. "He is due to call in thirty minutes. Is that sufficient time to initiate the surveillance and reclamation operations?"

"More than enough." Spencer picked up the phone and spoke softly for several minutes, consulting the biographical pages of Parker Chase and Erika Carr as he spoke. "It's done." The phone clicked down with finality. "If Ms. Carr does in fact have intelligence reports written by Paul Revere, we will have them shortly."

Stirling saluted him with an upraised glass. "I am most interested in their contents. Also, I hope that this Mr. Flood is not a vital member of your team?"

"No one who can't be replaced."

"Glad to hear it. If he is more involved than we suspect, Mr. Flood and his collegiate associates may soon meet with an untimely end."

Apparently the old codger wasn't getting soft on him after all.

Chapter 22

At nine o'clock the next morning, millions of televisions tuned in to hear the president's announcement regarding the untimely death of Treasury Secretary Gordon Daniels. Little was known other than that Daniels had collapsed while playing golf and paramedics had been unable to revive him. A nation waited for answers, citizens concerned for the future and wary of who would lead them there.

One man who was not worried, however, was Spencer Drake. He and his associates had received a message from Gerard Webster confirming what they had hoped. The president was going to appoint Webster as secretary of the Treasury. The news had come immediately following their call with Sheik bin Khan, who had agreed to proceed with the plan.

It was all coming together. When Drake and Stirling had presented their plan to Gerard Webster, the lynchpin to the entire operation had been securing the cooperation of Sheik bin Khan. At first, they had been stumped. How do you persuade a man who has everything? Only after Drake's research team had done some digging into bin Khan's background had they uncovered the truth about his past, about how his parent's deaths were indirectly tied to the United States' support of Israel. Once they discovered that bin Khan did indeed blame America, actually harbored a great hatred for the Western superpower, their course had been set. To obtain his aid, Drake had given him an opportunity that money couldn't buy.

Revenge.

A chance to avenge his parents' death, to strike a blow to the great

American machine that, bin Khan believed, had run rampant over his countrymen and destroyed their way of life. Drake personally thought the man was crazy, but he wasn't going to argue.

The plan was beautiful in its simplicity. As chairman of the UAE, bin Khan controlled one hundred billion barrels of proven oil reserves. All he had to do was make sure the oil kept flowing at a measured pace and that production didn't increase. As long as he ensured that the amount of oil produced remained constant over the next several months, America would experience a financial crisis the likes of which had not been seen in generations. The sheik had assured Drake that his influence extended well beyond the borders of the UAE. If he wished the supply to remain at certain levels, it would.

Drake's thoughts were interrupted as the president appeared on his television.

"Ladies and gentleman, President Harrison Knox."

Harrison Knox walked on stage, his lanky frame instantly recognizable. The former naval officer was a veteran of three tours in Vietnam. Knox's salt and pepper hair was longer than in his days at the Academy, but he hadn't gained a pound. A jaw chiseled from stone was his defining feature, the blaring pronouncement that preceded him through every doorway. Movie stars dreamed of jaws like that. You could crack rocks on it.

The president carried himself like a man who knew exactly what he was doing, an easy self-confidence born of experience and success. On the screen, his other distinctive feature demanded your attention. Icy gray eyes grabbed you in a chokehold, demanding to be heard.

"Good morning. As you are likely aware, Treasury Secretary Gordon Daniels passed away yesterday. The cause of death is still unknown, though at this time foul play is not suspected."

Drake grinned. Whoever he'd hired had been damn good.

"Secretary Daniels' unfortunate passing necessitates the need for a new Cabinet appointment. After careful consideration, it is my pleasure to announce that Deputy Secretary Gerard Webster has been chosen to fill the position, effective immediately."

Before his words finished reverberating through the air, a dozen hands shot up. The president's chief of staff pointed to one. "Go ahead."

"Mr. President, considering how Gerard Webster has been critical of your financial reform programs, will you and Mr. Webster be able to jointly address the issues America faces as we rebound from the recession?"

President Knox didn't flinch. "Mr. Webster is committed to doing what's best for America, not what's best for one man. He and I share many core beliefs regarding our nation's economy, and I will value his advice as we tackle these tough issues."

A second hand clamoring for attention was rewarded.

"Mr. President, would you care to address the inevitable accusation that Gerard Webster's appointment is merely a ploy to appease certain voting blocks in this country?"

Shards of anger flew from his polar eyes.

"I don't care what accusations you make, sir, but know that Gerard and I are working together to ensure America remains as strong as ever."

As the president continued to take questions, Drake wondered for the life of him why anyone would want that job. Sure, the power was enticing, but to have your every move scrutinized, your every decision questioned? No thanks. He'd take the private sector and the freedom to do as he pleased any day.

Gerard Webster was known in political circles as a quiet critic of the recent financial bailout. He had not been in favor of keeping the struggling financial institutions afloat via a government lifeline, but not many people knew it had nothing to do with his political beliefs. No, his reasoning was far more personal than that.

On screen, Secretary of the Treasury Gerard Webster took the stage.

"First of all, let me say how honored I am by the president's appointment. I look forward to working with him to better this great nation."

A shouted question cut him off. "Do you still believe that the bailout was a mistake, Treasurer Webster?"

Two upraised hands deflected the query. "Now is not the time to address such issues. Again, I thank the president for believing in me, and look forward to serving my country in the wake of Gordon Daniels' tragic passing."

Webster walked offstage amidst the reporters' continued shouting, waving politely as he disappeared behind a curtain. Drake killed the screen, waiting. Five minutes later, his phone rang.

"Not bad, Mr. Secretary. Those vultures were out for blood."

"I hope the press bus crashes into a minefield. They're all bastards."

Webster's tone was much harsher than the pleasant man Drake had watched on screen minutes ago.

"That was nicely done, ignoring the bailout. Should give them plenty to worry about."

A woman's muffled voice came through the phone. "Yes, yes, in a minute," Webster shouted. "I'll be out in ten. Shut the door." His voice returned to normal. "Sorry about that."

"Not a problem. You are the Secretary of the Treasury, after all."

"More importantly, I'm finally in a position to bring this country to its knees. As long as the sheik follows through, America is in for a surprise." Webster changed gears. "Have you had a talk with your traders yet?"

A single piece of paper was on Spencer's desk; he studied it as he spoke. "The meeting is scheduled for today. I've invited them to have lunch with me in our conference room. No one knows what the agenda is, but I can tell you they'll be falling all over themselves to do whatever I request, as long as there aren't any layoffs."

"Will they follow through on your orders?"

"If they like the fat paychecks I sign they will. Each of them will be assigned to purchase the oil futures for one of the shell corporations we established. The money to purchase these futures is coming from our reserves, and I'll make it clear this has my full backing."

Voices once again sounded in the background. Apparently, Webster was in demand. "I said five more minutes. Thank you. As I was saying, I believe that should you hint at a personal relationship with Sheik bin Khan, no one will worry when the supply of oil remains at normal levels despite the uptick in futures purchases."

"I had considered floating word of our association."

A woman now shouted for Webster. "I'm coming. Sorry, Spencer, but I have to run. Give those traders a good show."

Webster clicked off, leaving Drake to consider the upcoming presentation to his in-house traders. His gaze drifted to an oil painting on the wall adjacent to his desk. An eighteenth-century original, the man bore a passing resemblance to Spencer. It was fitting, as the man was Drake's cousin, albeit seven generations removed. Drake enjoyed delivering his practiced monologue about the piece, inevitably astonishing his guests when he mentioned the blood relationship and the fact his ancestor had worked at the first government bank on American soil.

Liz poked her head through his door. "Mr. Drake, the traders are waiting in your conference room."

Spencer stood, ready to implement the next phase of their plan for

America's destruction. He was most interested in seeing one trader in particular: Benjamin Flood, the young man whose phone calls he had been listening to for the past day.

It may be the last time he would see Mr. Flood alive.

Chapter 23

The sky was every shade of gray imaginable, some clouds colored by a pencil, light and airy. Others threatened rain at a moment's notice, so black they sucked every bit of light from the air.

Inside Erika Carr's office, the room's sole occupant was hunched over a desk on which an oversized viewing lamp shone brightly. Erika was studying one of Paul Revere's reports, searching for any further clues written between the lines. Or anywhere else on the page, for that matter.

A harsh sigh escaped her lips.

"There's nothing else here."

Erika had been studying the documents for five solid days since she and Parker had returned from Boston. Her first goal had been to ascertain the documents were in fact legitimate. Each of the three letters had been subjected to a battery of tests which compared them to extant examples of verified eighteenth-century documents. Each had passed with flying colors.

Erika had also put on her graphologist's hat and compared the three documents with known examples of Revere's handwriting. They had been perfect matches in every case. After the paper was positively dated from Revere's lifetime, there was no question of authenticity. With those issues settled, Erika was left with a much more daunting question.

What was the scheme Revere spoke of?

Erika had decided to take what little she knew and work from there. Revere had known the plot involved America's budding financial system, specifically mentioning a man named George Simpson.

A quick search revealed that one George Simpson had been the cashier at the First Bank of the United States, which had been the central tenet of

100

US fiscal and monetary policy created by Alexander Hamilton. Despite intense resistance from Secretary of State Thomas Jefferson, the bank's charter had been signed into law by George Washington for a twenty-year term. Unsurprisingly, the bank had been located only several miles away, on South Third Street right here in Philadelphia.

Erika couldn't find exactly when George Simpson was first employed by the bank, but upon the expiration of the charter in 1811, Simpson was working as the head cashier, apparently playing an important role in the bank's development. In that era, the head cashier was a powerful figure inside a bank, one step below the owner or director. Unlike modern banks, which were normally top-heavy, burdened by the crushing weight of legions of executives with hollow titles, a head cashier in this era carried considerable clout.

"That's not good," Erika murmured to herself as she read. "If he really was a traitor, he could have done some damage."

However, she had been unable to locate any reference to a collapse or crisis involving Simpson at the First Bank. After the expiration of its charter, which was supported by the federal government, the First Bank had been purchased by legendary financier Stephen Girard. Quite the contrary, Girard Bank had, over time, morphed into Citizen's Bank, the institution whose name was plastered all over the Philadelphia Phillies baseball park. They had been anything but unsuccessful.

As she searched for any disasters that were even remotely associated with Simpson, an interesting tidbit flashed across her screen.

"Girard Bank was the principal source of government credit during the War of 1812? That doesn't sound like a group that's trying to undermine the economy."

Her cell phone buzzed, interrupting the research.

"Hello?"

"How's my favorite professor in Philadelphia?"

Her cheeks warmed at his voice.

"Lonely and frustrated, Mr. Chase. Are you here?"

"Just landed. I'm headed to the taxi line now. Should be at your office in thirty."

Parker had taken the forty-minute flight from Pittsburgh early this morning to spend the next week in Philadelphia, partly to relax and partly to help her investigate these letters.

"See you soon."

What felt like an hour later, she heard a soft knock on her office door. The sight of his boyish grin never failed to send her heart racing.

"I'm interested in some one on one tutoring."

"Maybe later. Get over here."

His muscular arms wrapped around her, drawing her close to his chest. She breathed in deeply, enjoying the soft hints of the cologne she'd bought him for Christmas.

"So what's the word on our buddy Paul? Any idea what he was talking about?"

"Well, you already know that as best I can tell the letters are authentic." She pushed him into a chair across from her and sat down. "The handwriting, the paper, everything checks out. The more important aspect of these letters, though, is a bit murkier."

"As in what Revere is talking about?"

"Exactly. Now, I've done some research on George Simpson, the man mentioned in the last letter, but didn't find much."

Parker lounged back in her visitor's chair and kicked his feet on her desk.

"So what's the deal with this Simpson guy? I've never heard of him."

"You might find this interesting. George Simpson was head cashier at the First Bank of the United States. He later worked for Stephen Girard, who started Girard Bank, which today we know as Citizen's Bank."

When she glanced up to gauge his reaction, Parker's eyes were burning a hole through her skull.

"You're kidding."

She was thoroughly confused. "About what? I'm dead serious."

He didn't respond, too busy grabbing for his phone.

"Parker, what are you talking about?"

"Hold on. I have to call Ben."

What did Ben Flood have to do with this? Parker had spoken to him in Boston, said he and Erika had found some amazing artifacts, but other than that he wasn't involved.

"Ben. What's up? Nothing. Listen, remember that story you told me the other day? About your boss and that painting he was bragging about? Tell it again, to Erika."

Parker laid the phone on her desk.

"Erika?" Ben Flood's distinct Boston accent came through the speaker.

"Hi Ben. What's Parker talking about?"

"Yesterday we had an interesting meeting with our CEO, Spencer Drake. He's a character, blue blood, educated at Eton, the whole nine yards. Anyway, during the meeting he made it a point to show us an oil portrait hanging in his office. To me it's just some old geezer, but apparently not only was the portrait an original, painted by some semi-famous artist, it was also Drake's relative."

"That's interesting. What was the guy's name?"

"You know, I don't remember. That's not important, though. The whole point of the story is that this guy was supposedly the first cashier in the United States. You should have seen Drake's face. He thought he was the coolest cat in town."

Her back went rigid. "And you say that your boss is related to the man in the painting?"

"Yeah, claims he's a cousin or something like that. I'd never heard of his supposed cousin, but Drake was all about it."

"Ben, if I told you the man's name, would you remember it?"

"Maybe. You've actually heard of this guy?"

Her nose almost touched Parker's as they leaned over the phone.

"Was it George Simpson?"

Silence for a few beats, then, "You know what, I think that was it. Damn, Erika, you should be on *Jeopardy*. You're right, it was George Simpson."

"Ben, thanks for the call. I really appreciate it."

She could hear the confusion in his voice. "Sure, glad to help. Hey Parker, you have a minute?"

"Sure. What's up?"

Parker picked up the phone and held it to his ear. Erika didn't notice him anymore, her mind whirring at fantastic speeds. Within seconds a myriad of information about Ben's boss filled her monitor.

Spencer Drake was the CEO of Aldrich Securities, the largest investment bank and securities firm in Boston, and on par with the larger New York firms. Educated at Eton independent school in England, he'd completed his collegiate studies in the States at Yale, a classmate of future president George W. Bush.

Piercing green eyes stared back at her, contained within an angular face that was well complemented by the severe black suit he wore. A full head of sculpted hair covered his head, no doubt dyed to keep out the gray. Most telling of all were the razor thin lips bearing just a hint of a smirk. Spencer

Drake appeared every bit the arrogant, stately CEO who controlled over a half trillion dollars.

Erika immediately disliked him.

His organization was the oldest financial firm in Boston, founded in 1838. According to the company's website, they had been chartered by Aldrich Drake, who was an enormously wealthy entrepreneur of the time, with holdings in shipping, logging, mining and railroads. Aldrich had shrewdly invested in the burgeoning manufacturing industry and made a fortune supplying the Union Army during the Civil War.

Over the next century and a half, Aldrich Securities had experienced consistent growth, expanding their influence to include investment banking, management, securities and other services. Amongst their institutional clients were several of the largest corporations in the country. It appeared Spencer Drake was a powerful man.

"Let me know if you hear anything else. I'll keep an eye on it." Parker dropped his phone on the desk and interrupted her research. "Can you believe that? You know what this means, don't you?"

She had dealt with his enthusiasm before. "No, we don't know what it means. We may suspect what it means, but we don't know for sure."

His arms flew into the air. "How can you say that? Paul Revere writes a letter that specifically identifies George Simpson as a traitor. Lo and behold, we find out Simpson is related to the CEO of a securities firm in Boston. First of all, do you have any idea how much money it takes to start a bank? Even in 1838 you're talking about a fortune, maybe a million dollars, which in those days was an enormous amount of money."

She loved his energy, but the problem was controlling it. "I'm not saying you're wrong. In fact, I hope you're right, and this is the link we need. But right now I have to do some research to verify these claims. It won't do us any good to jump into anything without being sure."

"Stupid academics. No excitement about anything."

She suppressed a grin as he flopped back into the chair across from her. "Do you know anything about this Spencer Drake character? He's one wealthy man, for starters."

Parker shot back up in his chair. "You reminded me. Ben told me about some unusual stuff that's going on at Aldrich."

"Such as?"

"The meeting he had with Drake was about the futures markets, specifically which areas Drake wants the traders to focus on."

A blank stare was her only response. "Try it again, in English this time."

A playful grin flitted across his face. "All right class, today's lesson is about futures trading. Please be seated."

She was not amused.

"We'll start at the beginning. Ben is a trader with Aldrich Securities. You know what the stock market is?" A pencil flew at his head. "Thought so. Futures are basically like stocks, except they are based in the, wait for it...future. For example, if Ben thinks the price of oil is going to go up in the future, he may choose to buy oil futures now at a price that he predicts will be lower than the actual price of oil down the road."

Math was a subject she hated because, simply, it was boring. "So if he's buying the oil now, he plans on using it later, right?"

"Not exactly. Ben's never going to use the oil he bought. He's only buying it to make a profit."

"All right, so he buys these oil futures today, for some fixed date in the future, correct?"

"Yes."

"And in the future, whenever that is, he will own a stock, or future, of oil that is actually lower in price than the current market value?"

"More or less. You see, Ben probably won't hold on to that specific future until that day comes around. In all likelihood, he's going to sell it to someone else, another trader who's looking to make money on it."

That was a curveball. "Why would he sell it to someone else if he thinks that he'll make money on it in the future? That sounds like he's giving away guaranteed profits."

"Not really, for a couple reasons. First, nothing is guaranteed. Just ask your real estate agent. Second, you have to remember money is fluid, and no trader wants all their capital tied up in one stock or commodity. If Ben thinks he found a better deal in a different area, he might sell his oil futures to a new trader, take whatever profit he can get, and re-invest."

"I guess that makes sense. So what's the big deal about this meeting he had with Spencer Drake?"

Parker stood from his chair and began pacing back and forth. "All that stuff about futures was just background. Here's what has my attention. The meeting Drake presided over was about oil futures, a subject on which you are now a certified expert. What was interesting, and bear with me, is that Drake, who you must remember is a highly respected financier, has just instructed his traders to do something very unconventional."

"What do you mean by unconventional?"

Parker struggled for the right words. "As in the implications of what the traders have been instructed to do are that Drake either knows something that no one else does, or he's up to some shady business. Here's why." Parker grabbed a piece of paper and drew a rectangle. "Imagine this is the United States. Right now"-he put a dot in the upper right corner-"we're here, in Philadelphia. Ben is just above us, in Boston."

So far she followed.

"Ben has just been told that he is in charge of investing money for a company that didn't exist last week. It's incorporated here, in the Bahamas." Parker put a dot below the rectangle.

"Thanks for the geography lesson, but what does this have to do with anything?"

"Maybe nothing, maybe everything. When you hear the rest of the story you can decide for yourself. I just wanted you to see that the money he's using, and the profit he hopes to generate, is stationed offshore."

Her face lit up with recognition. "You think he's skirting the IRS?"

"It's how I would do it. Not saying that I would, but if I were a crook, I'd use the Bahamas."

"Remind me to start opening your mail."

"Anyway," Parker continued, "Ben has been told to invest money which belongs to an offshore corporation that didn't exist last week in oil futures. Not just invest, mind you, but to invest aggressively. As in spend every dollar he has on futures."

The fog of confusion had again descended. "Why is that noteworthy? Maybe Drake thinks that the price of oil is going to go up soon."

"He very well may, but logic would dictate that the price of oil will never get too high or too low, a theory which I'll explain in a moment. For now, just trust me. What I'm worried about is that a financier of Drake's caliber would never do this without being absolutely certain he was right."

The light in her head turned on. "You think he has inside information."

He put his hand out for a high five. "Correct again. It just doesn't make sense for Drake to do this. Of course, I don't have any proof, but there are unwritten rules to investing, and he's breaking one of the basics. And you can be damn sure I'm not the only person who's going to notice."

"But you yourself are working with insider information. If Ben hadn't told you about the private meeting he just attended, you'd have no idea what was going on."

His face dropped. Score one for Erika.

"One other thing you should know," he continued, ignoring her comment, "is that this isn't the first strange news I've seen about oil futures recently. Just after we returned from Boston, one of my trading buddies here in Philadelphia told me his firm had noted an unexplained up-tick in futures purchasing. I did some research, and guess who's doing the vast majority of the buying?"

"Aldrich Securities," Erika said.

"Bingo. Now put that together with what Ben just told us, and you have one company investing a boatload of cash in the oil futures market. Which, not to confuse you, isn't crazy because of the amount of money. It's crazy because, as any good gambler will tell you, it's smart to hedge your bets. All of Aldrich's money is predicting the price of oil will go up and up."

Here she was on more familiar ground. After the recent explosion in gas prices, she'd learned a little bit about the industry. "Is it bad because, contrary to what you'd think, the oil companies don't want the price to get too high?"

"Well done, Dr. Carr. Oil companies like it high, but not too high. If the price of oil gets too high, people and companies begin to curb their usage and purchase less of it. When people aren't buying oil, the oil companies aren't making any money."

"Which is why it doesn't make sense for Aldrich to gamble so much on the price going anywhere but up."

"Correct again. If the price of oil gets so high that consumption declines, the prudent course of action for suppliers would be to increase their output so that oil is plentiful. More available oil should slow any rapid increase in price. Once they stabilize the price, more oil will be sold, and their profits will rise."

Which in Erika's mind brought them back to square one. "So why is Drake doing this?"

His arms spread out wide. "That's the billion-dollar question. I have no idea. I doubt anyone outside of his inner circle does. However, what I want to know, more than why he's investing money so foolishly, is what relation does Aldrich Securities have with the letters we found."

She considered his question, her gaze falling to Paul Revere's espionage reports on her desk. Right now, she didn't have a clue.

Chapter 24

Overhead, the sun was shining on Boston, another beautiful summer day beckoning the legions of suit-clad business warriors out of their corporate prisons. Spencer Drake wasn't exactly working in a cell, but even he felt the warm weather's irresistible pull and was considering whether or not to jump into his helicopter and head up to Martha's Vineyard for the weekend.

Liz and her brilliant raven hair poked through his office door to interrupt his thoughts. "Tom Becker is outside. Says it's important."

"Send him in."

His head of security appeared, mouth pinched, eyes slits on his weathered face.

"Tom, what's the matter? You appear troubled."

A thin sheaf of papers was held in one hand. "I've brought you the latest correspondence from Mr. Flood. Sir, I'm not sure what it means, but he's been speaking with Parker Chase again, and the subject matter is very, well, very unusual."

Spencer tore the papers from Becker's hand. His face grew hot with anger as he read.

"Thank you, Mr. Becker. That will be all for now."

Becker heard the overt menace in his tone and disappeared.

"This cannot happen," Drake muttered, head resting in one hand.

Before he dialed Nigel Stirling, Drake reread the report on his desk, the implications of what Parker Chase and Benjamin Flood had discussed hitting him like a prizefighter's uppercut.

It was only a few short days ago that he had called Flood and a group of other traders into his conference room, detailing their instructions for purchasing oil futures in record numbers. Each man had been given primary control of a newly established offshore entity along with two hundred million dollars to spend on the commodity as they saw fit. Not only had he instructed the group that this was to be a private venture, with secrecy taking top priority, he had also explained that if word leaked about their plans, profits would be decimated.

It was all a charade, but the mere fact that one of his employees would so quickly and blatantly disregard his instructions infuriated him. Now Parker Chase and Erika Carr not only knew of Aldrich's plans, they were aware that several hundred years ago a covert mission had been undertaken by agents of the Crown to decimate the American economy. The likelihood of them connecting the two events was infinitesimal, but there could not have been a worse time for this to occur. Not when their plans were in motion, when they had finally secured a place within the halls of American power strong enough to effect truly disastrous consequences.

He only hoped Stirling would agree with his drastic proposal.

"Nigel. We need to talk. Immediately."

Stirling must have been on his boat, as seagull cries were audible in the background, along with the giggling of his overpriced escorts. They might have been stupid, but Nigel certainly had an eye for the pretty ones.

"Spencer, what's the matter? You should be out enjoying yourself."

"I'm not joking around. We have a problem."

Five minutes later, Stirling agreed. "It defies belief. What do you think we should do?"

"To me, there's no question. First, we obtain the letters. I want to see what is written in the reports, verify their legitimacy."

"Agreed."

"Two, we must eliminate Mr. Flood," Spencer continued. "He is too close to this operation, has too much access. An unfortunate accident would seal the leak nicely."

"I trust you can handle it. Call the asset we utilized earlier."

"I'll do so immediately."

Stirling clicked off, leaving Drake with a sense of unease in the pit of his stomach. Few men could make Spencer Drake nervous. A professional assassin was one of them.

Drake's office was swept for bugs every morning. The phone lines on which he spoke were secured with the best encryption system money could buy. He had bulletproof windows specially coated to disrupt the sound waves emanating from within, eliminating the chance his words could be intercepted with laser vibration microphones. Despite all this, he punched a button on his desk, lowering the window blinds. He also locked his office door. The slip of paper on which he'd written the assassin's contact number was locked in his wall safe, hidden behind the oil painting of his ancestor, George Simpson.

Steady yourself, old boy. It's just a phone call.

Chapter 25

Boston, Massachusetts

Two days ago, Ben Flood had been given the most unusual assignment of his career, and he was starting to wonder if his CEO was off his rocker. He'd just spent an entire day scouring the market for places to spend a brand new company's money, and there had been no shortage of takers. It didn't even seem like Drake cared how much the shares cost, just that the money was spent and the market was stimulated.

Out of curiosity, Ben had done some research, combing through his usual channels in search of any indication that oil was going to go up. Every single person he'd spoken with, people he trusted, people with decades of experience, had been unable to validate Drake's message. Same story with all the websites he'd checked and projections he'd run.

Nothing indicated an imminent rise in the price of oil. Calling Drake's directive strange was an understatement. In fact, and this is what he needed to tell Parker about, the spike in future oil prices could be directly attributed to Aldrich's massive spending. No one outside of the company would know it, but Spencer Drake had single-handedly sent the value of these futures skyward. Right now the price change wasn't drastic, but it wouldn't take much more for the media to get wind of the shift, and once they started cranking out doomsday stories to sell papers, watch out.

When Ben had last spoken to Parker, he'd been fascinated with his story, straight off the big screen. If Ben hadn't known the guy since their college days, he'd have a hard time believing that Parker and Erika had unearthed a series of long-lost espionage reports prepared by Paul Revere. How they'd found themselves in the business of unearthing lost artifacts he had no idea, but it sure made for entertaining conversation.

He thought Parker would find his latest bit of insider information just as juicy. His old friend picked up after one ring.

"Hello?"

"Hey bud, what's up?"

"Not much, Benny boy. I'm getting ready to head to Philadelphia. Took next week off to spend time with Erika."

"Find any more hidden letters from our forefathers?"

"I wish. No, Erika's been researching those letters, but hasn't made much progress. I pretty much leave that stuff to her. She's the Ivy League professor, after all."

"Do you remember what I was telling you about the meeting I had with Spencer Drake, our CEO?"

"For a billionaire, he has some strange ideas about investing."

"You don't know the half of it. I was talking to one of the other traders about this whole operation, and guess what he told me? When he was waiting outside Drake's office for another meeting, he overhead Spencer on a conference call. Drake likes to shout on the phone, so even though the door was closed my friend could still make out what was being said."

Ben's theatrical pause was met with silence and finally a long sigh.

"All right. Who was on the phone?"

"A who's who of the financial industry. The CEOs of Bank of America, Goldman Sachs and J.P. Morgan."

That grabbed Parker's attention. "Wow. It doesn't get any bigger than that. What were they talking about?"

"Get this. My buddy said Drake was playing salesman, encouraging all of them to invest in oil. Apparently he thinks oil is going nowhere but up, and he was convincing all of them they'd make a fortune if they invested heavily in the futures and derivatives markets for black gold. And you know what Warren Buffet said about derivatives."

He could hear a tapping noise come through the phone as Parker considered this.

"*Derivatives are financial weapons of mass destruction.* Boy, was he ever right. I didn't see that coming, but I guess if Drake believes he has a winner, he'd exploit every angle. I suppose it's not that strange for him to share the information. Maybe he has a vendetta against foreign investment firms and wants his buddies to make a killing while everyone else misses the boat."

"I'd agree with you, except for one thing. My buddy said Drake was encouraging all of them to use depositors' money."

The silence that ensued spoke volumes.

"Are you certain?"

"My friend has done this for twenty years. He's positive."

"But that's crazy. Proprietary trading is going to be illegal soon."

Ben knew Parker would never have suspected that little nugget. Proprietary trading, which was using depositors' money to buy securities or make trades, was scheduled to be illegal in the near future after passage of the Dodd Frank Act, a piece of reactionary legislation born out of the recent recession. Every institution that practiced commercial banking was steering clear of the practice.

"Questionable ethics aside, it's not technically illegal yet. However, I agree. Unless they plan on selling any accumulated assets quickly, there's no reason to do it."

"That's not even considering the mess they'd be in if they lost money. Ben, you know as well as I do that there aren't any guarantees in this business. If Drake and his CEO cronies lose depositors' money, they'll have to replace the lost funds from company coffers. Not a great way in impress investors, and you can be damn sure banking clients don't want their money invested in anything as risky as oil futures or derivatives."

"Which is why I called you. There has been some seriously strange stuff going on over the past few days. What it means, I have no idea, but I thought you'd want to know about it."

"I definitely do. Thanks for the update."

Ben had been out to lunch, and as he navigated the crowded sidewalks in Boston's financial district, the gleaming steel edifice of Aldrich Securities headquarters loomed in front of him. "Hey, I have to go, but let me know if you guys learn anything else about those letters."

"Will do."

Ben slid the phone back into his suit jacket, his mind racing as he tried to make sense of his current assignment. He didn't know what Spencer Drake was up to, but as long as the paychecks kept rolling in, he would follow orders.

Thirty stories above the sparkling glass door that Ben had just walked through, Tom Becker summarized the phone call. A list containing two names was on Ben's file. If any phone conversations involving Parker Chase or Erika Carr were intercepted, Becker was to hand deliver a summary of the call to Mr. Drake immediately.

Like a good soldier, Becker dashed upstairs and found Drake in his office, engaged in a heated discussion via teleconference. Without a word, he laid the summary on Drake's desk and departed.

"Gentlemen," Spencer Drake cajoled, his voice smooth as silk, "I understand this is an unconventional method. Before you write it off, I suggest you have a look at my track record. Have I steered you wrong before?"

"No, Spencer, we can't say you have."

"So there's no reason to think I'd start now."

Drake picked up the report and scanned the first few lines. His eyes nearly flew from his head. "I must apologize, but something has come up. Perhaps we can continue our discussion this afternoon?"

"We'll be here."

Drake stabbed the phone, cutting off his counterparts. The trio of CEOs had been hesitant to follow his lead when he'd first broached the subject of proprietary trading, but they seemed to have come along over the past twenty-four hours, as he'd known they would. However, that discussion would have to wait.

An agreement had been struck with the hired gun to eliminate Mr. Flood, though the arrangement had been open-ended. It seemed that Ben Flood needed to be dealt with in a timelier manner.

Once again, the assassin's phone number was in his hands. After several rings, the call was connected. Soft breathing, but no words.

"Hello?"

"What do you want, Mr. Drake?"

The man's total neutrality was unsettling.

"I need to know when I might expect completion on our latest contract."

"The job will be finished when I am able to do so."

The guy sounded like a damn machine.

"Would it be possible to accelerate the timeline? Something has come up, and I'd prefer that this be completed as soon as possible."

The silence stretched on for so long that Drake thought they'd been disconnected. Just as he was about to repeat himself, the man responded.

"For this inconvenience, the fee will be doubled. Payable immediately."

Another million dollars was outrageous, but he didn't argue. "Agreed. I'll deposit the balance in your account today."

"Don't forget."

The connection was severed. He stared at the phone in his hand like it was a live grenade. With any luck, that would be the last time he had to talk to that lunatic, and today would be the last day Benjamin Flood worked at Aldrich Securities.

Chapter 26

Boston, Massachusetts

By the time Ben Flood left his office, the moon was full overhead. Ever since this new assignment had come down from the CEO, Ben and his counterparts hadn't been able to get away until after dark, no small feat in late May. At this hour, few people were on the streets near Aldrich Securities headquarters, most having either made it home for the night or found their way to a local bar. It was toward the latter option which Ben was headed, where he had a date planned with an enticing young lady he'd met recently.

The only problem he had was a paucity of cash. Lunch had cleaned him out, and with the legendary temperament of Boston cab drivers when a fare tried to use their credit card, he'd rather avoid the hassle. He thought there was an ATM several blocks ahead, near his favorite coffee shop. The daytime crowds had disappeared, so much so that Ben's footsteps echoed off the skyscrapers all around him. Two men walked past, headed in the other direction. The only other person on the street was an elderly man walking behind him, his cane tapping out a staccato beat on the sidewalk as the old guy marched onward, face hidden beneath a fedora.

It was kind of nice to be all alone in the middle of so much humanity.

Ahead, the darkened windows of his local java joint reflected a solitary streetlight. The massive buildings on either side kept out the moonlight, rendering his surroundings a thick shade of gray, each alley and doorway a subtle outline in the dark.

The keypad beeped as Ben entered his security code, whirred for a few seconds, and then spit out a handful of twenties.

While he waited for his money, the sharp, short taps of the old man's cane continued behind him. The noise stopped abruptly, but Ben didn't realize the old guy was right behind him until he felt the cold steel of a gun barrel against the back of his skull.

Frozen with shock, Ben's hesitation cost him his life.

He never heard the shot, but neither did anyone else. Not a single person was within two blocks when the suppressed pistol fired a round into Ben's brain, the bullet exiting through his forehead to spray blood all over the bank machine.

When police reviewed the machine's camera, they would be at a loss to explain why the elderly man who carried a cane had shot the young banker. After he pulled the trigger, the old man shuffled away, not even bothering to take the money.

Chapter 27

Philadelphia, Pennsylvania

Three hundred miles south of where Benjamin Flood's corpse lay cooling, two men sat in a parked car, eyes glued on the building in front of them.

Tonight, they planned to break inside, specifically into the office of Associate Professor of History Dr. Erika Carr. Their supervisor had instructed them to retrieve three letters from the office, each one a single sheet of paper that was several hundred years old. They didn't know why the letters were important, nor did they care. Both men worked in the security industry, and both had served in the military under Captain Thomas Becker.

After each was dishonorably discharged for different reasons, employment prospects had been bleak until Captain Becker had contacted each man separately with a unique job offer. Becker had found work in corporate security, and he was in need of a few men with a talent for acquiring information. It just so happened that these two had been trained by the government in that specific field. They may not have been the most trustworthy or honorable men, but they could crack a locked safe in short order.

Five years and several dozen "liberation" operations later, the two men sitting outside Dr. Carr's office had become Aldrich Securities' go-to option for white collar espionage. Intelligent and articulate, a large reason for their success was that these two men didn't look like criminals. Tonight each was dressed as a professor, sporting rumpled slacks and mismatched blazers. Thick glasses completed the outfit, and no one gave them a second glance when they walked inside.

Dr. Carr's cell phone had been tapped for several days now, and they knew she was out to dinner in Old City with her boyfriend. The pair of thieves ambled slowly down the hallway, pausing only briefly outside Dr. Carr's door. Shielded by his companion, one fraudulent academic used a set of lock picks to open the door lock in ten seconds, and they slipped inside, unseen.

Careful not to disturb anything, one stood watch while the other searched the office for three letters written by Paul Revere. He spied a small safe near her desk, and a grin spread across his face. The man relished a challenge.

Five minutes later, the electronic coding mechanism he carried discovered the combination. The keypad chirped softly, and a faint whirring noise told him the deadbolts had retracted. Inside the safe was a small stack of cash, maybe five grand, and several sheets of paper in protective sleeves. The top three pieces all bore the signature of one *P. Revere.*

He gently pulled the documents from the safe and slipped them in a folder. One glance at his partner confirmed they were still in the clear. Back in the hallway, the door locked behind them, they moved at a languid pace toward the parking lot. Several minutes later the pair sat in silence, headed to the airport, where a private plane waited to ferry them back to Boston.

Chapter 28

Boston, Massachusetts

A full moon sat high in the evening sky above Aldrich Securities headquarters. Yellow light bathed the city in a midsummer evening glow, most denizens of the storied town asleep. Inside a gleaming skyscraper, Spencer Drake dismissed his security chief with a wave, eyes glued to the letters on his desk.

They had been taken from Erika Carr's office less than three hours ago and were now in front of him, a first hand, detailed account of the spy who had discovered their plot to destroy America. Drake had never heard mention of Revere's presence during the formation of their forefathers' plan, though the silversmith wasn't nearly as well known then as he was today. Fortunately, for whatever reason, the documents had remained undelivered for two hundred years.

Spencer punched a code into his videoconferencing system, and a flat-screen monitor slid noiselessly from inside his desk. A secure connection was established with Nigel Stirling, who had been waiting for the call ever since Drake informed him of their successful evening mission in Philadelphia.

Nigel dispensed with any formalities. "What do they say?"

Drake read the text from each letter verbatim. Stirling's face was a stone mask as he listened, one finger tapping slowly on his own desk. After Drake was finished, Nigel finally spoke.

"Where were these letters located?"

"We liberated them from a professor's office in Philadelphia, but originally they were found scattered throughout Boston."

"Do we have any idea how she learned of their existence?"

"No, I'm afraid not. If it weren't for the intercepted phone call between her boyfriend and my employee, we would not have known about them."

Nigel's eyes turned on him with a laser focus. "What is the status of your employee?"

"It wasn't cheap, but the process has been accelerated. As soon as I hear anything, I'll pass it along."

"Suddenly his elimination has taken on some importance, wouldn't you agree? Right now, the professor and her companion could conceivably uncover our existence with the aid of Mr. Flood."

The old man must be kidding.

"Surely you don't think they would be able to follow the trail from these three letters to my office? That's over two centuries of activity, and all they have, excuse me, all they *had*, were these letters."

"The connections exist, if only one knows where to look. You know that as well as I." Nigel was right, but the odds had to be astronomical. It would be like looking for a sunken ship in the ocean without having any idea where it went down. "Simply because their chances are small is no reason to take unnecessary risk. I would advise you to ensure Mr. Flood meets with an untimely end posthaste."

"Agreed. I've also taken the liberty of accessing Parker Chase's cell phone along with Erika Carr's. With any luck, Flood's murder should derail their inquiries."

"We cannot afford any missteps now. I see that the price of oil is continuing to rise, even as we speak. This bodes well for our operation."

"It closed at just over eighty dollars per barrel. That's up twenty percent in the past week."

"And how are your efforts proceeding with convincing your colleagues to engage in proprietary trading?"

"I don't have to convince them anymore. All I do is remind them how much money I've made while they hesitated, and they dive in headfirst. If they invest their clients' billions, and at the rate they normally spend, we could be seeing record prices in days, especially once others in the market see the action and follow suit."

A vengeful tint filled Nigel's eyes. "You realize what this means, Spencer? That we will finally fulfill our obligation to king and country, putting the wretched Americans in their place."

The thought warmed Drake's heart.

"And with that in mind, I suggest that you eliminate any and all threats to our success. Two hundred years of work cannot be undone by a meddlesome teacher."

Drake had considered the idea himself. "I would have to agree. For the right price, I'm certain our man will handle it."

"Tell him to make sure those two are never heard from again."

Chapter 29

Philadelphia, Pennsylvania

A red sun was beginning to crest the horizon on a warm summer morning. Even at this hour, traffic was heavy, every main artery in and out of Philadelphia clogged. Fortunately for Erika, her apartment was less than two miles from Penn's campus, and she went against traffic the whole way. Ten minutes after she last heard Parker snoring in bed, she pulled into her office parking lot.

Last night had been wonderful, dinner out and then an evening watching movies on her couch with Parker. Not a single moment had been devoted to studying centuries-old writing, a welcome respite from the daily grind that had consumed her since they discovered the letters. Reinvigorated, her batteries were recharged for another run at uncovering the evolution of Revere's discovery.

Keys in hand, her mind was already on the hunt when she pushed the thick wooden office door open. The lights clicked on, her feet moving to the coffee machine of their own accord. She was a creature of habit, and Dr. Erika Carr began every day with the same routine. Coffee on, computer fired up, get to work.

With a steaming cup on her desk, she knelt in front of her office safe, fingers tapping out the code.

Erika's heart stopped.

Revere's letters were gone.

She fell to her knees, scraping soft skin across threadbare carpet. This wasn't possible. She'd put them away yesterday, just like she did every day when she left.

A quick inventory confirmed her fears. The letters were nowhere to be found.

Erika searched again, refusing to accept the truth. She had several thousand in cash stashed in the safe that hadn't been touched. Her passport and birth certificate were in the fireproof box, but that was it.

She didn't move until the dull ache in her knees turned to razor sharp pains shooting up each leg. A teary sigh escaped her lips as she stood, her entire body numb.

This wasn't fair. It wasn't right. She and Parker had worked so hard, had found the priceless artifacts on their own, and now they were gone.

Right now she wanted to cry, wanted to curl up in a ball and scream, but that wouldn't solve anything. Instead, she decided to take a page out of Parker's book and get angry. He always said that harnessing his anger was what helped him, focusing the energy to help achieve his goal.

Well, right now she was pissed off to the point she could run through a brick wall.

Parker's voice was thick with sleep when he answered her call. "Tell me you're playing hooky today."

"Parker."

That was all it took, and he knew it was serious.

"Are you all right?"

"They're gone."

"What? What's gone?"

"The letters. All three of them are gone."

Silence filled the phone. "It appears Paul Revere was right."

She related the story of her discovery, of both her office and the safe being locked, letters missing but the money left behind.

"So whoever took them knew what they were looking for. This isn't good."

"Of course it's not good. No one will ever know what we found. I have pictures of the letters, but that won't mean anything."

"No, Erika, I mean this isn't good for us. Think about it. Someone knows what we found. Other than Ben, who did we tell? I sure didn't say anything."

"Neither did I. None of my colleagues knew about it."

"So that means that either Ben spilled the beans, or we're being spied on."

She flashed back to several months ago, to the discovery that her office, the same one from which Revere's letters had been stolen, was under surveillance by an unknown group. Listening devices had been on her desk phone, her computer, and even on her coat.

Her chest tightened as she spoke.

"How could that be? Why would anyone care about these letters enough to steal them?"

Ever the analytical one, Parker asked, "How much would those be worth on the open market? Would people pay for them?"

"Well, they were signed by Paul Revere and written to Alexander Hamilton, so yes, collectors would be interested. But the type of people who would want those letters aren't going to burgle my office to get them. My guess is they'd bring around ten thousand at auction, maybe a little more."

"So not enough to risk a jail sentence over."

"Not at all. And more to the point, how did anyone even know they existed?"

The sound of sheets rustling came over the phone.

"Erika, I'm on my way over. Hang up, lock your office, and get around other people. I'll be there soon."

The hair on her neck stood when he clicked off. Suddenly doubting the security of her professional sanctuary, Erika grabbed her purse and rushed out the door, only pausing to lock it. Outside the building, a steady stream of students and faculty scurried about the manicured grounds, and it was to this comforting assembly that she headed.

Ten minutes later a taxi roared up, tires squealing to a stop. Parker threw several bills at the driver and ran to her.

"Everything all right?" Genuine concern radiated from his eyes.

"Yes, I'm fine."

"Show me your office. We need to call the campus police and report a break-in. Does your building have security cameras?"

"I know they have them at the entrances, but I'm not sure about inside. There aren't many crimes committed in the history building."

"At least not many that are reported. This is twice in the past year that people have broken into your office."

Above the main building entrance, Erika spotted the telltale black orbs containing cameras. Inside the hallway, they found nothing.

"Damn. Maybe those things took a picture of whoever did this."

She picked up her desk phone and dialed zero. A robotic operator answered.

"Directory."

"I need to speak with the police."

"Hold please."

Seconds later a much more serious voice answered.

"University police."

"Hello, my name is Erika Carr. I'm a professor in the history department, and I need to report a robbery."

"Is the robbery in progress, Dr. Carr?"

"No, I discovered it this morning when I arrived."

"When and where did this robbery take place?"

She relayed the details, and the officer promised to send someone over immediately.

"Hey, before the cops get here, is there anything you don't want them to find?"

What kind of a question was that?

"What do you mean?" She cocked her head to one side and studied him. "Do you think I have something illegal in here?"

"No, that's not what I'm getting at. The police are going to go over this office with a fine-toothed comb, and I'm just wondering if there's anything from earlier this year that we should keep to ourselves."

He actually had a point. One night, several months ago, there had been a large duffel bag filled with automatic weapons, ammunition, and high-tech espionage equipment on her floor.

"No, nothing's still here. Nick took everything with him when we left for Mt. Vernon."

The thought of Nicholas Dean's towering clean-cut visage carried with it a sense of security, and she wondered if it would be prudent to call their friend. He was a CIA agent, after all. If anyone could help, it was him.

"Good. The last thing we need is for the cops to find a loaded weapon in here. We have enough problems as it is."

Outside of her office door she could see the parking lot, and a University squad car pulled up, lights flashing. Two very serious-looking officers parked on the sidewalk and headed inside.

"I'll stay quiet. You do the talking, and tell them the truth. If they don't offer, I'd suggest checking the cameras to see if we can get a look at the burglars."

A heavy knock sounded on her open door.

"Dr. Erika Carr?"

"Yes, that's me. Thank you for coming."

She offered each officer a seat across from her desk, which they declined.

"Would you please tell us what was stolen?"

She launched into a brief description of the artifacts, describing them vaguely as Revolutionary documents. Parker remained quiet the entire time, gaze locked on the uniformed patrolmen.

The younger of the two, broad-shouldered with a square jaw, took notes as she spoke. His senior partner, whose thick mustache brought to mind Burt Reynolds, asked the questions. He inspected the safe intently, questioning her repeatedly about the large amount of cash inside. The fact that it remained obviously puzzled the man.

"Well, Dr. Carr, I think that's everything we need. My partner will check to see if anything was caught on the surveillance system, and if we identify any possible suspects, I'll need you to come down and view the footage."

"Certainly. Thank you for coming."

"I suggest you put in for a new door lock. The maintenance team can give you an upgrade on this old thing."

He rattled the lock as they departed.

"Have a nice day. If anything else happens, call us immediately."

Parker had remained silent the entire time, but as soon as the officers were gone, he shot from the chair like he'd been bitten.

"We should leave. Get everything you'll need for a few days, anything that might help us figure out what the hell's going on with those letters, and let's go."

His energy flowed through the room, sweeping her back from the valley of self-pity and reinvigorating her spirits. Parker was right. Now wasn't the time to be afraid. It was time to get angry and do something about it.

"I have some high-resolution pictures of the letters." Erika flitted about the room, gathering what she needed for the search. "I also have a few ideas about what to look for next. Give me a hand."

Against police orders, she opened the safe and removed several thousand dollars.

"You never know when we might need it."

The money went into her purse, along with a thumb drive containing photos of the letters. Her document preservation and inspection tools were shoved into Parker's arms, and they were ready to roll.

"What do you think about heading back to my place? I need a computer, and my gun is there."

After they'd nearly been killed a few months ago, Parker had insisted she buy a handgun and learn how to use it. A lifelong sportsman himself, Parker had been impressed with how quickly she had picked up the sport.

"Good call. We might have to get Nick involved with this if things get hairy."

Outside in the warm sunlight, surrounded by carefree adolescents headed to class, what had minutes ago seemed innocuous passersby suddenly took on a sinister tint, every person a potential threat.

They made it to her car without incident, and ten minutes later had locked her apartment door behind them, Parker already heading to the bedroom closet where her gun was stored.

"Look at you, listening to me."

In one hand were the three extra magazines he'd instructed her to buy.

"I have two more boxes of ammo in there as well. I hope that's enough."

A humorless grin crossed his face.

"If we need that many bullets, we're not getting out anyway."

Ignoring his gallows humor, she fired up her laptop and pulled out her handwritten notes on Revere's letters.

"I spent the past week inspecting those letters for any errors or inconsistencies. Everything checked out, so the next step is to follow up on Revere's intelligence."

Parker's eyebrows jumped. "You really think you can do that? That report is a little out of date."

"Don't doubt me just yet. I have an idea where to start."

Parker looked expectantly at the monitor as her fingers danced over the keyboard.

"The part that grabbed my attention was Revere's mention of George Simpson," Erika said. "At first, I didn't make much of it, but after you spoke with Ben, it's been stuck in my head."

"You mean because Simpson was related to Ben's boss, that Drake guy?"

"Correct. Seeing as how we have literally nothing else to go on, it's as good a place as any to start."

"Do you think Drake could be tied in with this?" Parker asked.

The thought had crossed her mind. "I love the enthusiasm, but hold on a second. You realize you're talking about a conspiracy stretching over two centuries, which would involve one of the largest financial institutions in the country? I love a good story as much as you do, but we have to be realistic."

Parker muttered to the ground. "It could happen."

"We'll see. But for now, let's focus on Simpson, the only person we can associate with the plot with any certainty."

"A plot of which we don't even know the details."

"Yes, but that's what we're going to find out."

The Internet, in all its glory, provided scant information on Mr. Simpson. Beyond some minimal background regarding his service as Head Cashier at both the First Bank of the United States and its successor, the Girard Bank, there was little to be found.

Parker leaned over her shoulder as she read. "Hey, look at this." His finger stabbed the screen. "Simpson went to college at Eton."

No bells went off in her head.

"Why's that important?"

Here his normally confident tone diminished. "Well, maybe it's nothing. Didn't Ben tell us his boss went to Eton?"

She opened a second browser and found Spencer Drake's corporate profile. "Good memory. Spent half his teenage years there before coming back to the States. He was born in Massachusetts, though. He's an American citizen."

"I'm not sure if it means anything. Just throwing it out there."

"We can file that one away for now. But it's an idea."

Thirty frustrating minutes later she was ready to give up.

"This is awful. There's nothing out there about George Simpson. The guy was basically a nobody as far as history is concerned."

Parker had pulled out his own laptop and was peering at the screen.

"Well, since you're striking out, take a look at this." He brought the computer over and presented a screen shot from Aldrich Securities website.

Erika said, "Don't tell me they list George Simpson as a founding member."

"Not quite that obvious, but it's something. Look at the first board of directors."

"Who has your eye?"

He indicated the first name.

"Henry Stephen Fox? Who's that?" Erika asked, her forehead wrinkled.

"In 1836, he was appointed as the British Ambassador to the United States. His posting lasted through 1843."

It took a few seconds, but then it clicked for her.

"Which includes 1839, the year Aldrich Securities was established."

Parker held out his hand, which she begrudgingly slapped. "Two points for Erika. Now, I know this doesn't prove anything, but guess where he was educated."

His finger traced over the now-familiar school.

"Eton College," she murmured. "Interesting."

Erika took a deep breath. "Do you really think that one of the foremost educational institutions in the world is connected to a two-hundred-year assault on America?"

"I'm not saying that." His shoulders reached towards the ceiling. "I'm just saying that in the sea of uncertainty that we've floated through this past week, Eton College has been a shining beacon of consistency. It's a fact, and a damn strange one."

"Well said, and you're right. I can't argue with it. However, by no means does it establish that Eton is a center of evil. If you listed every notable Briton over the past two centuries, I'd bet at least fifteen percent of them attended that school."

"You're probably right. This could be nothing, but I say we take a hard look at British and American economic relations during the time period. Who knows what else may turn up?"

She had to admit, it made sense. Her interest piqued, Erika got down to business. "I'm going to call Ben and tell him about this. He was supposed to keep his ears open for me. Maybe he learned something."

Erika asked, "Keep his ears open about what?"

"Do you remember the diagram I drew about Ben's offshore activities with Drake's money? The funds he had to use to buy oil futures?"

Parker reached for a pen and paper.

"Yes, yes," she said hurriedly. No need for another lesson. "Did he get any more mysterious directives?"

"No, but Ben was told about a very strange conversation. Apparently Spencer Drake was on a conference call with the CEOs of some heavy hitters in the financial community. The gist of it is that Drake is encouraging these men to engage in proprietary trading, which is using depositors' money to purchase stocks, bonds or other financial items."

That didn't seem so strange.

"Isn't that what banks do? Invest money to make money?"

"Yes, but not with deposits. Investing money is risky. People don't put their money in the bank so fat cats like Drake can play the market. If he loses his shirt, theoretically, those savings could be gone forever. Now, the practice isn't illegal. Yet."

She looked up.

"I'm waiting for the other shoe to drop."

"It will be illegal soon," Parker continued. "After the financial crisis, Congress passed an act outlawing proprietary trading. It is supposed to go into effect within the next year."

"If it's not illegal, then what's the big deal?"

"Think about it. If Drake and his cronies invest all this money that isn't theirs, they face two major problems. One, they could lose everything if the market crashes. You'd think they would be smarter than that, but no one saw the housing collapse coming."

"That makes sense."

"Two, once all of the money is invested, even if they turn a profit, they'd have to pull out of the market almost immediately. With the way financial instruments work, especially derivatives, you can't just undo all that activity overnight. It would take months to unravel everything and get the depositors' money back into the proper accounts."

Her face screwed up in thought. "Why?"

"It's not as though each dollar they invest has a tracking chip to identify where it came from. All of the funds that are invested go into a pool of money from a variety of investors, depositors, and other sources. Unwinding hundreds or thousands of those trades would be an immense undertaking."

Parker held his hands far apart for emphasis. "And this doesn't even begin to address the issue of insider trading. If Drake had advance knowledge of oil pricing, which he almost certainly did given how he is manipulating the market, he could go to jail for using this information for personal gain."

That phrase rang a bell in her mind. "You mean like what happened to Martha Stewart?"

"Same idea."

This new information washed over her. The world of banking was not her forte, but what Parker was saying made sense. It certainly didn't prove anything, but with everything they'd learned in the past week, Aldrich Securities was practically screaming for their attention.

Parker continued, "That's what I need to speak with Ben about. I hope he's not out with one of his women."

"Plural? I thought he had a girlfriend?"

Erika could have smacked the smirk off his face.

"No, he's one of the lucky ones. He has quite a few girlfriends."

She waited until he turned around before firing a pretzel at his head.

A moment later, Parker's voice jerked her from the computer screen.

"Hello? Yes, this is Parker Chase. Who's this?"

Every speck of color drained from his face.

"No way. You can't be serious. What does he look like?"

More silence as he ignored her pleading looks.

"Oh no. What happened?"

Finally he mouthed the words.

Ben's dead.

Erika's breath caught in her throat and tears sprang unbidden. It couldn't be.

"Thank you."

Parker was completely crestfallen as he hung up.

"That was the police. A Boston patrol officer found Ben last night, lying on the street near his office. He was shot in the head."

A single tear welled in one eye, the liquid diamond sliding down his face. It was the first time she'd ever seen Parker cry.

"He's dead."

Chapter 30

Boston, Massachusetts

Michael Brown lost fifty years in five minutes.

One shot, and it was done. Benjamin Flood was eliminated. In no hurry, he shuffled away from the ATM, cane clicking on the sidewalk. Three blocks later he turned down an alley filled with darkness, and more importantly, a speck of light in the distance.

During the minute-long walk around Dumpsters and over one sleeping bum, he took off the thick scarf and fedora, his limp disappeared, and the cane retracted in on itself and slid up his coat sleeve.

Whereas a withered old man had entered the alleyway, a trim and unassuming businessman exited with a briefcase in one hand. Moments later, a cab fortuitously rolled by, and Michael Brown settled in for a short ride across town.

He paid in cash and was dropped off several blocks from his hotel. On the street, a homeless man panhandled for change. Michael gave the man a dollar and set the briefcase down as he walked past. By tomorrow the old man's coat, hat, scarf and cane would be lost amongst Boston's underground community of vagrants.

One hour later, after a wonderful dinner of lobster and clam chowder, Michael prepared to depart for the train station and a two-hour ride into the blessed anonymity of New York City. His lone bag packed and all evidence discarded, he walked into the hallway. Unfortunately, his cell phone began buzzing in his pocket.

That infernal man was calling again. Michael didn't like to be bothered.

"Spencer Drake." Time to send a message. "Spencer, I know where you live. I know what kind of car you drive and where you like to eat."

Michael let the silence stretch on.

"What do you want?"

Drake was flustered, his words clipped before they finished.

"Well, Mr. ..."

"You can call me Mr. Smith. Please get on with it."

"Yes, of course. Mr. Smith, I'm not calling about our recent arrangement, as I trust you will complete the agreement in due time."

"Then what are you bothering me about, Spencer?"

"I would like to engage your services again."

Well, this was a pleasant surprise. Michael had assumed Drake was growing impatient and checking up on him. If Spencer wanted to give Michael more of his money, he'd be happy to take it.

"Who would you like me to meet?"

"It's actually two people. They are currently in Philadelphia."

"I trust this is your private line? The one in your office that is checked daily?"

"Of course, Mr. Smith."

"Then please continue."

Drake described a man and a woman, the latter a professor in Philadelphia. Michael noted their names and occupations, mentally cataloguing other relevant details.

Before Drake had finished, Michael was calculating how much it would cost.

"Mr. Drake, I accept your proposal. The fee is ten million, payable immediately."

Drake didn't even flinch. "Agreed."

"Send it to this account."

Michael read a long string of digits written on the slip of paper he held.

"I'll deposit the money immediately."

"I will contact you upon completion of the agreement. And as I'm sure you're interested to know, our last arrangement was completed this evening."

Michael clicked off and walked outside, hand covered by his shirtsleeve when he closed the door. He'd wiped the entire room down as well. No sense in leaving any prints behind for the police, no matter how remote the chance they'd find his room.

Tonight, he would rest on the train. Tomorrow, he'd learn about his new assignments, Parker Chase and Erika Carr.

Chapter 31

Philadelphia, Pennsylvania

After an hour of calls, Parker finally learned what had happened to Ben.

"Thank you, and I'm terribly sorry for your loss."

He hung up, leaving Ben's sister sobbing on the other end.

"The cops don't know what to make of this. Ben was at an ATM, and surveillance footage shows an old man walk up behind him and shoot him point-blank in the head. Ben never saw it coming."

"An old man? How do they know that? Did they see his face?"

Questions started to tumble out of Erika's mouth.

"It was dark outside and there weren't any streetlights around, so they didn't get a look at his face. The shooter was wearing a fedora and scarf, and was using a cane. It's the summer, but you know how old people are always cold. Apparently the guy just shuffled off after he shot him. And get this; he didn't even take the money lying on the ground."

"He left it there? That doesn't make any sense. If he was mugging him, he'd at least take his wallet. And weren't there any witnesses, someone who heard the shot?"

"That's the thing. There was no one else around at that time of night. It's the business district, and everyone had gone home after work. His sister isn't sure, but she thought she overheard one of the cops say it looked like the gun had a suppressor attached. That would explain why no one heard the shot."

Erika had fallen into her desk chair, the laptop in front of her now showing a black screen.

"Erika, I don't think there's any question this is related. Ben's sister said

135

it was a safe part of the city. There shouldn't have been any muggers around there."

"This can't be happening again," Erika mumbled, her head shaking back and forth. "Do you think it's the same people who were after us before?"

She was referring to the group of men who'd murdered Parker's uncle earlier that year. Joseph Chase, Parker's uncle, had been a world-renowned scholar when he worked with Erika at Penn. After the murder, Parker had unwittingly stumbled into the group's path, and both he and Erika had nearly been killed.

"No way. Nick killed that guy and all his men. There's no one left to come after us."

"Maybe we should call him. Nick has access to every database on the planet."

For the first time, Parker considered the idea. Nicholas Dean was a CIA field agent based in Philadelphia, less than five miles away. At the time Parker's uncle was murdered, Nick had been investigating some missing plastic explosives. The men who had stolen the explosives were the same men who had murdered his uncle, and eventually Nick had run across Parker and Erika, usually while they were running for their lives. If it weren't for him, they'd be dead.

"I hate to say it, but you're right. We're in way over our heads. Again."

Parker still had Nick's number in his phone.

"While I call him, why don't you follow up on that guy we found on Aldrich's board? The more we know, the more likely Nick will be able to help us."

He dialed Nick's number, moving into the bedroom to give Erika some quiet. The call was answered immediately.

"Dean."

The gruff voice was good to hear.

"Nick, it's Parker Chase."

"Parker? This is a surprise. You in trouble or something? Because I'm not going to stick my neck out if you did something stupid."

"No, Nick, it's nothing like that. Well, actually it is."

"I knew it. What did you get yourself into this time? And the short version if you can manage it. I'm kind of busy."

"Erika's office was just robbed, one of my friends was murdered tonight, and it all started after we found three letters Paul Revere wrote about a plot to destroy the American economy."

That did the trick.

"Hold on a second." Parker heard a door slam shut. "Did you say Paul Revere?"

"Yes. They were letters Revere wrote to Alexander Hamilton while he was spying on King George."

"Only you, Chase." Nick let out a heavy sigh. "Start at the beginning, and tell me everything."

Ten minutes later, Nick was up to speed.

"You two have to be the most interesting people I've ever met in my life. You couldn't make this stuff up. First of all, are you in any immediate danger?"

"I don't think so. We came back to Erika's place, and I'm fairly certain we weren't followed. I have a gun here with plenty of ammunition."

"Glad to hear you're not totally helpless. Do you have anywhere else you can go, maybe a hotel or a friend's place?"

"A hotel would work."

"Do it, and don't tell anyone where you're going. I'd also get a new cell phone. You have no idea how easily those calls are intercepted. We do it every day."

"I'll do that tonight. Do you think you can find out what happened to my friend?"

"I have a contact in our Boston field office. He should be able to dig up the report. While I'm at it, give me the name of that banker again. You never know what we might have on him."

Parker recited Spencer Drake's name and company.

"I'll get on this right now. And listen, Parker, you guys better not do anything stupid like get yourselves killed. Go hide somewhere until you hear from me. I'll send you an e-mail. You still have the same account?"

"Yes."

"Keep your head down and your eyes open. If you get in trouble, go to the cops. They're better equipped to handle this than you two."

"Thanks, Nick. I really appreciate it."

"No problem. You guys did save my life."

He hung up, hope swelling through his chest. Nicholas Dean was one tough agent, and it felt good to have him on their side.

He walked into the main room and found Erika hunched over the computer.

"Nick's going to look into Ben's death and get back to me."

"Good. He still owes us one. We did save his life, after all."

"He also said we should get out of here, get a hotel for the night while he checks things out."

She finally looked up at him. "What do you think?"

"I think Nick Dean knows what he's talking about. It wouldn't hurt to lay low for a bit."

Erika didn't put up a fight. "If you think so. But before we leave, come over here and look at what I found."

He leaned over her shoulder, the lingering scent of her perfume pleasant in the air.

"Henry Fox wasn't the only British ambassador associated with Aldrich Bank, which is what it was known as in the nineteenth century. After Fox left the board, a new guy named Richard Lyons joined."

On the screen a biography popped up. Erika continued. "Richard Lyons was also the British Ambassador to the United States during the Civil War."

This was getting stranger by the minute.

"What is it with these British people and Aldrich Bank? I'm starting to doubt that this is a coincidence."

Erika rubbed one red eye as she listened. "I'd have to agree with you. I logged onto my university account, which allows me to access Penn's archives. Every single piece of paper the history department possesses has been digitized so I can access them without having to physically be at the school. We also have reciprocal agreements with institutions around the world, so I have literally billions of records at my disposal."

She pulled up yet another web page as she spoke. "I did a search on this guy Lyons, and found some interesting material from an archive in London."

Several handwritten letters popped onto her screen. "Now, it appears that these are of questionable provenance." She glanced at him with skepticism.

Parker fired back. "I know what provenance means. You're saying no one can guarantee where it came from or, in this case, it's authenticity."

"Not bad, football boy."

"I did more than just play football at school. Even managed to take a few tests."

"Anyway, there have been a bunch of papers written discrediting these letters."

She seemed to have skipped the explanation.

"That's great, but what do they say? I can't read those scribbles."

"I'm getting there. These are all letters that bear the signature of Richard Lyons, dated when he was in America serving as the British ambassador." She abruptly stopped and turned to face him. "How much do you know about the Civil War?"

"Enough. Would you please get on with it?"

"No, this is important. I'll give you the short version." Parker rolled his eyes to no effect. Erika went on. "Around 1860, right before the first Southern states seceded, industrial economies across the globe depended heavily on textiles derived from cotton. This included Britain and France, the two largest economies at the time. And guess who had the best cotton?"

"America."

"Correct. As I'm sure you're aware, the vast majority of cotton grown in America was grown in Southern states, which had the climate for it. What's in these letters that grabbed my attention deals with cotton, particularly how American cotton affected the world's industrial markets."

"What did Richard Lyons write that is so interesting?" Parker asked.

"It's right here." The writing was in the middle of the page, a tiny mass of scribbles.

"Read it to me, please. I can't see it."

"It's addressed to someone named Stirling, no first name listed."

Dear Mr. Stirling,

I have recently spoken with Mr. Davis, a leader amongst the Southern contingent. While he is a capable military leader, he lacks the sophistication necessary to properly understand and evaluate commerce on a global level.

In America there exists a concept known as "King Cotton." Certain Americans, specifically those in the southern regions, believe this crop to be a panacea that will provide nourishment like manna from the heavens in times of need. Unfortunately, the notion is pure fallacy. It was but a simple matter to convince Mr. Davis of what he already believes, which is that their beloved crop will sustain them throughout a costly war.

Mr. Davis does not realize that neither we nor the damned French require his cotton to continue our industry. I have personally seen textiles produced from Egyptian cotton, which is readily available, that are comparable to those produced with the American version.

This is relevant as I predict the Southern states, which have taken to calling themselves the Confederacy, will be subjected to a naval blockade of their ports during the coming conflict. Alas, this new Confederacy has no navy to speak of, and as such, will be unable to export their beloved cotton to any country. Contracts for the delivery of cotton from Egypt are already in place. My dear friend, I believe that our time is finally at hand.

Truly yrs,
R. Lyons, Viscount

The implications were clear.

"It sounds like the British ambassador was actively encouraging the South to secede from the Union."

"Well done, Mr. Chase. If it weren't for the fact that these letters have been discredited, British and American relations might be quite strained right now."

"How do you know they're fakes?"

"Richard Lyons himself denied ever writing them, claiming that a member of his staff had forged the letters on his personal stationary. The man was hung for his crimes."

He wasn't buying it just yet. "I'll bet you a dollar the guy who was strung up denied the whole thing."

Erika confirmed it. "If you were going to be killed, wouldn't you do anything to save your neck? The man who was responsible had been Lyon's servant for years. I doubt Lyons would allow him to be killed without cause."

"You can't be serious. Do you really think a powerful man wouldn't throw his subordinate under the bus to save his own skin?"

She opened her mouth to argue, but said nothing.

Parker pressed his point. "Or are you just going to believe what you've read, go with the prevailing theory? Five hundred years ago most people thought the world was flat."

Erika had the look of a stunned prizefighter. "But if that's true, then ..." Red nails ran through her silky blonde hair.

"Then we just found another piece of evidence connecting Aldrich Securities to Revere's letters."

He had to give her credit. It couldn't be easy to dismiss a widely accepted theory on the letter, but she was trying.

"If what you say is true," Erika continued, "then the British government, or at least a faction of it, was actively encouraging Civil War in the United States."

As she sat and pondered the implications, Parker's phone buzzed. He looked down and found his inbox overflowing with e-mails. He also remembered it was time to ditch the phone.

"Pack whatever you need for the next few days. We have to get out of here and into a hotel. Bring a few changes of clothes, your money and your computer. Take the battery out of your phone and leave it here."

As she moved to comply, he glanced over the messages beeping for his attention.

His eyebrows touched as he read, the lines on his forehead growing deeper.

"What's wrong?" Erika asked. "Did Nick send you anything?"

"No, it's not that. I've received twenty-five e-mails in the past few hours relating to the rising price of oil."

"So? You're in the financial business. That stuff matters to you."

"Yes, but listen to this. A barrel of oil is going for a hundred ten dollars. That's up twenty percent in the past twenty-four hours. Do you have any idea how crazy that is?"

"I don't buy barrels of oil."

"Very funny. Trust me, it's a big deal. On top of that, OPEC hasn't said a thing about it."

She shoved her computer into a shoulder bag. "I take it that's unusual as well? Parker, I don't know anything about oil. Tell me in plain English."

"OPEC should at least give an indication, even if it's off the record, that they're going to address the issue. Like we discussed before, it doesn't benefit them if the price of oil goes up too quickly."

"Because if oil is too expensive, people won't buy it. I know."

"Which is why I would expect them to at least hint at an increase in production. Those sheiks aren't stupid. They know how to make money."

Erika headed to the bedroom, talking over her shoulder. "And you think this is somehow related to what we found?"

That was where he was struggling. Their theories were nice, but they were just that. Speculation that strung together events over the past two centuries. There was no proof, nothing concrete he could point to as solid evidence.

"I don't know." He followed her to the bedroom and began repacking his travel bag.

"We can't prove anything right now," Parker declared. "For all we know, this could be a horrible set of coincidences. Revere could have been mistaken, Ben could just have been in the wrong place at the wrong time, and OPEC might be greedy. The one thing that sticks with me is Aldrich Securities. What they're doing makes no sense whatsoever." Her weary face turned back toward him. Weary, but beautiful.

"So you think we have nothing."

"No, I'm not saying that. What might be happening, and what makes sense if you look at this like a criminal, is that Aldrich Securities is manipulating the market for profit."

"In English, please."

Parker laid it out for her. "Spencer Drake could be using his client's money to earn profits for his bank. He won't have access to depositors' funds much longer, as the proprietary trading we talked about is going to be illegal. While he does, though, he may be buying oil futures at this incredible rate to drive the price up. Once it gets high enough, whatever number that is, he'll sell all the futures he bought at a lower price and turn a profit. How it relates to Revere's letters or Ben's death, I have no idea."

Her duffel bag zipped shut. "Then I guess we'll have to keep moving forward. You talk to your friends, see if you can figure out what Drake may be up to, and I'll see if there are any other links between Aldrich Securities and Richard Lyons, the British instigator."

A moment later Erika held a much more sinister type of bag. The metallic black handgun case was light, even filled with the firearm and plenty of ammunition.

"Why don't you hold on to this?" She held it out. "I have my registration and concealed carry permit in my purse."

"Is it loaded?"

"You told me never to do that."

A mischievous grin cracked his countenance. "Good answer. Guns are dangerous. I'm also glad we have one."

Erika leaned into his body and squeezed tightly. He could tell this was getting real for her, with the need to leave her apartment and Ben dying. She was keeping it together pretty well, but underneath it all she still was a girl with feelings and emotions, trying to be tough.

"Don't worry. Everything's going to be fine. Nick's going to help us out, and I'm here for you. I won't let anything happen, I promise."

She pulled away and walked toward the door, his shirt wet where her tears had fallen.

Chapter 32

Early morning sunlight broke through the thin curtains on Amtrak's Acela Express train as it left Penn Station, New York, headed south to 30th Street Station in Philadelphia. Michael Brown felt the warmth on his face, both eyes snapping open like a camera shutter. The seat adjacent to him was occupied by a sleeping young woman, an oversized purse clutched to her chest. Slender and petite, her flowing black tresses were immaculately curled and smelled faintly of lavender. She hadn't made a sound since boarding almost two hours ago in New York, and he appreciated the silence.

With feline grace, Michael extracted a razor thin computer from his black leather travel bag. In seconds, biographies of Parker Chase and Erika Carr were on-screen, complete with recent photos. Spencer Drake had provided satellite maps depicting the location of every phone call or electronic transaction they'd made in the past three days, all in and around the Graduate Hospital neighborhood or just across the Schuylkill River in University City.

Of all the information with which he'd been provided, only one item was worrisome. Last night, while Michael had been on his way home from Boston, Parker had called a number that Drake's people had been unable to identify. They had no idea if the call was ever connected, who Parker had spoken with, or where the number was registered. Michael had never seen anything like it. It was as if the phone call never happened.

Ahead, the skyline of Philadelphia loomed large, sparkling glass of the Comcast Tower rising above all. Despite its proximity to New York, Michael had only been to Philadelphia twice and wasn't familiar with the area.

The maps on his screen also provided real-time updates of any electronic transmissions or transactions Parker or Erika made. The last call from either of their phones had been the mysterious unidentifiable number yesterday evening. Since then, no ATM withdrawals, no check card purchases, nothing. He assumed they were sleeping at Erika's apartment. It would be the first place he visited on his mission, and if all went well, the last.

Metal screeched as the train slowed for arrival at 30th Street Station, a towering edifice adjacent to the unique, slanted glass tower that housed Amtrak's headquarters. The sun hid behind a stray cloud, and Michael could see a display of lights shine through Amtrak's windows, the red-tinted bulbs forming a stylistic "*P.*"

Pneumatic springs hissed and train doors opened to expel a tide of humanity. Michael waited patiently, moving through the mass of people toward an exit, outside of which he found a string of yellow cabs.

"Rittenhouse Square." The cabbie nodded and took off, all the while murmuring into his earpiece in Greek.

Within minutes, the fertile green oasis appeared in front of them, materializing as they rounded a soaring apartment building. Rittenhouse Square was one of the most desirable parts of Philadelphia. Similar to Central Park, albeit on a much smaller scale, the square block boasted beautiful landscaping, brick-lined walkways and dozens of trees, all surrounded by some of the finest restaurants in the city.

The symphony of life filled the air. Pedestrians jammed the sidewalks around him while cabs honked at the bicyclists who risked life and limb on these hectic streets. On his smartphone, Michael found walking directions to Erika's apartment. Dressed in blue jeans, running shoes, and a windbreaker, Michael disappeared into the crowd, a leather satchel slung over one shoulder.

Less than a mile away, Erika's apartment was to the southwest, toward the river. As he neared his destination, the sidewalks emptied noticeably, with only a handful of other people in view. He passed churches, corner shops and restaurants, some busy, most empty. A warm breeze ruffled the leaves far above his head.

One block from her building, Michael stopped outside of a massive school building which a concrete cornerstone indicated had been built in 1927. The place appeared empty, another victim of city budget cuts.

Stooped to tie his shoe, he pulled the .9mm Jericho 941 pistol from the black leather shoulder bag and confirmed a steel-jacketed hollow point was racked and ready to fire. The gun vanished into a holster under his left shoulder.

Like most blocks in the city, Erika's apartment was buried in a long stretch of row homes, no alleys in between. Michael walked leisurely past a red brick church that had been converted into a retirement home. Across the street, an abandoned candy factory stared back, the boarded windows like closed eyes, resting after a hard journey.

Connected to the candy factory was her apartment complex, a three-story yellow brick structure, two apartments on each floor. Drake's report indicated Erika's apartment was on the east side of the second floor. A lone metal door provided access to the building. Each window in her unit was closed, blinds on all. Next to the door was a box with call buttons. Beside each button a label identified the occupant. Next to the button for apartment 2D was a hand-scrawled *E. Carr.* Michael tried the handle. The door didn't budge.

A glance to either side revealed several people moving around, some on the sidewalk, a few sitting on their porch steps, phone in hand as they jabbered away. None paid him any attention.

In addition to Erika's call button, five other black dots bore the names of occupants.

What the hell.

He pushed the first button, marked *W. Groves.* A loud buzz could be heard, but there was no answer.

The second button yielded a similar result. However, he struck paydirt when he pushed the call button for *S. Fleet.*

A chirpy female voice came through the speaker. "Yes?"

"Delivery for Erika Carr."

"Who's that? Does she live here?" Apparently they didn't have community dinners.

"Yeah, second floor."

"Hold on." A second later, the door clicked open. Michael didn't even blink, long ago having accepted that most people were naïve and trusting. Too bad for Dr. Carr.

Gray industrial carpeting lined the floors, a sharp contrast to the vivid white hallways and harsh overhead lights. A gunmetal door to his left and one down the hall were closed, silence coming from each.

Soft steps took him up the wide staircase, thick rails on each side. At the second floor landing, Michael found himself facing a freshly painted door bearing the designation 2D.

To his right was another apartment. He crept over and leaned close to the door, ears open. Several seconds of quiet, and he was satisfied. He slid back to Erika's door, a suppressor now attached to the Israeli-made pistol in his hand.

There were no peepholes on any of the apartment doors. Still, he stood to one side and knocked heavily. One finger on the trigger, his back pushed against the wall.

After ten seconds without an answer, he knocked again, just as strongly. No one answered.

His ear close to the door, Michael heard nothing. No television, radio, or shower running. It appeared Ms. Carr was not home.

Michael removed a roll of clear material from his pocket which looked like clear tape. The material contained microfilaments that carried an electrical current generated by exposure to light. Inspired by photosynthesis, the overhead hall light would service nicely as a substitute for the sun.

Several inches of the material peeled off, sticky on one side. The adhesive gripped the gray door nicely, in the upper corner where it met the frame. When the door opened, the current would be disrupted, and a signal would be sent to his cell phone.

Down the stairs and back outside, Michael drifted toward a grassy lot he'd passed on his way over. After taking up residence on one of the community benches, all that remained was to wait for either the electronic surveillance net Drake had in place to register a hit, or for Erika to return home.

If Michael was fortunate, Parker would accompany her, and two bullets from his pistol would be the last thing they ever saw.

Chapter 33

Philadelphia, Pennsylvania

Panic alarms blared. Acrid black smoke poured from damaged engines, the helicopter suddenly transformed into a black angel of death plummeting from the sky. Parker stared up as the burning metal carriage fell, his feet rooted to the ground.

Just as the helicopter was about to crush him, Parker shot up in bed. Sweat coated his chest and face, lungs heaving. Ever since he'd nearly died in a gunfight that had taken place near one of the whirling birds, the airborne device had played a role in his nightmares.

Erika was staring at him from the bathroom, sympathy in her eyes. "Easy, Parker. Everything's fine."

Mid-morning sunlight slanted through the windows, shadows flying up the walls as Erika opened their hotel room curtains. He must have dozed off after they'd checked in.

"Want to get some food after we check out?" She was wrapped in a towel, her blonde hair soaked.

"Yeah, sure. Give me ten minutes to shower."

"Also, I need to go back to my apartment."

"What? You know Nick told us to stay away."

"I know, but I left my university keycard there. I need it to access the university archives from my home computer. It'll only take a minute."

He didn't have the energy or the ability to argue right now. "Fine. We'll grab it before we get lunch."

Arms stretched high overhead, a spine-rattling yawn got him going. Ten minutes and one steaming hot shower later, temperate summer air whistled past his ears as they headed to a nearby coffee shop.

"So what's on your radar for the rest of day? Any idea where to look next for a connection between Aldrich and Revere's letters?"

They chatted softly in line at Starbucks. No one gave them a second glance. Well, at least no one gave him a second glance. Two guys sitting at a corner table had given Erika a third and fourth one.

"I'm hopeful that Aldrich's website will point us in the right direction," Erika said. "They claim to be one of the oldest banking institutions in America, and they have their lineage on display for everyone to see."

"And if you find a few likely characters, you'll run them through Penn's archives for any hits?" Hot coffee burned his tongue. Happened every damn time and he never learned.

"You're not as dumb as you look."

Next to Starbucks was an electronics store. "Wait here. I need a new phone."

A few minutes later he had the new device, along with several pre-paid cards that he loaded onto the phone. As they walked, Parker turned to Erika.

"Listen, you get in and out of that apartment. I doubt anyone's around in the middle of the day, but I'm not trying to get into a gunfight."

He was surprised when she answered in an equally serious tone. "I hate to say it, but you're right. I'll only be a minute."

It was a short walk to her apartment building, the streets peaceful, foot traffic sparse. On her front stoop, Parker's gaze flashed to and fro. A stare held too long. Anything that signaled trouble. The street behind them was empty, and nothing seemed amiss inside her building.

"I'll be out in two seconds." Her apartment door opened, and Erika disappeared inside. He chose to wait out in the hall, one eye on the stairwell as she retrieved her card.

Her voice called out from the bedroom, "I can't find it. Can you check on the table?"

Erika was one of the smartest people he knew. At certain times, she could also be the most air-headed, infuriating woman on the planet. Parker stood on the bamboo kitchen floor, just inside the apartment door. As he searched for the missing keycard, Parker heard the outside buzzer go off, and moments later, the front door open. Someone had been buzzed in.

"Erika, we need to go. I don't see the card anywhere." Sure enough, the kitchen table was empty.

"Never mind, I found it." She appeared from inside the bedroom, keycard in hand. He held the front door open with one hand, ready to leave.

"I left it—"

Her eyes saved his life.

As she spoke, they grew to twice the normal size, locked on something behind him. Without thinking, he hit the deck, twisting around as he slammed the door shut. A puff of air, and the bullet shattered her microwave.

"Get back," he shouted at her. An arm was stuck in the door, the suppressed pistol still locked in its grip. Two more bullets ripped out, the shooter firing blindly.

One foot against the door, Parker grabbed the arm and wrenched it backward. A painful shriek, and the gun clattered on the bamboo just as the door burst open, Parker's weight no longer keeping their attacker at bay.

Into the apartment came a total stranger. As he fell, Parker was struck by how *gaunt* the man appeared. Tall, but not exceedingly so, facial skin stretched tightly across his skull. Shocked at the raw power this skinny apparition of death could generate, Parker tumbled to the ground, the attacker's wrist still firmly grasped in two hands.

The man's free arm came down on Parker's throat as they landed. He never would have thought a skinny guy could hit with so much force. Parker twisted to dodge the blow. Flat on his back, he had no leverage to shatter the bony wrist in his grasp.

Everything happened in seconds, and as Parker pushed desperately against the ground, struggling to gain the upper hand, his attacker's eerily calm face never changed. What the man did was pull a knife from inside his windbreaker, arm flashing so quickly that Parker barely saw his hand move. One moment it wasn't there, the next it was streaking toward his chest.

As he struck, the man's head jerked, and the gleaming blade whispered past Parker's chest to stick in the bamboo floor. Warm blood spurted from a gash on the man's cheek, courtesy of the, and he almost laughed, the *frying pan* in Erika's hand.

Before he could thank her, the guy bounced up from the ground and stood back, his black, dead eyes searching for an opening.

Parker had just gained his feet when the man, expression never changing, spotted his lost gun behind where Parker stood. He darted toward Erika, knife outstretched.

Parker grabbed for the gun in his waistband, only to realize it was unloaded. With no time to fix that problem, he took the more direct route. Parker launched himself into the slender man with practiced ferocity.

Head up, lead with the shoulder, just like he'd been taught, Parker nailed the guy square in his chest, the skinny body wrapped in both arms.

The pair crashed to the ground, and Parker spread his legs wide, searching for balance to keep their assailant pinned. Parker sensed movement as Erika ran to his side, the shiny metal skillet raised overhead. She searched for an opening to strike, but Parker had the man completely covered.

Just as Parker looked back down, a flailing knee found his crotch, and lightning bolts of pain shot through his body. Parker reacted without thinking, releasing the man as he shriveled up in pain.

Like a snake, the man slithered free, and Erika's pan slammed to the ground where his head had been a moment ago. He was going for his gun.

Parker lashed a kick at the pistol, his toe connecting to send it skidding across the floor and under Erika's couch. The man slid over, his belly on the floor as he reached underneath her furniture.

"Come on," Erika shouted as she dropped the pan and grasped his arm, "let's go."

He didn't need to be told again. Parker hopped gingerly to his feet and followed her out the door while their attacker dug under the couch.

They flew down the stairs, footsteps pounding.

"Who was that?"

Erika's hair streamed in her face as they raced out of her building and onto the sidewalk.

"I have no idea, but let's go. Watch where you're walking."

She turned just in time to avoid plowing into a stop sign.

Behind them, the building door slammed open. Parker risked a glance and saw two muzzle flashes.

The car windshield next to him exploded in a spider's web of broken glass. Across the street, an old woman sporting a head full of curlers screamed and ducked for cover.

"Follow me. Keep your head down." Parker darted to the right, down a side street that put a building between them and the gunman. Every block in this neighborhood consisted of uninterrupted row homes, essentially rendering them rats in a maze.

Momentarily in the clear, he reached into his waistband, where Erika's pistol was still stashed. It had to be, because his back ached like an anvil had struck it where he'd landed on the unforgiving steel.

Unfortunately, the gun wasn't loaded.

"Get onto Christian Street. There might be cops out."

She overtook him as he fumbled for the magazine in his front pocket. "You can't shoot out here. There are people every—" Her words were cut off as two more shots peppered the brickwork beside them. The gunman was gaining.

"Screw it. Shoot back."

Amazing how a few bullets could change your mind.

Christian Street was much more heavily trafficked than Carpenter Street, on which Erika lived. Parker decided to head left, toward a massive generation plant that occupied over a square block of real estate. No reason to endanger any more innocent people than necessary.

The magazine locked into place and Parker racked the slide. He turned and squeezed off two shots at the man, who was gaining on them. Without a suppressor on his gun, the effect was instantaneous.

Anyone within fifty feet, and there were plenty of people on the sidewalk, began to run. Once they started moving, each person the crowd passed joined them in terror, and Parker found himself sliding between screaming mothers and crying children. He kept his gun hidden as they moved, not wanting to risk any heroes taking him down.

"Cross the street." Erika nodded, and they cut between two parked cars, running blind in front of moving traffic. A taxi whizzed past in front of them, horn blaring. A moment later, its rear windshield exploded.

They'd been spotted again. Two more bullets slammed into the parked car beside Erika. Like scared rabbits, they each tore down the rapidly emptying sidewalk toward the ominous towers of the electrical generation plant.

Parker had always referred to the engineering monstrosity as Gotham City, and right now he could have used an appearance from the Caped Crusader. He and Erika darted back and forth, moving erratically, offering as small a target as possible. Even still, several shots pinged off the sidewalk and buildings around them as they ran, their mysterious attacker in hot pursuit.

Two excruciating blocks later, Parker ducked onto a street that encircled the generation plant. Next to him ran a steel wire fence meant to keep trespassers away from the massive generators that hummed inside.

When he visited Erika, he liked to jog around this area, and it was during one of these midday runs that Parker found a hole in the fence. Barely large enough to crawl through, it was nearly invisible until you were right on top of it, the light gray metal of the fence blending with a turbine of the same color that sat a foot inside the wire loops.

Erika followed him through, and as they moved around the circular turbine, Parker spotted the skinny attacker poke his head around the street corner, wary.

"Don't say anything," he whispered, the sound of their feet moving over the loose rock concealed by the deep hum of the generators. "He won't expect us to be in here."

She nodded once, determination outweighing the fear in her eyes.

The slender man's head whipped back and forth as he crept down the short alley. With all the movement, he looked like a paranoid Ichabod Crane. Parker waited patiently as the man moved past the broken fence, his gaze flowing right over the hole, never stopping.

He was so focused on their attacker that Parker never saw the white-striped skunk appear from behind the adjacent generator. Erika did, however, and let out a clipped, piercing shriek.

Before Parker knew what had happened, the black-haired gunman twisted around and he fired. The bullet nicked Parker's right shoulder, a white-hot streak of pain when he dove away from cover. As Parker fell, his gun never left the man, firing twice to send a pair of slugs hurtling through the fence toward their assailant.

Parker slammed into the rocky surface, cutting his arms and face. His sight blurred on impact, and he blinked rapidly, knowing it was too late. Erika screamed again, once, then stopped.

She's been hit.

Murderous rage filled his body. Parker jumped up and ran blindly at the shooter, who must have dropped to the sidewalk, offering no target at all.

As his finger tightened on the trigger, Erika screamed again. She was alive.

In front of him, Parker saw why.

On the hot sidewalk, blood leaked from Ichabod Crane's head. Parker had shot him squarely between the eyes.

Without a word, he ran back inside the fence, grabbed Erika's hand, and pulled her onto the sidewalk after him. Sirens sounded in the distance.

"Don't scream and keep your head down."

Parker rapidly frisked the corpse. All he found was a slip of paper in one pocket on which several strings of numbers had been written. Parker pocketed it, hoping that it might reveal who this guy had been.

Parker's and Erika's footsteps faded down the sidewalk as approaching sirens filled the air.

Chapter 34

Boston, Massachusetts

The lead story on the evening news brought a smile to Spencer Drake's lips. On the screen, a perfectly coiffed male anchor stared at the camera.

"Thank you for joining us this evening. Tonight, the question that has exploded across the nation. Why is the price of oil skyrocketing? In the past week, the price of a barrel has risen eighty percent, to a high of one hundred thirty-five dollars. Only last week oil was trading at around seventy dollars per barrel. Almost overnight the price has nearly doubled, and there's no relief in sight. With us tonight is Dr. Horace Nance, Professor of Economics at Boston University."

Across from the square-jawed anchor sat a lunatic. He had to be, with his untamed shock of wild white hair, moth-eaten plaid jacket, and bright red bow tie. Thick, Coke bottle glasses were perched on his enormous nose, his eyes reminiscent of a monstrous bug.

The professor looked surprised. "Yes, why, of course I am. What we've seen in the recent weeks may appear to be complicated, but in reality is likely quite simple."

Spencer smirked at the bumbling educator. If this goon could unravel his plans, he didn't deserve to succeed.

"There has been a notable uptick in the price of oil as a direct result of several occurrences. One"-Nance held up a finger-"the volume of oil traded on the stock market has increased markedly. Why this has happened, I have no idea. Possibly some trader got the idea in his greedy head that oil was going to go up, told a few friends, and they bought all the oil futures. Or maybe not. The commodities market is a funny mistress. Her whims are known to no man."

Not bad. The professor was on the right track.

"Second, the amount of oil available for consumption has remained stagnant. This is somewhat unusual, as the oil-producing nations must be aware their product is becoming expensive, almost prohibitively so. Gasoline is becoming more expensive. If the average consumer has to think twice before filling their tank, they won't drive as much, and the people who produce oil lose potential profits."

"How long until Americans can expect relief from this crisis?"

The news anchor was deathly serious, which seemed to amuse the old codger.

"Well, I wouldn't call it a crisis just yet. You see"-and here the thick spectacles slipped down his nose, hanging precariously-"the men who produce the oil may decide to increase production tomorrow. If there is more oil being produced, the price of oil will soon return to normal, as one would expect. Supply and demand and all that good stuff."

The professor's host was tenacious, pressing the issue.

"What if the oil-rich nations do not increase production? Would we, as Americans who are dependent on their exports, be able to lead normal lives?"

The host's gelled hair nearly poked Dr. Nance as he leaned over the table.

"Ignoring the implications of our oil dependency, the answer is maybe." His obtuse nose finally lost the struggle, and Professor Nance's glasses dipped off his face.

"Oh dear. I must really get a string for these. Anyway, as I was saying, it all depends on what happens to production. If more oil is exported, we can expect things to return to normal. If production remains stagnant, then we may have a problem. It all depends on what the producers decide. We are truly at their mercy."

As the anchor spun that comment into a worrisome tirade of rhetorical questions, Drake flicked off the television. The old geezer had been completely on point, except for one thing. America wasn't at the mercy of the sheiks. They were at the mercy of Spencer Drake.

And his was not a benevolent soul.

The desk phone buzzed. "Yes?"

"Nigel Stirling calling for you."

Probably checking up on the status of their latest contract. The man had no patience.

"Nigel, how are you?"

"There is a problem in Philadelphia."

"What do you mean?"

Drake jumped from his chair. How did Stirling know about a problem? He was in England, for goodness sake.

"A man was shot to death two hours ago within blocks of where Dr. Carr lives. No mention was made of any female victims, and there is amateur footage on YouTube that shows the decedent."

Drake's stomach sank.

"Let me guess. He doesn't resemble Parker Chase."

"No, Mr. Drake, he most definitely does not. In fact, I've been told that police are having a hard time putting a name with their corpse."

"You don't think Chase was able to get the best of him, do you?"

"It bloody well looks like it. Get our man on the phone-if he's not lying in a morgue."

The connection severed, and Drake fumbled through his desk for the assassin's phone number. It went straight to voice mail. The room was suddenly a bit warmer.

No need to worry, old boy. He's probably finishing them off as you sit here. The man was a trained killer. A banker and a teacher wouldn't stand a chance.

It made for a convincing argument. Too bad Drake didn't believe it.

Chapter 35

Philadelphia, Pennsylvania

As they raced away from their would-be assassin, Parker and Erika blended in with all the other frantic pedestrians hurrying from gunfire. Police vehicles flew past, lights flashing. Parker also found his overnight bag on the street where it had fallen, an unexpected surprise. Two blocks later he spotted a taxi and they climbed in.

Erika's voice quivered. "Where can we go?"

Her apartment was out of the question. This guy might have backup, and they would know where she lived. They needed a place to lie low, somewhere off the radar.

The gun was jammed into Parker's coat pocket, half-visible, metal rattling against his keys.

He pulled out the small set and found his answer.

"Take us to Rittenhouse Square." The taxi driver nodded, tires squealing around a turn.

"We can go to Joe's old place," he said to Erika, his voice low. "I still have the key."

Her mouth dropped open. "Do you think it's safe?"

"Right now, we don't have much choice. We won't stay for long."

Ducked low in the backseat, Parker assessed their situation. Somehow they both still had their bags. They had Erika's gun, along with some spare ammo, and they were alive. All in all, not so bad.

The taxi dropped them off in front of his uncle's old apartment building. On the second floor, Joe's windows were covered, the blinds drawn the way Parker had left them several months ago. His only uncle had been a bachelor, and with both his parents dead, the downtown single-story

157

apartment in one of Philadelphia's most desirable neighborhoods now belonged to Parker.

Which would have been nice if he didn't live in Pittsburgh, three hundred miles away.

Inside he found everything as he'd left it, along with the scent of wood polish, courtesy of the cleaning company Parker had brought in to clear up Joe's study.

Inside Joe's old enclave, Parker studied the refurbished room.

Patched bullet holes lined the mahogany walls. Parker had thrown out the leather couch, which had been oozing stuffing from its desecrated hide, but kept the beautiful desk that dominated the room. Constructed of lumber salvaged from the bottom of Boston harbor, the desk had been one of Joe's prized possessions, a monstrous ode to his passion for all things historical.

Parker may have been hurtling down memory lane, but Erika didn't have time for such nonsense. She went straight to the chair behind Joe's old desk and sat down, her laptop blinking to life.

"I haven't been able to stop thinking about Aldrich Securities and their connections with the British ambassadors. You'd think that someone would have realized by now that they're basically supported by a foreign government, the next stop on a pre-planned journey that begins at Eton."

She was all business again.

"Do you think anyone would have the resources to identify a trend like that?" Parker asked. "And are we sure it's a trend, or did it just happen to be that a few of the retired ambassadors were chummy with Aldrich's board? That kind of stuff happens all the time, people getting hired somewhere that they're buddies with the bigwigs."

"Thank you, Captain Obvious. Now that no one's shooting at us, I can check the rest of Aldrich's records. If they're trying to hide anything, they're doing a terrible job. Everything we've found so far has been on their website where the whole world can see it."

For several minutes he stared absently at the floor, his mind racing with unanswered questions. Who had that guy been? How had he found them? And most importantly, why did he want to kill them?

Parker scratched his thigh and heard the rustle of paper in his pocket. "Wait a second. I forgot about this." The slip of paper he'd taken from the dead assassin's pocket was in his hand.

"What?" Erika's face darkened. "What is that?"

"It was in that guy's pocket. I grabbed it before we left."

She scrutinized the small sheet. Two strings of numbers, each around fifteen digits long, were written in concise script.

"Do you think it's a code?"

A nagging thought that had been buzzing in the back of his mind finally clicked.

"It's an account number."

"A what?"

"A bank account number." He was positive now. "And that's the password."

Her incredulous look spoke volumes. "How in the world do you know that?"

"Several of my clients have offshore accounts. Remember what we talked about, the offshore company Ben was running? Well, you can also have offshore bank accounts. Say you have a whole bunch of money, and for whatever reason, you don't want the US government to know about it. If you're paid off the books or from an account that's already out of the country, you can wire money to your non-American bank account and keep the IRS from ever knowing about the cash."

"So why would a guy who was trying to kill us have a bank account number and password in his pocket?"

"I have an idea. Let me use that computer."

"No way. I'm actually doing research that might save our lives. Use this for your wild goose chase." From inside of her bag Erika withdrew an iPad, handing the slender device to him.

Parker tapped the touchscreen and brought up his work e-mail account. "Here, look at this." He pointed to a string of numbers of the same length. "This account belongs to one of my clients. I send his profits here every month."

"Does that even help us?"

"It tells me that this account is from a Swiss bank, and there are only a few institutions that a hit man would trust with his money. A bank would have to be very discreet for a killer to trust them."

A quick search presented Parker with a list of the five largest banks in Zurich.

"Now what?" Erika asked. "If these banks are so secretive, no one will tell you if this guy had an account or not."

"Oh, I think I can convince them to share."

Parker dialed an international number for the first bank on his list. Once the signal traveled halfway around the world, a demure female voice answered.

"Guten Tag." Parker didn't speak German, so he got right to the point and rattled off the first string of numbers.

"Zugangscode?" He had no idea what that meant, so he read the second string of digits. A keyboard could be heard tapping. Several interminable seconds later, the woman spoke.

"Was kann ich fur Sie tun?"

He should really learn another language. "I'm sorry, but I don't speak German."

The response was instant. "I apologize, sir. How may I help you?" Gone was the harsh German accent, replaced by flawless English.

"I'd like to check the balance of my account." Erika's jaw had dropped wide open as he spoke, one hand on her chest.

More keyboard clicks. Parker put the phone on speaker.

"As of today, it is forty-nine million seven hundred eighty-six thousand dollars, sir."

The number literally took his breath away.

After several seconds, the woman asked, "Sir, are you there?"

"Yes, yes, I'm here." He scrambled to think while Erika sat immobile, her eyes unblinking.

"Thank you for your help. That's all I require."

"Have a wonderful day, sir."

The connection severed, he nearly fell onto the desk.

Erika exploded. "Parker, did you hear her? This guy had fifty million dollars." Her hands flew about, slicing through the air as she spoke.

To Parker, the next step was obvious. "He doesn't need it anymore."

"What are you talking about? Parker, no." As he considered the situation, she already knew where he was going. "You can't. You don't know where that money came from."

"And to be honest, I don't care. He was a murderer, Erika, and apparently a prolific one. It's not going to do him any good now."

"You want to steal it." Erika shook her head, which now rested in both hands. "What if they find out you're not the account holder? You could go to jail."

"That's the beauty of Swiss banking," Parker responded. "Half the time they never even see the person who opens an account. It's all done electronically or through personal representatives. Having a whole bunch of money can make people act in strange ways."

"But still, you don't know where the money came from. Doesn't that bother you?"

He thought about it for a moment. It didn't bother him one bit.

"Not at all. That guy might have killed people for a living. I shot him, so I can take his money. Aside from that"-and here he grabbed her hand-"I'm sick of people trying to kill us. With that kind of money, we can hold our own. Think about it. Now we won't have to rely on Nick to save us when things get tough. I'll hire an army of security to protect you, to figure out who's after us and how we can stop them."

"I don't know; it just doesn't seem right."

His resolve was steel. "Frankly, I don't give a damn. It's there, and we have access to it if we need it. That's good enough for now. Once we know it's safe, we can take a trip to Zurich and I'll make sure no one can ever trace it."

Obviously uncomfortable with the whole idea, she chose to avoid it. "Fine. We'll deal with it later."

Her hands turned to the keyboard and began banging out instructions. While she worked, Parker pulled up CNN, searching for any report of their recent shootout. Nothing was on the national news yet, as every outlet was busy trumpeting word of the impending oil crisis. Despite the fact he now found himself fifty million dollars richer, this oil business had grabbed his attention and wouldn't let go. Parker couldn't put his finger on it, but as he devoured article after article, the feeling that something about the whole business just didn't add up grew stronger by the minute.

Chapter 36

Philadelphia, Pennsylvania

The soft glow of the computer screen lit her resolute features, but Erika's mind caromed around like a rollercoaster as she sat behind Joe's old desk. Try as she might, she couldn't focus on the laptop in front of her.

It was the first time she'd been in her mentor's office since his death. Parker had visited several times since then, one of which ended in a shootout between law enforcement and two hit men sent to murder Parker. A Philadelphia homicide detective had been killed, and Nick Dean, the CIA agent who ultimately helped them survive the ordeal, had saved Parker's life.

Other than the formerly bullet-ridden walls and furniture, the place was fairly clean. If it hadn't been for the fifty-million-dollar discovery a few minutes ago, she would be getting some work done right now.

Instead, she struggled to accept that the man she loved was going to steal an ill-gotten fortune. It wasn't that she disagreed with taking the dead man's money. He had tried to kill them, after all. It was that the money was as dirty as it came, likely accumulated through years of calculated killing. The idea that his newfound riches were obtained on the backs of innocent victims made Erika shudder.

How did this ever happen to her? Six months ago she'd been an ambitious assistant professor at Penn studying under Joseph Chase, one of the most respected men in the field. The fact that he was also Parker's uncle had been interesting, but things had worked out. Now she was once again running for her life with Parker, albeit a much wealthier Parker than before.

She needed to focus.

"Screw this." Erika shoved the whole mess from her mind and focused on Aldrich Securities' home page. Their self-important lineage had so far proven to be a lucrative source of information.

The list of former directors stretched for miles, going all the way back to the early 1800s. The most recent hit she'd had, Richard Lyons, had served in the 1870s. Starting with the board members that came after Lyons, she punched their names into her university archives.

Thirty minutes later, she hit pay dirt.

"Parker, look at this."

He'd been glued to her iPad for the past half hour, completely ignoring her. "What's up?"

What had grabbed his eye? "Tell me what has your attention. You haven't moved since that phone call."

"I'm not sure. Seriously, I don't know. Give me some time and I'll have a better answer."

"Fine. One of us has to do some work. Check this out."

Parker leaned over her shoulder and studied a grainy, black-and-white photo. A half dozen white men, all clad in turn of the century fashion, stared back. "Who are these guys?"

"You don't recognize any of them? That guy, the one with the beard, is J.P. Morgan."

"They all have beards, and that has to be the grainiest photo I've ever seen." He had a point.

"This is a who's who of bankers and industrialists a hundred years ago" Erika explained. "The heads of Morgan Bank, Chase National and National City Bank of New York are there, as well as the head of Aldrich Bank, which is what Aldrich Securities was known as back then. His name"-and here she indicated one of the bearded participants-"was Quentin Waldegrave."

"What's so special about this?"

"This photo was taken in October 1929, the same month the stock market crashed and America fell into the Great Depression."

"I assume all these bigwigs were trying to prevent the crash?"

She opened a second window, this one displaying several news articles retrieved from Penn's archives. "You'd be correct. Do you know anything about Black Thursday?"

"Just that it's when the stock market crashed."

"Yes, but listen to this. Some of the more astute financial leaders of that era had read the tea leaves in the preceding week and knew the market was in trouble. This photo with all the big shots was taken a few days before

Black Thursday, at a meeting of the minds in New York, the purpose of which was to figure out how to stop a cataclysmic collapse of the market. Quentin Waldegrave was invited to the gathering."

"Their meeting didn't go so well."

"Well done, Sherlock. It failed, and failed miserably. Once the tumble began, with heavy trading on Thursday that led to even heavier losses, the game was over. However, the group had been trying to avert such losses for over a week, ever since they arrived in New York the prior weekend."

"How do you know they were in the city that early?"

"Because some of them were giving interviews to the news outlets, telling everyone that things would be all right, to hold the course."

Erika enlarged one of the news articles on her screen. It was what had grabbed her attention in the first place.

"So imagine my surprise when I find this." She watched his lips part and eyebrows reach skyward as he read the interview of Quentin Waldegrave. Printed in *The New York Times,* dated two days before the market collapse, Waldegrave had done little to assuage the fears of a skittish public.

"All he talks about is how bad things are going to get," Parker observed. "He didn't say anything about staying calm. In fact, everything he's quoted as saying is the complete opposite."

"And that's not the worst of it." A second interview she had located of Waldegrave the following day presented more prognostications of disaster. Not once in the conversation did the Aldrich Chairman imply the impending storm would soon pass or offer any calming words.

Parker began to pace around the desk. "Those two interviews sound like he *wants* to create a run on the banks, to scare people into withdrawing all their money. He sure didn't do his team of gurus any favors."

"That's the same thing I thought. This second interview was on Wednesday, and on Thursday the market tanked. It doesn't make any sense that Waldegrave would sabotage all their efforts at stabilizing the situation."

He parked his rear end on Joe's desk across from her. "Wouldn't the other guys have seen these interviews and called him on it?"

Her shoulders lifted. "You'd think so, but remember that this was a hundred years ago. Those men may have been so involved with trying to salvage things that they didn't read the paper. Which, by the way, was the most popular medium of communication, along with the radio. It's not like they could go to *The Times* website and check the headlines. With all the turmoil, a single interview could easily have slipped under their radar."

As Parker mulled this over, she brought up the most damning part. On the screen was a photo taken on the market exchange floor on Black Thursday. Waldegrave, along with his fellow industry leaders, stood together below the famed market bell, engrossed in conversation with the president and vice president of the exchange.

"Look at this. One day after his second negative interview, Waldegrave is singing a different tune." Several quotes below the black-and-white photo from Aldrich's chairman urged investors to remain calm and not pull out of the market.

"Why would he do that? If he really wanted to avert a disaster, he sure did a poor job of it. Those two interviews on Tuesday and Wednesday would have destroyed investor confidence."

Always a list person, Erika pulled out a notepad and pen. "I think we've found a pattern." Red ink carved out a series of names on the yellow sheet.

"Going back to when this whole mess started, the first person we found was George Simpson, when Revere listed him as a traitor."

From across the desk, Parker picked up on her line of thinking. "Which led us to Henry Fox and Richard Lyons, both British Ambassadors to the United States, and both members of Aldrich's board of directors."

"And both men were educated at Eton."

Those two names were scrawled below *George Simpson* on her pad.

"Which brings us to the latest suspect, Quentin Waldegrave."

Parker stood from his perch on the desk's edge. "Where did he go to school?"

Her humorless grin said it all.

"He went to Eton as well. What's up with that place?" Parker asked.

"That's a good question, one that I don't have an answer for. Waldegrave spent his teenage years at Eton, though he was an American by birth. After Eton," Erika said, "he came to America and continued his studies at Yale. Right out of college, it looks like he started working for Aldrich and eventually became chairman." From each name, Erika drew a line which led to the college's name, written in capital letters.

"Other than the fact they all attended this English prep school, what else connects these guys?" She felt herself being drawn into the mystery, anticipation trumping frustration and fueling a desire to unravel this mess.

"Well, we know that Simpson was a traitor, involved with some plot to undermine the American economy."

She turned toward Parker, who had gone rigidly still.

"Erika, I think that's it."

"What's it?" He could be so confusing at times. Typical man.

"The motive. Every one of them."

"What in the world are you talking about?"

One finger stabbed at her list. "George Simpson. American by birth, worked with the English, wanted to destroy our economy."

She nodded, allowing him to talk out his theory. "Fox and Lyons," Parker continued. "Both Englishmen who were in America. Both ambassadors, men with power. And both involved with the forerunner to Aldrich Securities." He leaned close to her, his hazel eyes dazzling as rays of sunlight streaming through the open window struck them.

"These two also encouraged the South to secede from the Union."

Finally the lightbulb clicked on. It had been in front of her the whole time.

"They both tried to destroy America," Erika stated. "To rip this nation apart at the seams."

Parker nodded, face alight. "And Lyons's position as the British ambassador allowed him to succeed. Who knows how much weight his promise of purchasing Southern cotton carried, but I'd bet Jefferson Davis was pretty excited to know there would still be a market for his cash crop."

"Too bad he didn't think about how to transport it."

"Which was lucky for the North. If the South had more money, maybe we'd only have twenty-five states today."

He pointed toward the final name, but no explanation was needed.

"And now we have Mr. Waldegrave, Eton grad, chairman of Aldrich, and from the look of these interviews, a man wholeheartedly determined to destroy confidence in the stock market and banking system."

Parker had returned to his perch on the desk. He favored her with a penetrating gaze. "Why would these men try to wreak havoc on the United States? They all must have come from privileged backgrounds, considering the positions they held, the schools they attended. What could possibly inspire them to do this?"

She knew the questions were rhetorical.

He continued. "As crazy as it sounds, Revere may have been right. Don't you agree?" Faced with the mounting evidence, she had little choice.

"I'm not sold yet, but it certainly looks like it. I've only made it to the early twentieth century of Aldrich Securities board members. Who knows what else there is to find?"

"In that case, I suggest you continue searching."

Parker plopped down onto the room's sole remaining chair, a dark leather club seat whose three matching companions had fallen victim to the gun battle several months ago.

"I'm interested to see what you find from Aldrich's more recent past. Specifically from a few years ago."

"You mean 2008?"

"That's exactly what I mean. The worst financial crisis since the Great Depression. Yesterday I would have said you were nuts, but it's right up their alley."

He traded the iPad for his cell phone.

"I'm going to call Nick and tell him what happened. Hopefully he knows how Ben was killed and if there's anything strange about the murder."

"Make sure to ask him what he learned about Spencer Drake. I have a feeling that guy has some skeletons in his closet."

While Parker dialed the phone, she realized that she should be frightened out of her mind. For the second time this year, someone was actively trying to kill her. Instead, the discovery of Paul Revere's letters and the thrill of the search left her with-and it was hard to explain-a feeling of satisfaction. All was not well, and she was starting to enjoy it.

Chapter 37

Philadelphia, Pennsylvania

"Dean."

The gruff voice of his CIA friend put a smile on Parker's face. The man was all business.

"Nick, it's Parker."

"Did you make it somewhere safe?"

"Sort of."

"What do you mean, sort of? You have any bullet holes in you or not?"

Parker recapped their narrow escape from the slender assassin. Nick said nothing until he was finished, though Parker could hear a pen scratching away as he spoke.

"Are you on a cell phone?"

Oops. "Yeah."

The anger in his voice was a tangible object. "Hang up and call me back on a landline."

The line went dead, and Parker redialed Nick's number from Joe's desk.

"What did I tell you about cell phones? I hope it's a throwaway."

"Don't worry, it is."

"Where are you?"

"We're at Joe's apartment. I still have the key."

"That's actually not a bad idea. About time you did something right." From Nick, that was a true compliment.

"What did this assassin look like, and where did you leave the body?"

Parker described the gaunt man and his final resting place.

"Parker, you have to be more careful. Nice work getting rid of him though. You know my offer still stands."

168

After their interaction a few months ago, Nick had offered Parker a job with the Agency, promising to keep him in Philadelphia to work on his team. Though he did seem to have a knack for staying alive under fire, Parker wasn't ready to give up his day job just yet.

"I appreciate that, but right now I want to figure out why this is happening, starting with who would want to kill Erika and me."

"As do I. I did some digging on your friend's murder. There's not much to go on, but it looks like an old man walked up behind him at an ATM and shot him. No one in the area saw this old guy, and forensics came up with absolutely nothing. No hair samples, clothing fibers, zip. We talked to every cab company, and none of their drivers remember picking up anyone fitting his description in the area. I hate to say it, but right now we have nothing."

Parker had suspected as much. If Ben's killing and the recent attempt on his own life were related, they were probably dealing with professionals.

"Thanks for checking. There's something else you should know, a common denominator Erika and I have been researching."

"What do you have?" Nick asked, an edge of intrigue in his voice.

"Those letters from Revere mentioned a single name, one man who Revere suspected was a traitor."

"His name was Simpson, right?"

"Correct," Parker confirmed. "We've found a trail leading from George Simpson to the twentieth century, and the trail may not have reached a conclusion." Parker summarized their findings, from Simpson's alleged betrayal to Henry Fox and Richard Lyons, the British ambassadors who served on Aldrich's board. He told Nick of their suspicions regarding Lyons encouraging the South to secede, and finished with Quentin Waldegrave, a past chairman of Aldrich who seemingly encouraged the investor panic that led directly to the Great Depression.

"So," Parker finished, "we have a link stretching from Revere's discovery of a plot to destroy the American economy to the chairman of Aldrich Securities giving contradictory interviews immediately prior to the Depression. And Erika's still working on the more recent Aldrich boards and presidents."

Nick was silent for so long that Parker worried he'd lost him. "You still there?"

"I'm here," was his terse response. "Chase, we need to meet. Now."

That was the last thing he'd expected. "Sure, we can do that. What do we need to talk about?"

"I'll tell you later. Can you be outside Reading Terminal Market in fifteen minutes?"

"I'll be there."

"Wait by the covered entrance. I'll pick you up."

Parker turned toward the desk where Erika was furiously tapping at her computer.

"Time to go. Nick wants to meet."

She was obviously not expecting that either. "What? Why does he need to see us?"

"He didn't say, but you know Nick doesn't joke around. We're leaving now."

Fifteen minutes later, Parker and Erika stood at the corner of Twelfth and Filbert, shrouded in the passing crowds of tourists and locals, many on their way into Reading Terminal. A Philadelphia landmark for over a century, each year millions of hungry people came to the market in search of food or merchandise. The market covered a square block and offered a nearly limitless variety of culinary options. The delicious smell of fresh-baked bread wafted outside, slicing through the stench of garbage on a hot summer day. It was only when a black Suburban nearly clipped their toes that they realized Nick had arrived. A window slid down to reveal the stern countenance and considerable bulk of CIA Agent Dean.

"Get in."

Parker hopped in the front seat, Erika in the rear, and the throaty growl of eight cylinders firing sent them shooting into the city's downtown area.

Parker remained silent as Nick drove, waiting for the ever-serious government man to speak first. Not until they merged onto the Schuylkill Expressway, the main traffic artery that desperately needed a Lipitor prescription, did Nick say a word.

"You two have no idea who you're messing with."

What was he talking about? Parker glanced over his should at Erika, who wore an equally bewildered expression.

"That stiff you left by your apartment is a ghost. Not Casper the friendly ghost. He's a nobody, a guy who doesn't seem to exist. We can't find anything on him. No prints, no tattoos, no driver's license, passport, nothing."

Erika spoke up from the rear. "What does that mean?"

"It means that whoever he was, he went to a whole lot of trouble to make sure he was invisible. If Interpol's database has nothing on him, he's either squeaky clean or dirty as hell. We're sending people around to all the hotels in the area and checking airport and train security footage to see if we can find someone who saw him or figure out how he got here."

Parker sensed there was more to this meeting than that. "Is that what you wanted to tell us?"

Nick went silent for a moment as he exited the expressway, turning into the Manayunk neighborhood of the city. About ten miles from downtown, it was popular with a younger crowd, as much for the abundance of bars and restaurants as the affordable rent.

"I did some digging into Spencer Drake. At first, there was nothing that would lead me to believe the man's a murderer. Filthy rich and fond of beautiful women, yes, but not a killer. It was only after you mentioned the trail of renegade British statesmen associated with Aldrich Securities that I found it."

Erika was leaning between them, her blonde ponytail tickling Parker's nose. "Did you find a link between Drake and Waldegrave, their chairman during the Depression?" Parker didn't have to see her face to know the intensity of her gaze.

"Not exactly." Nick had found his way onto Kelly Drive, arguably the most scenic roadway in the city. The curving four-lane thoroughfare paralleled the meandering course of the Schuylkill River, sheer rock on one side, a strip of grass with occasional parks that abutted lapping water on the other. It was into one of these small park areas that Nick steered the vehicle. On the river, a collegiate crew team rowed in unison, their elongated vessel gliding across the river's glassy surface.

When he put the car in park, the interior grew noticeably darker.

"What was that? Did you turn the tint up or something?"

"The windows automatically adjust the level of light that flows through based on outside conditions. Part of the vehicle's security system is keeping anyone from seeing who, or what, is inside."

Parker was impressed. "Are the windows bulletproof?"

"Rated to withstand a shotgun blast at point-blank range. Same goes for the body, and the undercarriage is hardened against explosive devices."

A low whistle escaped Parker's lips.

"I brought this car because what I'm about to share with you must never be repeated." A thin manila folder appeared from the center console.

"While researching Spencer Drake, I learned that one of his associates is a man named Sir Nigel Stirling, an English lord of some renown. His ancestor founded the East India Company."

Erika gasped. "You can't be serious."

Parker knew the company had been powerful several hundred years ago, but the most recent time he'd seen the name was while watching Johnny Depp in the role of Captain Jack Sparrow.

"In 1600, Queen Elizabeth granted a charter to Stirling's ancestor to commence operations," Nick explained, "and they were wildly successful until their dissolution in 1874. As you can imagine, the Stirling family accumulated an immense amount of wealth, which today is under the control of Nigel Stirling, the sole heir to the Stirling fortune."

Parker loved history as much as anyone else, but how was this information going to keep them alive?

"What does this Stirling guy have to do with Drake, or with who's trying to kill us?"

Nick removed several sheets of paper, though he didn't hand them over. "I don't know who's trying to kill you, but I can tell you that Nigel Stirling's grandfather may be the next link in your chain."

Erika's eyes locked onto the hidden papers when she spoke. "Was he on Aldrich's board?"

"He was, for the last twenty years of his life. Horatio Stirling died in 1958, and was soon followed to the grave by his son Arthur, who was Nigel's father."

Erika's voice was heavy with intrigue. "Were they murdered?"

"No, nothing like that. Horatio died of old age, and Arthur died in a car crash. The reason I had to speak with you in person relates to Horatio's activities in late 1941." The sheets of paper Nick held were still hidden from view, blank rear sides facing Parker. A group of joggers ran past the car, their conversation barely a whisper through the SUV's thick windows.

Nick scrutinized the group as they passed, and only when they were well down the road did he continue. "In December of that year, Horatio Stirling was on vacation in the Hawaiian islands. On December 7, Horatio's wife and children were at their home in Florida, supposedly preparing to leave for the island to meet him. Of course, that all changed when the first Japanese bomb fell on Pearl Harbor."

For what felt like the hundredth time that week, Parker was trying to connect the dots, but he didn't have the first clue where to start. "Was

Stirling involved with the bombing? Not to be rude, but that sounds crazy."

Agent Dean's look said it all. "It does. Until you see these." Nick turned the concealed papers around to display a color copy of what looked like gibberish.

Before Parker could respond, Erika blurted out, "That's written in Japanese. I can't read it, but I recognize the characters."

An intense squint at the paper confirmed his ignorance. He had no idea what those scribbles meant.

"Correct," Nick said. "Do you notice anything else?"

Finally, Parker was first at something. "There's one word in English, and it says *Stirling*."

Near the top of the single paragraph was the surname, clearly spelled out in English.

"Nice work, Chase. For your information, there is no Japanese form of the surname."

Erika asked, "What does the message say? And where did you get it?"

"This is a telegraph communication found in the cockpit of a Japanese fighter plane shot down over Pearl Harbor. Pilots would get these printouts with updated information on target coordinates, weather or mission plans. This particular update basically says that *Stirling* has confirmed the American naval forces were unprepared for an attack. The transmission is dated December 7, and was received at seven in the morning. The first bombs fell forty-eight minutes later."

He and Erika were speechless. Had a British citizen aided in slaughtering over two thousand American troops?

Parker finally found his voice. "Why have we never heard of this?"

"As I said before, this is highly classified. It hasn't been released, and probably never will be. There are some things that are too volatile for the public to know. Second, and more pertinently, we have no proof that the word *Stirling* refers to Horatio Stirling, or if it even refers to a person at all. Perhaps the word was a code name for some type of stolen technology, or a signal the Japanese developed. No mention was ever found of this *Stirling* again, so all we have to go on is a single transmission."

Erika was aghast at his explanation. "But if you know Horatio was in Hawaii at the time, and you can connect him to the Japanese, shouldn't he at least have been questioned?"

"Erika, you have to realize that this information didn't come to light until several weeks after the attack. Most of the naval base was destroyed, and it took months for it to recover from the damage inflicted by the attack. There just weren't enough people to dig through all the evidence to get anything done right away. And besides that, the fact that Horatio Stirling was in Hawaii at the time wasn't known until *a full year* after the attack. This wasn't, and still has not been, identified as high value information."

Parker was looking for holes in the story. "In that case, how did you find it?"

"Every year the CIA hires hundreds of interns whose sole job is to scan or manually enter old files into our database. One of those poor saps scanned and uploaded the file that contained this message, so when I conducted my search, it was able to be located."

A pack of cyclists pulled off the roadway into their parking lot, stopping several spots down from Nick's armored tank of a vehicle. He eyed them suspiciously, hard eyes unblinking.

"You know," Erika said, her head between them both, "this actually fits into what we've found so far, but on an entirely different level."

She was addressing Nick, but her gaze was on Parker. "If the message really did come from Horatio Stirling, then we would have evidence of a direct attack on American soil orchestrated in part by a British citizen. This is completely different than everything we've uncovered so far."

What she said made sense.

"None of the other Aldrich members we found were involved in a direct assault on America. Each of them was a behind the scenes operative who set the plan in motion and hoped it would work. Some did better than others, but they didn't help kill Americans."

The group of bikers hadn't left yet, so Nick turned the key and motored back onto Kelly Drive.

The muscular agent shared his plan. "I'm going to take a deeper look into Aldrich Securities, see if there's anything I can find connecting Spencer Drake and Nigel Stirling."

"Parker and I can keep digging through the past board members and see what we find."

"Whatever you do," Nick's voice was even more serious than usual, "don't go back to your apartment. It's not safe anymore."

He was interrupted by the shrill ringing of his phone. One look at the device and Nick nearly rear-ended the car in front of them.

"Guess who just went through customs at Logan International in Boston."

Their voices rang out in unison. "Nigel Stirling."
"His private jet landed ten minutes ago."

Chapter 38

Boston, Massachusetts

For the tenth time in the past half hour, Drake's call to his hired killer rang straight through to voice mail.

"Damn it, this can't be happening."

The number had been given as an emergency contact, only to be used if Drake uncovered the exact whereabouts of Parker Chase or Erika Carr. Drake doubted the assassin had gotten this far in his craft by ignoring such valuable information.

On his desk, the intercom crackled to life, Liz's voice ringing out. "Spencer, phone call for you."

"Put it through."

"Mr. Drake? This is Tom Becker." His head of security had contacts in law enforcement, and Drake had instructed him to call in whatever favors he had to identify the corpse in Philadelphia.

"Who's the dead guy?"

A heavy sigh sent Drake's heart into his throat. "I've confirmed it's not Parker Chase. I spoke to an officer who was on the scene, and the body didn't fit his description. He described the corpse as exceedingly thin, with buzzed hair. There was no identification of any kind on the body."

It had to be their man. Somehow, Parker Chase had gotten the better of a trained killer.

"I want you to gather a group of men you trust," Spencer instructed. "We have a major problem on our hands, and we need to take care of it before this gets out of control."

Becker responded without hesitation. "Will the elimination be permanent, sir?"

He knew his security chief had enjoyed his time in the military and was not averse to the more gruesome aspects of combat. It was one of the main reasons he'd hired the man. Tom Becker was not afraid to get his hands dirty.

"Without question. For a variety of reasons, this problem must be buried immediately."

A hint of pleasure tinged Becker's reply. "I know just the men, sir."

"Good. You have my personal authority to spend whatever it takes to get them on board and ready to roll. Once the team is assembled, I'll pass along further instructions."

"Multiple targets, sir?"

"Yes. And these targets may prove to be formidable. I trust you are capable of handling any adversity that may be encountered, Mr. Becker?"

"I look forward to it, sir."

When he hung up, Drake found his spirits had lifted. Becker was a hard man, had cut his teeth in the sands of Desert Storm and honed his skills in Somalia hunting warlords. With his skills, Spencer hoped that the last thing Dr. Carr and her boyfriend ever saw was the smoking barrel of Tom Becker's pistol.

The red light on his desk phone blinked. "Lane Peterson on the line for you, sir."

Just what he needed. The head of JP Morgan calling for some reassurance. Weren't people like him supposed to have self-confidence?

"Lane, how are you?"

The short, clipped tone coming through his speakers oozed privilege, though Drake suspected that the blue-blooded New Yorker was all nerves right now.

"Mr. Drake, how are you? I hope all is well at Aldrich Securities."

"Swimmingly, Lane. What can I do for you?"

"Well, I'm calling to discuss your recent predictions regarding oil prices, which I must say have been spot on."

Drake had encouraged Lane Peterson, along with several other heads of New York's largest financial institutions, to invest heavily in the oil futures market, predicting that the price of oil would rise.

"I appreciate your gratitude."

"I just wonder if what you suggest regarding our clients' money is wise. Depositors and investors don't expect our bank to take excessive risks with their funds."

The man had no backbone to speak of. Risk-averse and conservative, he sounded like a frightened child.

"Lane, you old dog, have I led you astray yet?"

"No, not at all. Though, I do have to admit that I'm a bit worried about what could happen if the price of crude doesn't continue to rise as you predict."

"I stand by my recommendations. While we are still able, I believe that in order to maximize profits, Aldrich and every other financial firm should use all available funds to invest in oil futures."

"Yes, but don't you feel that some of our clients, particularly the depositors, would be upset to learn that we were taking such risks with their money?"

"I would agree if I thought it was a risk. Lane, this is a guarantee. Look at how much money we've made. Would I send you on a path to ruin?" Drake failed to mention that the only reason he was certain the investments were sound was because Sheik Khan had assured him oil production would remain stagnant. That would be his little secret.

"You've certainly been correct so far. My only concern is that if oil prices plummet, I would be overextended. As it is, and I've spoken with several of our colleagues who are in the same position, I have more of my assets invested in oil than I normally would. Far more, to be truthful."

That was music to Drake's ears. The more money Lane and his foolish counterparts dumped into the oil market, the greater their losses when Sheik Khan flooded it.

"Lane…" Drake dropped his voice. "Trust me on this. So far, I've made tens of millions, and I'm just getting started. I have it on good authority that OPEC has no intention of increasing the supply of oil. A close friend of mine tells me that the kings and sheiks over there are concerned that by abating this mini-crisis, by helping America and other oil-dependent, predominately Christian nations, they risk losing the support of their local religious leaders, the vast majority of which are Muslim. I don't have to tell you how influential a cleric can be. It's a matter of survival."

Nothing from Peterson. Would he buy that line of nonsense?

A few tense moments later, he did. "Then I suppose there's nothing wrong with making a profit, wouldn't you agree? After all, men such as us with the vision to foresee these opportunities would be remiss were we to let them pass by unrealized."

The pompous buffoon. He had no idea what was happening.

"Exactly. One should take one's chances when presented."

"In that case, I will personally handle the investing of our clients' deposits. Return the money in a few weeks, minus the profits, of course, and perhaps I will soon build a new yacht to challenge your own beauty."

"Now, you know I couldn't let that stand for long. Consider yourself forewarned, sir."

Peterson let out a nervous chuckle.

"Oh, I almost forgot," Spencer said, setting the hook. "I would recommend you keep an eye open for some 'internal' Aldrich e-mails that may soon find their way into the public domain. These e-mails, which I can assure you would never be intentionally leaked, will likely speculate that the price of oil will continue to rise in the foreseeable future."

Which would make any other hesitant investors confident enough to jump into the speculative oil futures market, further increasing the coming losses.

"In that case, I have some investments to make. Spencer, it's been a pleasure, as always."

After ringing off, Drake felt an uncouth urge to jump about the room. It had all been so easy. These greedy Americans were so obsessed with profits, with pillaging their fellow citizens' pockets, that they never stopped to consider the consequences of their actions.

If one of the largest investment institutions in the country would risk their clients' money with such a cavalier attitude, what did that say about the people who comprised such a nation?

Whatever his feelings on American morality, Drake turned to another matter. He needed to update Nigel Stirling as to his plans for eliminating Parker Chase and Erika Carr.

Phone in hand, Drake dialed Nigel's private line, only slightly leery of the fact that two hundred years of work was now dependent on Tom Becker's lethal hands.

Chapter 39

Boston, Massachusetts

Inside the elegant dining room of Del Frisco's, Boston's power brokers rubbed elbows over perfectly seared prime rib and long-stemmed glasses of Pinot Noir. A setting sun lent sparkling red diamonds to the glassy water's surface, the perfect complement to sweeping views of Liberty Wharf and downtown that greeted patrons as they entered the stylish modern establishment. The one-of-a-kind art collection complemented a unique, vibrant atmosphere which housed curving booths and intimate table settings. In the main room, an impressive circular bar boasted several thousand vintages of hand-selected wine.

Built to showcase the unique beauty of Boston's waterfront, Del Frisco's had incorporated other, more secluded areas into the open layout. On the upper floor were several private dining rooms, each accessible via staircase, the entire floor concealed behind additional wine racks open enough to allow some ambient light through while keeping each private room hidden from view.

Inside the private level's lone corner room was a single table, around which two people sat, candles glimmering on the red tablecloth. A woman laughed demurely, one hand resting just above the plunging neckline on her red evening dress.

Spencer Drake found that he was enjoying himself, this evening with Liz doing wonders for his over-burdened mind. Liz was sharp and witty, a devilish beauty. Qualities a man could appreciate.

After speaking with Nigel about eliminating the troublesome Dr. Carr and her boyfriend, Spencer had tossed his phone into the plush center console of his Aston Martin DBS, ready for an escape. With primal excitement, his foot slammed down and the V12 engine responded instantly. Over five hundred horses roared to life and he rocketed ahead, Liz losing her lipstick as she was thrown back into her seat.

It was cliché, but Drake secretly loved tooling around in James Bond's vehicle of choice.

"What do you say to a second bottle? The sommelier was spot on with our first selection."

Liz was radiant in the soft candlelight. "Are you trying to get me drunk, Mr. Drake?"

"Never, my dear."

Her pouting lips sent an electric thrill down his spine. The moment was lost, however, when the maître de appeared at the door. "Mr. Drake, please excuse the interruption, but you have a call."

Who could be calling? No one even knew they were here.

"Take a message." He'd left his phone behind for a reason.

"I tried, sir, but he was most insistent. The gentleman's name is Stirling, and he said it is of the utmost urgency."

Drake froze in his chair. Nigel was not given to hyperbole. "Bring me the phone."

"Of course, sir."

Their elegantly dressed host hurried away, only to reappear moments later bearing a handset resting atop a silver platter. He disappeared after setting the tray on Drake's table.

"Nigel, what in the world is going on? How did you know where to find me?"

"You are a creature of habit, Spencer. There are only certain establishments you favor."

The man was unbelievable. He had informants everywhere.

"What's the matter?"

"I've received some most distressing news. Do you recall my grandfather, Horatio?"

"Of course. A lovely man."

"Yes, he was. He had a fondness for travel, particularly to the Hawaiian Islands. Did I ever tell you about his visits there?"

The breath caught in Drake's throat. "Perhaps we should continue this conversation later."

"Spencer, the file has been accessed. By a man connected to our friends in Philadelphia."

Drake clenched the phone so hard he thought it might shatter. Across the table, Liz's eyes grew wide. "I'll ring you in half an hour." Spencer threw the phone down and stood from the table, his chair falling to the ground behind him.

"We have to leave."

"Is something the matter?"

Drake threw a stack of hundred dollar bills on the table. "Put your coat on. I have to get home immediately."

She knew better than to press the issue. Twenty-five minutes later, the graphite gray English sports car squealed into his driveway, having covered the fifteen miles to his home in record time.

Leaving a sullen Liz in his wake, Spencer barged through the towering front door and went straight to his private office. Inside the mahogany-paneled room, which he'd personally designed in the classic style of a nineteenth century English men's club, Drake punched the speed dial button for Nigel Stirling.

Several rapid clicks confirmed the call was being routed through an encrypted line.

Nigel dispensed with the pleasantries. "The CIA just accessed the file."

"Bloody hell. How do you know?"

"I have a contact within Interpol, and as part of their cooperative agreement with the Americans, they have access to certain levels of intelligence reports. The file containing my grandfather's transcript is among those files, and I was told that it has been accessed by an internal agent for the first time in forty years."

"That's just perfect. Who's looking into it?"

"An agent by the name of Nicholas Dean. He's based in their Philadelphia office."

Which was where Erika Carr lived.

"Are you certain he's interested in your grandfather? The file on Pearl Harbor must be simply massive. There's only a single piece from Horatio in the whole stack."

"My informant told me Agent Dean specified the name Stirling in his search query."

Icy fingers skittered along Drake's spine.

"Bloody hell. Are you certain?"

"Of course I'm certain, you fool. I don't have to tell you what this means."

Drake recalled another piece of information regarding Agent Dean, passed on in Nigel's earlier message.

"Did you say this Dean fellow has some connection with the pair in Philadelphia?"

"That's the worst part, Spencer. Earlier this year Agent Dean was involved with the Philadelphia police investigation into the murder of Parker Chase's uncle. The dead man was a professor at Penn, actually mentored Erika Carr. He was shot in his apartment, and for some reason Nicholas Dean became involved. He's listed on the blasted police report. No idea what he did, but he's on there."

Only a fool would assume this was coincidence.

Spencer's mind rapidly filled with numbers, calculating the profits he could realistically expect to keep once their oil charade was over. The rough estimate quickly approached a half billion dollars.

A fair sum to pocket while the American economy collapsed all around him.

"Nigel, I believe we have pushed this as far as I dare. If in fact Agent Dean is somehow aware of our existence, our window of opportunity is rapidly closing."

"My thoughts exactly. My plane will be landing at Logan International in thirty minutes. I suggest we rendezvous at your office to discuss the final phase of this operation and to monitor the situation with Agent Dean and his two youthful companions."

"Agreed. I'll be there in one hour."

The line went dead, and Drake stood silently for several moments, gazing through the cherry surface of his bar, fingers drumming idly on the polished wood. Beneath his feet, the teak floor seemed to hum with energy, a sensation that climbed from his legs, coursed through his torso, and tingled past his cheekbones.

The time was upon them. Events set in motion two hundred years prior would finally be realized, and England would have her revenge against the rebellious colonists, the cause of the once mighty nation's fall from her rightful perch atop the world order.

Chapter 40

Bright sunlight filled the room, birds chirping outside as dawn asserted itself, blue sky stretching to the horizon promising another beautiful summer day in the city of brotherly love.

On a couch in his late uncle's apartment, Parker cracked open one eye, disdain for nature's alarm clocks written on his tired face.

He'd been up until well past midnight, working with Erika to uncover a connection between the mysterious telegram found at Pearl Harbor and Aldrich Securities. Erika had scoured Penn's database for any further clues, but her search had failed to unearth anything of value. Nothing else that linked Aldrich with either Horatio Stirling or any other suspicious events was located.

Parker soon tired of being her lackey and decided to conduct his own line of inquiry, focusing on what he knew best. He dug through the financial records for Aldrich Securities, which as a publicly traded company was required to disclose a wealth of information to the federal government. After eight fruitless hours, Parker had fallen onto the couch in his uncle's study, exhausted. It seemed that just as his eyes closed, the sun had appeared to wake him from a deep slumber.

Now vertical on the brown leather, which he'd always thought resembled a shrink's treatment couch, Parker realized that he'd drooled on a pillow.

A lovely start to the day.

Parker rose to the soundtrack of every joint in his body popping like fireworks. A lifetime spent smashing into other large men in pads had left its mark. His joints may have ached, but at least football had paid for school.

The wooden floorboards creaked sporadically as he padded to the bedrooms. In a guest bed, he found Erika curled into the fetal position, apparently unaffected by the streaming sunlight that splashed onto her face.

"Hey, sleeping beauty. Wake up."

She jolted up in bed, hair flying like a modern Medusa. "What is it? Where are they?"

"Where's who? It's me, crazy girl."

She rubbed her eyes vigorously, both hands kneading the sleep from her body. "What time is it?"

"Just after eight. I think I fell asleep around three."

For some unknown reason that elicited a glare from Erika. "I know you did. I was up for another hour after you bailed on me. However, I didn't find anything."

"Same here," Parker said, spirits quickly dimmed. "I can't believe the trail would go cold right now."

"It didn't go cold." She rose from the still made bed, having never burrowed under the covers. "We just haven't found it yet."

"How can you be so sure?"

She brushed past him, softly moving toward the kitchen where a coffee machine waited.

"Think about it. What we've found isn't a coincidence. For the past two hundred years, people associated with England who also have a connection to Aldrich Securities have been actively attempting to undermine the United States. It's a fact, and now we have to find out why it's been happening."

Parker wouldn't go so far as to call their suspicions *factual*, but he liked her enthusiasm. "And how do you propose we do that? I looked through every available record on Aldrich for the past decade and haven't found a thing."

She dumped a full pot of water into the machine and fired it up. "Then keep looking. There's a connection out there, waiting for us to find it. Oh, and in case you forgot, someone tried to kill us yesterday. A man the CIA can't identify. You think that's a coincidence?"

She had a point. He may have agreed with her, but proving it was a different ballgame altogether. Try as they might, the mystery surrounding Aldrich Securities was reticent to reveal its most recent secrets.

"I have a few other ideas I can follow up on," Erika offered, opaque as ever. "But that's not happening until after we eat."

Parker flipped on the television, looking for any updates on the futures market. An excited female anchor was on screen, lips moving rapidly without sound. Beside her perfectly styled brunette hair was an oversized photo of a metal barrel.

Once the sound kicked on, Parker's jaw dropped.

"To reiterate, we've just received word that OPEC, whose twelve members allegedly control eighty percent of the world's oil reserves, has announced a nearly one hundred percent increase in daily oil production, from fifty-eight million barrels per day to one hundred million barrels per day. No reason was given for the increase. This news was met with astonishment, as the twofold increase is far and away the single largest daily jump in oil production in world history."

"Erika, get in here."

"Hold on a second."

He raced into the kitchen. "OPEC just announced that they're doubling oil production."

She was less than impressed. "Oh, that's nice."

"Don't you get it?"

She finally seemed to hear him and looked up from the coffee pot.

"Spencer Drake and all his cronies are screwed," Parker told her. "Completely, utterly screwed."

He saw the gears begin to turn, and realization slowly dawned.

"You're right. They put all their money into futures, assuming that the price of oil would go up. Is this bad?"

"It's beyond that. For starters, Aldrich Securities may no longer exist after today. If they overextended themselves, Drake could go to jail."

"Why would he go to jail? Investing is a risk and sometimes you lose your money."

"Because from what Ben told us, Drake and his cohorts were using funds they shouldn't have to fund their investing. Aldrich may go bankrupt, and if people who put all their money into Aldrich's banking services lose everything, they'll be swimming in lawsuits. Drake won't have the shirt on his back when the lawyers are through with him."

"But isn't that money insured by the federal government? I thought the FDIC prevents people from losing their money like they did in the Great Depression."

"They do, but it only applies to deposit accounts, up to a quarter million per. If you have money in something other than a deposit account, you're probably out of luck. The program assumes that banks won't take unnecessary risks with your money. "

She took a step back, bumping into the counter.

"So you're saying it could all happen again?"

"I don't want to believe it, but it's looking that way," Parker confirmed. "And if you think about what Treasury Secretary Webster might do, the situation doesn't get any better."

Erika lifted a wayward strand of blonde hair behind her ear. "What are you talking about?"

"Gerard Webster opposed the bailouts from 2008. He believes that no company is too big to fail. If Aldrich Securities or any other investment firms get in over their heads, I doubt he'd throw them a lifeline."

"Well, that doesn't sound like such a bad idea. If you screw up, you should have to deal with the consequences," Erika responded, arms crossed. "I know personal responsibility is becoming something of a joke these days, but making people accept the consequences for their actions is the right thing to do."

He agreed, but there was so much more to it than that. "I think you're correct, but remember that customers who put their money into Aldrich deposit accounts expect that money to be there when they need it. A checking or savings account isn't an investment, it's a deposit. Banks aren't supposed to take risks with deposits."

"In that case, why wouldn't the government just refund the money and throw Drake and his buddies into jail?"

He barked a harsh laugh. "One, it's not technically illegal yet. Why it took this long to outlaw proprietary trading is beyond me, but it has. Two, do you realize how much money these men have? They're each worth billions. They could put together a team of lawyers and legal experts that would make O.J.'s crew look like a bunch of scrubs. And he got away with murder. Putting Spencer Drake in jail for an offense of any type would be almost impossible. Men like him are almost above the law."

She opened her mouth to respond, but stopped short. In a small voice devoid of hope, she asked, "So what can we do?"

"I don't know."

He hadn't felt this drained in a long time. Whoever they were up against had more money, men with guns, and if they were correct, hundreds of years of experience. What could two people do against a force such as that?

"We can't do anything right now."

He headed back to the bedroom and changed into a fresh shirt.

"I need to get out of here and clear my head. Maybe Nick will have new information for us, a lead on Drake or this Stirling guy."

She followed him in, jumping into a tight pair of curve-hugging tan shorts, the high-cut bottoms frayed ever so slightly. "Good idea. I'm getting so bogged down in my research I can't think straight."

Before exiting the apartment, Parker slipped her gun into the waistband of his jeans. With his T-shirt untucked, it covered the weapon from view.

"I don't want to take any chances even though we'll be right back. Whoever came after us could do it again."

Parker locked the door behind them, the hallway already growing warm courtesy of the large bay windows at each end. They took the stairs, and emerged from within the converted schoolhouse to find the sidewalk empty. It was a few moments before he remembered it was a weekday, and most people would be at work.

Across the street, two men sat in a black Lincoln Navigator, sipping coffee with the windows down. He almost missed them, with their seats tilted back and faces partially obscured by the doorframe.

As Erika started to talk, his internal alarms were blaring at full volume. Each man's hair was close cropped, and, not to put too fine a point on it, they didn't fit the stereotype of two lovers enjoying the day.

When the passenger briefly locked eyes with him, Parker knew.

"Listen to me," he interrupted Erika, grabbing her elbow tightly as they walked, "and keep looking ahead. There are two guys across the street in a black Lincoln who are looking at us."

To her credit, Erika never flinched. "Are they coming?"

He glanced back over one shoulder and saw nothing. For a brief second, he wondered if he was overreacting. Then both doors swung open and the men hopped out. When they started running toward them, Parker shoved her away and reached for his gun.

Chapter 41

Boston, Massachusetts

Inside the executive boardroom atop Aldrich Securities headquarters, Spencer Drake kneaded his temples, his eyes closed. For the past twelve hours he had been dealing with the fallout from Horatio Stirling's telegram, the discovery of which had forced his hand. Whether or not Agent Nicholas Dean had any idea of what he'd read, Nigel had been right. Now was not the time to take chances, so he and Nigel had decided to move forward with the final phase of their operation.

Slightly less than six hours ago, Spencer and Nigel had finished their call with Sheik bin Khan, who had been less than pleased to learn that this supposedly foolproof plan may have been uncovered. The sheik was not used to taking orders, but when Drake told him it was time to send the American economy into a tailspin from which it might never recover, he'd gladly agreed.

Today, the sheik had promised, oil production would double. Aldrich Securities and any other corporation, firm, or person who had overextended themselves to purchase oil futures assuming the cost of a barrel would continue to rise was in serious trouble.

Trouble of the bankruptcy variety.

"I suppose this calls for a celebration, Spencer."

Nigel Stirling stood and moved to the bar, and moments later two drinks appeared.

"Not now. We still don't know what happened to Mr. Chase and Dr. Carr. As long as those two are on the loose we're not safe."

Stirling waved one hand dismissively. "They're good as dead. Your head of security and his men are close on their tails. They won't survive the day."

189

Drake's fist smashed on the table, which sent whiskey shooting across polished mahogany. "Don't be a damn fool. They've already escaped one attempt and killed a professional hit man. Do you really believe that they're good as dead? I won't be satisfied until I see their bloody corpses in a morgue."

Stirling said nothing, sipping his drink.

Nigel's wrist casually turned toward the ceiling, shirtsleeve sliding up to reveal his Patek Philipe watch. "I believe that the news may be out."

The television flashed to life. An extremely stern-faced analyst confirmed Nigel's supposition.

"It has begun."

The sharp buzz of Drake's cell phone emanated from his pocket. It was Tom Becker.

"Have you found them?"

"They were just spotted outside Joseph Chase's apartment. Our backup team is after them now. I'm on my way."

Drake's reply was clear. "End this. Now."

Chapter 42

Philadelphia, Pennsylvania

Both men dove to the ground when Parker's gun appeared. He grabbed Erika's arm, already racing down the street. "Come on."

Their feet pounded on the sidewalk. Parker kept his gun aimed at the men, but didn't shoot. He still didn't know who they were, but if they gave chase, he wouldn't be asking first.

Erika's face was ashen as she kept pace with him, veering down a side street. "Who are those guys?"

"No idea, but one of them was on a cell phone. They might have friends on the way."

"Are you sure they're not cops? Maybe they need to talk to us."

Two sharp *cracks* resounded off the brick walls surrounding them. "Maybe not," she decided. "Come on."

Erika shot ahead of him with a burst of speed.

Parker turned and saw the pair of suited men, each holding a gun. A muzzle flashed twice, and the car window beside him shattered.

Who were these guys? And how did they find him?

Parker whipped off a shot, which slowed them for a moment. As he raced across a lot that was under construction, Parker struggled to connect the dots. Unless these guys had been following them since their escape yesterday, which he highly doubted, there was just no way. He and Erika had ditched their phones. The clothes they'd been wearing from yesterday were gone, tossed in the trash. He'd learned the hard way several months ago how tracking bugs worked.

Stacks of two by fours littered the lot. A dumpster was parked in the alley, nearly filled with debris. He spotted Erika's blonde hair disappear around the scuffed blue metal. Hidden by the dumpster, they crouched

191

down, eyes peering underneath the massive container for any sign of pursuit.

Behind them was an apartment building, yellow brick stretching to the sky. Parker hoped the men would race past without stopping, focused on gaining ground.

Two sets of feet slapped on the asphalt, the sounds becoming muffled when they hit the dirt lot, still moving fast. The men weren't stopping.

Side by side, they rounded the dumpster's edge, passing within a foot of Parker's upraised gun. Faced with the brick wall, the pair stopped, glanced right and left.

They never saw it coming.

From inside of twenty feet, he put a shot squarely in each man's back with ease. The bursts of concentrated fire sent them sprawling to the ground, their guns falling uselessly aside.

Parker was on them in an instant, but they weren't getting up. "Grab those guns, and check their pockets. I want to know who the hell these guys are."

Erika complied, cool under pressure as always. After what they'd been through, this was a regular day at the office.

Pockets turned inside out, all Parker found was a cell phone. No wallets with any convenient identification cards. A sharp gasp from Erika grabbed his attention.

"What is it?"

She held up a photo, a color snapshot of two people.

Two people he knew very well.

"It's us. He has a picture of us."

This wasn't good at all. The picture was recent, a shot of them out to dinner one night.

"Parker, this is barely a month old. Our waiter took this with my iPhone."

"They must have hacked into your phone before you ditched it."

Erika retied her ponytail, which had come loose during the chase. Parker saw her hands shaking as she twisted the flaxen strands.

"Did you find anything? We have to figure out who these guys are."

"Just this cell phone. He doesn't have—wait a second."

The phone in Parker's hand began to vibrate. A local number flashed across the screen.

"Don't do it, Parker."

She knew him too well.

"Why not? I want to know who the hell these guys are."

Before she could protest, he connected the call. He answered in a harsh, gruff tone.

"Yeah."

"What's your status? Did you get them?"

"No."

"What happened? Where are they? We're in the car now."

Parker said nothing.

"If Becker finds out we let Chase and his girl get away, it won't go easy for you. We have to end this today."

He ended the call, his mind racing.

"What did he say?"

Erika's blue eyes were wide, fierce yet fragile.

"Some guy named Becker is their boss. The one I just talked to is on his way, and he's not alone. We have to move."

Without waiting for an answer, he bolted from behind the dumpster, headed toward a busier street to find a cab. Erika was right behind, a pilfered gun in each hand.

"Put those away. The cops will be here any minute. Someone had to hear all those shots."

Even as he spoke, the high-pitched whine of emergency sirens could be heard only blocks away. Erika tucked the guns under her shirt as Parker held one hand in the air.

Ahead, a yellow taxi screeched to a halt. "Take us to the Liberty Bell."

The driver gunned it, tires squealing, never stopping the conversation in Arabic he was having with his Bluetooth.

"The Liberty Bell?" Erika whispered with anger. "Are you crazy? They just found us at Joe's old apartment. It won't be a stretch to look near Independence Hall." She was referring to the fact that while they'd been running from his uncle's killers several months ago, they'd caused quite a scene at the venerable bell's complex.

"You might be right, but there are going to be tons of people there and it's not far from Nick's office. We need to get him involved, and I need time to think. Those guys wanted to kill us, and anywhere is better than here right now."

She said nothing, anger blazing across her soft features.

Parker continued. "Would you be surprised if this had something to do with what we saw on the news? Maybe what's going on with oil forced their hand in some way."

A light clicked on. She stared into space for a moment, and then slowly nodded.

"It's a possibility. You know more about the financial side of this whole mess than I do, but it seems plausible."

Her mouth screwed up, forehead lined. "One question, though. Why would Aldrich, if they are somehow involved with this oil production thing, purposefully lose so much money? And besides that, how in the world could they influence whether or not oil production increased? They don't own any oil facilities, do they?"

Even amidst this disaster of a day, she was sharp as ever.

"Both valid points. As for answers, I don't know. I'm hoping Nick can help us."

The taxi stopped outside of Independence Hall, which was across the street from the Liberty Bell Center. On the grassy lawn that surrounded the newly constructed building, hundreds of tourists milled about, most snapping pictures.

They hurried to a nearby payphone.

"You know, I haven't used one of these in years," Parker said.

"Neither have I. Do you have any quarters?"

"No, but Nick's office has a toll free number. This call's on Uncle Sam."

A minute later, Nick picked up. "Chase, what's going on? I told you guys to stay put."

Parker brought him up to speed while Erika kept her eyes on the surrounding crowds, searching for any unfriendly faces.

"You sure keep things interesting. What did you do with the guns?"

"We still have them."

"All right, I need to meet you guys. Bring the guns, and maybe we'll get lucky and get a hit on them. Are you safe right now?"

"There are tons of people around here. I think we can last for a bit."

"Stay put. I'll be there in fifteen minutes. Try not to shoot anyone."

Parker hung up. "Nick's coming here."

Erika was silent, her eyes never leaving the crowds.

With nothing to do for the time being, Parker figured he may as well check his messages and see if any of his industry contacts had called about the oil trading.

He punched in his office number and had the secretary connect him to voice mail.

The first six messages were all from clients, people with questions about their investments. Those could wait.

The seventh message could not.

"Get over here."

Erika's head jerked around, one hand reaching for a gun.

"No, no, the phone. Listen to this message."

He punched a button, and the message started over. Erika pressed one ear to the receiver as Parker listened in.

"Parker, my name is Craig Fisher. I worked with Ben Flood at Aldrich." The voice was soft, hesitant. "We've never met, but Ben mentioned your name a few times." A deep breath, and Craig's voice was even shakier. "I don't know if this matters, but I thought you would want to know. A few days ago, when I was in our chairman's office, I saw your name and photo on his desk."

Erika jumped a few inches off the ground, her mouth shaped like an oval.

"I couldn't see what was on the file, but I saw your name written on some papers attached to the picture, so I checked out your company profile photo. I have no doubt it was a photograph of you." Craig sounded like he was about to lose it. "There was also someone else's photo in the file, a blonde girl. All I could see was her first name: Erika. After that, Spencer Drake walked in. If you want to call me, here's my cell."

Neither of them spoke for a few seconds. While they stood, pondering this latest development, Nick's government-issue sedan pulled to the curb. "Toss the cell phone you found and get in."

Parker dropped the phone on the sidewalk before hopping in Nick's sedan with Erika. Tires chirped as he cut off the car behind him, merging with traffic.

"What happened to the badass SUV?"

"Someone else is using it. What—"

Parker cut Nick off. "I think we just found out who's after us."

While Parker relayed the story to an astonished government agent, none of them noticed the black Suburban that trailed behind, shadowing their every turn.

Chapter 43

On a crowded street in downtown Philadelphia, traffic inched along. Amidst the exhaust fumes and orchestrated chaos, a black Suburban carried three men, each silently focused on the dark blue sedan four cars ahead, in the back of which sat their two targets.

One of the dark-suited trio spoke rapidly into a cell phone. "Yes, we found the other two. Both were shot. No, we didn't have time to move the bodies. Because the police were coming, that's why." He listened for a moment, face unmoving.

"The two of them are ahead of us. We have visual contact. They're now with a third man, identity unknown. I've never seen him before. We'll follow them until an opportunity presents itself. I'll notify you before we move on them, Mr. Becker."

He replaced the phone in his pocket. Each member of his team carried an identical device, including the two who were now lying in a dirt lot, shot to death by Parker Chase. Fortunately for these men, each phone was equipped with a real-time GPS tracker. Without it, the three men would never have been able to locate Parker, Erika and their driver outside of Independence Hall.

"Once we get into a less populated area, we move. One hit from this tank"-he patted the dashboard-"and that sedan won't be driving anywhere."

For several miles, they remained just back of the sedan, hidden in heavy traffic. It was only once their target entered the Fairmount neighborhood of Philadelphia that traffic began to thin. Located near the world famous art museum, the area was mainly residential, with relatively few cars on the one-way streets.

Ahead loomed the gothic facade of the infamous Eastern State Penitentiary. Stone walls stretched over forty feet into the air, constructed in the manner of a medieval castle and spanning an entire block.

The passenger made a call. "We're moving in. Eastern State Pen, south wall."

He dropped the phone and pulled out his gun. "Get them."

Without a word, the massive eight-cylinder engine growled, and their oversized vehicle shot forward, on a direct course for the blue sedan.

Chapter 44

"Craig Fisher, please." Parker rode shotgun in Nick's car, talking on the agent's speakerphone. After he'd explained to Nick about the message they'd received, Nick wanted to speak with Fisher immediately.

"Fisher speaking."

"Craig, this is Parker Chase. You left me a voice mail about Ben Flood."

The voice coming into Nick's car dropped so low it was scarcely audible. Nick cranked the volume knob in frustration.

"Parker, wow, you must think I'm nuts."

"Not at all. I can't explain right now, but trust me, I believe you and I appreciate you calling. I have someone on the line who wants to speak with you."

"This is Central Intelligence Agent Nicholas Dean, Mr. Fisher. I need your help."

"Did you say CIA?"

"That's right, son. Where are you right now?"

"I'm in my office."

"Good. Do you have access to your company's main database?"

"Yes, of course," Craig replied. "Why?"

Nick ignored the question. "You'll be receiving a phone call in the next ten minutes from one of my colleagues. I need you to do exactly as they tell you. Mr. Fisher, you may have just stumbled onto one of the biggest conspiracies in our nation's history, and we need your help to stop it."

Craig's response was incredulous. "What are you talking about? Are Parker and that blonde girl in trouble?"

"Yes, Mr. Fisher, they are. However, that's not important right now. Let me ask you a question. Are you having an interesting day at work?"

Craig sounded taken aback. "Well, yes. Actually, that's an understatement."

"What we are investigating is directly related to the recent news regarding oil production."

Craig didn't say anything, but Nick wasn't biting on the silence.

There was a long pause.

"Oh," Craig Fisher finally continued. "In that case, I suppose I can help. Is Parker still there?"

"I'm here," Parker replied. "We think that whoever killed Ben is somehow tied in with the people responsible for today's oil announcement, and we need your help to find them."

"You think the Arabs killed Ben?" Craig shouted.

"Craig, keep it down. No, I don't think it was anyone from the Middle East. Listen, we need your help now. I'll explain everything later."

Craig didn't sound happy, but he agreed to do whatever they requested. Nick called his office and arranged for one of the Agency's electronic surveillance experts to send a virus through Craig's computer that would allow the technician to access Aldrich Securities' database. Once the CIA technician was able to get into Spencer Drake's computer, they may be able to locate a link between Aldrich and either the attempts on Parker's and Erika's lives or the oil fiasco currently unfolding.

"Will you be able to use any of that information in court?" Erika asked as soon as Nick hung up. "It can't be legal to hack their database like that."

Nick's eyes were rock hard. "I don't plan on giving Mr. Drake his day in court. Neither should you if he sent those two killers today."

She said nothing, her expression mirroring Nick's stony visage.

"Maybe we'll find out how those two guys knew we were at Joe's," Parker said as a terrible thought flashed into his head. "You don't think they have us bugged, do you?"

"I've had a sweeping device activated since you sat in this car. It hasn't found anything, and it's a damn good one, so you're clean."

"Then how did they know where to find us?"

"My guess is they either found the police report from your uncle's murder or searched property records. Think about it. Whoever is doing this knows you're with Erika. They stake out her apartment and her office in case you go there. She has no relatives in the city to worry about. You, however," Nick said, pointing at Parker, "are the proud owner of an apartment in Rittenhouse. Any idiot with half a brain could find it and send a stakeout team."

Parker smacked the dashboard. "I never even considered that. So you think they were waiting for us?"

"I think you two dodged a bullet. You have to be more careful until we figure out what's going on, which is why I'm taking you to my place for the time being. No one knows you're with me, so you should be safe there."

Ahead, the towering walls of the Eastern State Penitentiary loomed over the road.

Parker shared a glance with Erika. What did they have to lose?

"Where do you—"

Parker's skull slammed off the window. Glass shattered into a thousand tiny pieces as his head filled with a roaring pain. Erika shrieked from the backseat as they slammed into a row of parked cars that lined the street. A small convertible in front of them was pushed aside. Parker didn't understand why Nick was hammering the gas.

It was only when he realized the roar in his ears was coming from a massive Suburban behind them that he knew this was no accident. Nick twisted the wheel, fighting to regain control. "Hang on. They're trying to crush us!"

Nick was right. The massive black vehicle was still pushing, tires squealing on the roadway as Nick's much smaller sedan was pushed toward the thick stone walls ahead. He was standing on the brake pedal to no avail.

Three rapid blasts filled the car. Parker's ears rang, and he turned with a sense of dread, expecting to find Erika bleeding in the rear seat.

Instead, she was twisted around to face their attackers, gun in hand, firing rapidly. The rear window had shattered, and several spider web cracks blossomed on the Suburban's windshield.

As he watched, a gun appeared from the Suburban's passenger window. "Get down," Parker shouted, just as the muzzle flashed twice.

One rear window shattered. Fortunately, no one was hit.

"I can't stop," Nick yelled. "That thing's too big."

Nick was struggling with the wheel in one hand, his pistol in the other.

"Parker, follow me."

"Where?" They were all stuck in this car. There was nowhere to go.

Nick ignored his shouted question. Through the gunshots, he could barely make out the next words.

"Bring Erika."

The sedan's engine roared as Nick let off the brake and punched the gas. As he did so, the gear shifter was slammed into reverse. Now pushing back, the mangled sedan was able to put up a fight and their inevitable progress to the unforgiving stone wall slowed.

Nick immediately twisted the wheel sharply to his left. With the engine screaming, Nick's sedan shifted so that the Suburban's front end scraped across their passenger side, Parker's face only inches from the screeching metal.

Without the sedan pushing back, the black vehicle behind them shot forward and slammed into the prison walls. Parker turned to see Nick dive out of his door, hitting the sidewalk in a barrel roll.

"Come on."

Parker grabbed Erika's shoulder just as her magazine ran out of bullets. They followed Nick out onto the sidewalk and crouched behind the battered sedan for cover.

"You guys all right?" Nick asked, back against his ruined car.

They each nodded.

"I think I hit the driver." Erika ducked her head under the car, looking for feet. "Right before we got out."

"That's why he's still gunning the engine."

A tremendous roar came from the wrecked Suburban as it continued to push against the massive stone wall.

"Two of them just got out. Both on the far side."

As she spoke, the engine cut off, deafening silence filling the void. Parker shook his head to clear the ringing from Erika's shots inside the government car.

His voice a whisper, Nick motioned to the stone wall on their right. "I'll go that way. You two head left, sweep around their rear. If you have a shot, take it."

Parker took the lead, Erika trailing behind. "Stay behind me and keep your head down."

Erika could be reckless, but she wasn't stupid. Parker had been shooting his entire life and had a much better chance of hitting their target.

Crouched low, Parker darted from behind Nick's bullet-riddled car onto the road, keeping the smashed-up convertible between himself and the Suburban. Two kids on skateboards who had been inspecting the vehicular carnage saw his gun and bolted, their wheels skimming across the sidewalk at high speed.

Fortunately, those were the only other people Parker saw. The last thing they needed was some nosy neighbor catching a stray bullet in the chest.

It was hot outside, and beads of sweat slid down Parker's face, his chin a foot from the sticky asphalt. Shallow breaths filled his chest as he strained to catch any sound of their assailants, a soft footstep or kicked pebble. He could sense Erika mirroring his moves, directly behind him.

There.

A barely audible scraping reached his ears. It came from the car to his left, parked in front of the convertible they were using for cover.

One hand went up, and Erika froze. He pointed in the direction of the sound and then motioned for her to stay put. On all fours, he spotted two feet moving on the street, about to round the front end of the car.

Arms steady on the ground, Parker fired two shots.

Blood poured from a shattered wingtip. A scream filled the air, and the injured man fell forward, torso coming into view. As he fell, Parker was shocked to see the gun still grasped in one hand. Before he could react, the man fired.

A searing hot pain ripped through Parker's right hand. Sticky red fluid oozed from the gash that appeared below his knuckles, and the pistol in his grasp clattered to the ground. Reacting on pure instinct, Parker dove toward the falling man, desperate to cover Erika and to close the distance.

When the suited man slammed onto the hot roadway, his gun jarred loose, clattering on the ground out of reach. Before the guy could move, Parker slammed a shoulder into his chest with a fury born of fear and white-hot anger. Momentum carried him head over heels, latched onto his quarry with a vise-like grip.

"Get out of the way!" He heard Erika's shrieking voice, but wasn't about to disengage. The guy was thick with muscle, and one hand grabbed for Parker's throat, seeking his windpipe.

His palm shot up and knocked the guy's arm away.

Damn, that stung. The guy's arm was like a pipe. Time to fight dirty. He glanced down to confirm which foot had been shot. It was the right one, which he'd been aiming for. Before he could kick at the bleeding appendage, a fist like concrete slammed into his already woozy skull and brought the ringing noise back.

Parker's neck twisted with the blow. His hands slipped, and the suited man fell from his grasp. The man jumped to his feet. Unfortunately for him, one of them now had a bullet lodged in it and was useless. He fell to his knees with a cry of pain.

A gun blast ripped through the air, and Parker heard the supersonic whistle of a bullet whiz between them. Erika's face was ashen as he glared at her, the pistol in her grip smoking.

The guy in the suit didn't stop to look, instead diving at Parker. That backfired, however, when Parker's fist slammed into his stomach, doubling the man over. Knees flexed, Parker shoved the man, keeping a tight grip on his shirt.

Half afraid Erika was going to fill them both with lead, he drove the helpless man into a parked car. With a sickening thud, the back of his skull cracked against the trunk, skin ripping open on contact. He was out cold and slumped to the ground.

Lungs heaving for air, Parker heard two rapid shots. Using the unconscious man for cover, he twisted his neck and saw Nick standing on the sidewalk, a gun in both hands.

Before he could blink, an engine roared behind him. Tires screeched, and a scream of pure terror ripped his chest apart.

In slow motion, he saw a door open on a second black Suburban that had just arrived. One hand reached out to Erika, who couldn't get her gun around fast enough. A sharp burst of blue light flashed on her neck, and her body instantly went limp. The man inside hauled her unresisting form into the vehicle, which shot down the street and disappeared from view.

Erika was gone.

Chapter 45

Boston, Massachusetts

On every floor of Aldrich Securities, pandemonium reigned.

Phones rang nonstop, petrified traders desperately trying to salvage any modicum of profitability from their over-leveraged portfolios. Other investors, men who had risked everything based on Aldrich personnel's advice, were in a panic, suddenly faced with losing billions. Everyone wanted to know what was going on, and no one had any answers.

No one, that is, but Spencer Drake. He knew exactly what was happening, because he had orchestrated the entire fiasco. Today was the culmination of two centuries of work, a final jeweled dagger from His Majesty George III to the infernal peasants responsible for Great Britain's fall from power.

Ensconced within the opulent confines of Drake's office, Nigel Stirling raised a glass to the television they both faced. On screen, one of the talking heads speculated wildly as to why OPEC was injecting such a massive amount of oil into the world economy.

Drake's phone had not stopped ringing for hours, and he'd spoken with the panicked CEO's of Merrill Lynch and Goldman Sachs. Each man was on the verge of a breakdown, alternately berating Drake for encouraging their reckless investing or plotting how to avoid the coming fallout. It was a testament to their hypocritical, self-serving nature that these supposed leaders were already searching for a way to avoid taking responsibility for their actions.

However, such was the state of America. Personal responsibility was a myth. When things went wrong, blame someone else.

Those bastards deserved everything they got.

"Well done, Spencer. This is more than I could have ever hoped for."

Despite himself, Drake's mouth twitched slightly at the corners. He and Nigel had done some projections, and it appeared that Goldman Sachs and JP Morgan would be bankrupt barring a bailout. Merrill Lynch was teetering on the brink, and Drake had little doubt they would soon fall as well.

All told, losses were projected to exceed two trillion dollars.

"It's not over yet. We still have to contain those two in Philadelphia."

"Any word from Mr. Becker?" Nigel asked.

"No," Spencer said just as his cell phone began to vibrate silently, "but here is Secretary Webster right now."

He connected the call, Gerard Webster's smooth voice filling the air.

"Mr. Secretary, good morning."

"I trust you have seen the news. This is most distressing."

Webster had been kept apprised of every step in the process. He knew exactly what was happening, and was going to play a vital role in the coming hours.

"I agree. In fact, I'm quite worried about the solvency of America's financial institutions if they have in fact overextended themselves in the recent oil speculation."

"A valid concern, Mr. Drake. As I've stated time and again, the American government will not come to the rescue of any business again. The United States is the beacon of capitalism, and in that economic model, the strong survive."

The irony was not lost on Drake. "I understand, Mr. Secretary. A hard decision, but a necessary one."

"Indeed. I apologize, Mr. Drake, but I have matters that require my attention. Specifically, the drafting of a speech addressing that very subject. I have a strong suspicion my views on the issue of a bailout will need to be made crystal clear in the near future."

The line went dead, and Nigel Stirling coughed out a throaty chuckle.

"A remarkably similar viewpoint to the one expressed by Chancellor Moore."

Several hours ago, Drake and Stirling had spoken with Chancellor of the Exchequer Colin Moore, the final member of their organization. His support of Secretary Webster's refusal to bail out any floundering institutions would be the American economy's death blow. Any financial institution that had invested too heavily in the oil futures Drake had recommended was on its own.

Oh, the beauty of capitalism.

This thought warmed Drake's heart more than the dram of whiskey he sipped on in celebration. Aldrich Securities was on the verge of ruin and he couldn't be more excited.

If it weren't for the couple in Philadelphia, there would be no stopping them. Even so, those two had little chance of surviving the day, and if by some miracle they were breathing come nightfall, Drake doubted they had any type of incriminating evidence.

In his pocket, a cell phone vibrated silently. His heartbeat accelerated when he saw Tom Becker's number flash on.

"Tell me you've handled the problem."

"I'm afraid not."

"What?"

Across the room, Stirling caught the tone of Drake's voice and froze.

"Three of our team members are down," Becker stated in a clipped tone. "Chase and Carr were with an unknown male who assisted them in repelling our assault."

"Are they still alive?"

"Affirmative, sir. However, we do have Dr. Carr in our possession."

"You *kidnapped* her?"

"That's correct, sir. Shall I dispose of our guest?"

Drake's mind raced, seeking some way to turn this disaster to his advantage. The very last thing he needed right now was to have the police digging around his offices. If the cops knew where to look, they could find dots that, once connected, would paint the entire picture of his plot in bright colors.

"No, don't kill her. She's more useful to us alive."

Nigel spit amber whiskey all over Drake's authentic Persian rug.

As he spoke, a plan took shape. Drake could use Erika Carr, use her to silence Parker Chase and their mysterious companion forever.

"What should we do with her, sir?"

"How many of your team members are alive?"

"Two of us. We're leaving Philadelphia now."

"Come back to Boston. I'll have a car ready for you at the airport."

Becker and his team had flown to Philadelphia on Drake's private jet. Barring complications, Becker could be at Drake's compound outside of Boston in under three hours.

"Understood, sir."

Stirling was staring at him, mouth agape. "Spencer, tell me this is a terrible misunderstanding."

When he didn't respond, Nigel began yelling.

"Do you have any idea what could happen to us?! We're on the verge of destroying the United States' economy, which we've been working on for *two hundred years*, and you're engaging in kidnapping?"

"Trust me, Nigel, I won't jeopardize the operation." As Spencer explained the idea blooming in his mind, Stirling's face gradually regained its color.

Five minutes later, he moved back to the bar and poured a new drink.

"I believe that we may yet celebrate our success today. And bid a permanent adieu to Dr. Carr and Mr. Chase."

Chapter 46

On the fourth floor of a nondescript office building in downtown Philadelphia, people ran about, shoes clicking sharply on the tiled floor. Phones rang constantly, demanding attention. However, inside one corner office, a man sat on a worn couch, his gaze drifting far beyond the confines of those four walls.

Parker Chase had barely moved since arriving at Nick's office. Over and over, the image of Erika being grabbed from the street ran through his mind, an overwhelming feeling of helplessness sapping his remaining energy. The contained chaos unfolding outside Nick's door never caught his eye.

A fresh bandage encircled his right hand, the bullet wound having been treated by an Agency physician. Parker had been lucky. It was only a flesh wound.

Cold coffee grasped in his good hand, Parker fought an urge to race from the room and stage a solo assault on Aldrich Securities. Getting himself killed would accomplish nothing except to guarantee Erika followed him to the grave. Slouched on the rock-hard government couch, the sense of despair that had settled on his shoulders was unlike anything he'd ever felt.

Plastic blinds smacked on the office door as Nick's massive frame burst through.

"We have some of our best in-house techs working on Aldrich's database. With Craig's password they should be able to hack the mainframe shortly. Problem is, once we get in, there's no telling what kind of additional security Drake has installed on his personal computer."

Nick's voice brought him back to reality. "So how long will it take?" They needed to find Erika before Drake killed her.

"If he has some heavy duty programs protecting his hard drive, it could take days."

A flame lit his steely glare. "We don't have days. Erika's in trouble, and we have to save her."

"Believe me, Parker, I understand. Right now, we simply have nothing to go on."

Parker shot up from the couch, irrational anger fueling his tirade.

"Why don't you send the cavalry into Aldrich's building and find her? You're the CIA, Nick. You can do whatever you damn well please."

"It's not that simple," Nick barked. "I can't just send a hostage rescue team onto private property without evidence."

Parker's arms flew out, cold coffee splashing on the wall. "What do you mean, *evidence*? We know it's Drake who's after us. We found the connection, all the way from Revere's letters to the telegram sent by Stirling's grandfather. Drake and Stirling are buddies, and it just so happens that on the *same day* OPEC floods the market with oil, Nigel Stirling shows up in Boston."

Even as he said it, Parker realized the futility of his argument. Every piece was circumstantial at best. They didn't have one shred of concrete evidence to show Drake was involved.

Nick laid a heavy palm on his shoulder. "I know how you feel." The sympathy in his voice was genuine. "But you have to understand, I can't authorize an operation like that without proof. Right now, all we have is a preliminary investigation with circumstantial evidence. My bosses don't even know about this yet, because quite frankly, I'd sound like a fool if I came to them with that theory."

Argument sprang to his lips, but Parker remained silent. Nick was right. "What if you find evidence of Drake's involvement on his computer?"

"Then we're in business." Nick tucked his towering frame behind the tiny government desk. "If we have anything that directly links Drake to these attacks on you and Erika, we'll move in. Until then, we wait."

The television in one corner caught Parker's eye. He needed a distraction before he lost it. "Mind if I turn that on? I haven't heard anything about the oil shipments all day."

Nick flipped him the remote, and Parker soon found one of CNN's seemingly endless supply of experts postulating as to why OPEC had ramped up production. Several citizens were interviewed, their reactions overwhelmingly positive. Most people equated more available oil with cheaper gas, and they were right.

Despite this, Parker couldn't shake the nagging feeling that something about this was off. If Drake had really invested an immense amount of Aldrich's capital in oil futures, he was in danger of becoming insolvent.

An organization with the resources of Aldrich going under would have been unthinkable a few years ago, but that was before Lehman Brothers and the 2008 mortgage crisis changed everyone's perception of being too big to fail. And he hadn't even begun to consider what could happen if, as Ben had told him, Drake convinced his peers in the investment community to invest depositors' funds. If billions of dollars of investors' money suddenly disappeared, America might be staring at the next Great Depression.

Across the room, Nick whipped out his cell phone. "Dean." A heartbeat later, his voice sent pure adrenaline through Parker's veins. "Erika?"

Parker shot up from the couch. "Is it her?"

Nick said nothing for a moment, and Parker almost grabbed the phone from his hands.

Almost. He thought better of it when he remembered Nick was a force of nature.

"Hold on, he's right here."

Nick put the call on speakerphone, and the most beautiful sound Parker had ever heard filtered through.

"Parker?" Timid and scared, but definitely Erika.

"Are you all right? Where are you?"

Silence, and then a robotic voice said, "She's in a safe place, and she's fine."

It sounded like Stephen Hawking, but deeper.

"Who is this? I swear, if you so much as—"

"No need for theatrics, Mr. Chase. Dr. Carr is perfectly healthy, but if you wish for her to remain that way, I suggest you listen very carefully."

Nick was waving at him, making a rolling motion with one hand. *Keep him talking.*

"All right. Who is this?"

Nick raced from the room, faster than a man his size should be able to move.

"We are who you have been searching for, Mr. Chase. You've been on

210

our trail for some time now, ever since Dr. Carr stumbled across a letter from Paul Revere."

"Am I speaking with Spencer Drake?" Maybe catch them off guard, get a reaction.

The disembodied, mechanical laugh was an eerie sound. "You certainly have an active imagination. Do not concern yourself with the who, Mr. Chase. You should concern yourself with how. As in how are you going to keep your girlfriend alive for the next twenty-four hours."

Where was Nick?

"What do you want?"

"Very simple, Mr. Chase. We don't want anyone concerning themselves with our business, because until a few weeks ago, everything was fine."

"What's the big secret? We don't have any idea who you are. You're the ones who came after us."

"That is irrelevant. Dr. Carr is with us, and if you want to keep her alive, you'll do exactly as we say."

Nick finally reappeared from the hallway, and a pair of thick fingers sprouted from his palm. *Two more minutes.*

"What exactly do you want from me? I don't have anything to give you."

"Incorrect. Dr. Carr informed us that you possess a copy of three letters written by Paul Revere."

"You have the originals."

"We require the three copies in Joseph Chase's apartment. We also require Dr. Carr's office and personal computers."

"How about I mail them to you?"

The robotic laugh again. "I'm afraid that would be unacceptable. You will deliver them in person, and after we are certain that no further record of the letters exists, we will part ways."

They must take him for a fool. "What's to stop you from killing both of us when I show up?"

"Nothing, Mr. Chase. You'll simply have to trust us."

"Why would I do that when you've tried to kill me three times already?"

"Fortunately for you, circumstances have changed, and you are no longer our primary concern. Besides, Mr. Chase, it is too late."

"Too late for what?"

Nick held up a single finger.

"You will learn soon enough. An address will be e-mailed to you within twenty minutes. Be there tonight at ten o'clock. Bring the items we requested, and if you want Dr. Carr to live, come alone."

"Where—" The line went dead.

Chapter 47

Parker stood frozen. A harried technician, glasses askew, rushed through Nick's door moments later. "We couldn't get a fix. They were using a satellite phone with some heavy duty encryption."

"Did you get anything?"

Even from across the room, Nick towered over the man.

A stutter appeared in his hesitant voice. "Well, uh, we ..."

"Yes or no?"

"No. We couldn't even identify what country he was in."

"Damn. For all we know she could be aboard an airplane right now."

While the interrogation was going on, a light went off in Parker's head. "Nick, it doesn't matter where they are. That e-mail will give a location, which should at least give you a basic area for where she's being held."

One massive hand waved dismissively, and the tech disappeared like a magician's assistant. "But will it give us enough time to set up proper surveillance measures? I doubt it. It's two o'clock right now, which gives us less than eight hours."

"They can't be telling me to go very far. It's not like I have a plane I can just hop in and jet around the world."

"You're probably right, but what has me worried is the attack they carried out. Those guys were professionals. The coordination, the organization, it was way too good for a bunch of thugs."

That didn't sound right.

"We killed half their team, Nick. How good can they be?"

His response was cold as ice. "We're good too, Parker. We have to be."

A Blackberry flipped through the air, landing softly in Parker's hands.

"Use this to check your e-mail. The sooner we know where you're meeting them, the better prepared we'll be. And don't forget, you still have to get those copies and Erika's computers before you leave."

Parker tapped out the password for his private e-mail account, mind still running through what the robotic voice had said. "Do you think that was Drake? He said it was already too late to stop whatever they were up to. What else could he have been talking about?"

Years of experience darkened Nick's face.

"One problem at a time, Parker. First, we worry about getting Erika back. After that, we can deal with whatever that guy was talking about. And do I think it's Drake? I'm not sure. All that circumstantial evidence you guys gathered could point to someone in his organization, but right now I can't say." The big man made no noise as he walked over and put a hand on Parker's shoulder. "I know you're angry. You need to channel that anger, focus on what we can control, and worry about the rest later. Erika's our first priority right now. The rest can wait."

Such words of wisdom from a battle-hardened operative like Nick buoyed his spirit. They would do this. Erika would live, and whoever had her would die.

On the screen, a new message popped up:

25 Louisburg Square, Beacon Hill, Boston.

Nick scribbled the address down. "It's six hours by car. Which gives you two hours, max, to get everything they want."

Parker stood to go, but Nick was ahead of him. "I'm coming with you. I doubt this is a trap, but you never know. Let's move, Chase."

Nick thundered down the hallway, people dodging left and right to avoid the speeding freight train. Parker followed in his wake, an iron resolve building as they moved to save Erika.

It was going to be a long night.

Chapter 48

"Well done, Dr. Carr. An excellent performance."

Erika was aboard Spencer Drake's jet, currently flying off the coast of New Jersey. It was the nicest plane she'd ever seen. Oversized leather captain's chairs dotted the interior of the Gulfstream G550, interspersed with several long bench seats, various tables and workstations, and even a flight attendant. The girl was kind, if robotic, and hadn't even blinked at the handcuffs that locked Erika's left arm to her seat.

It had been a whirlwind few hours. When she'd been standing in front of Eastern State Penitentiary watching Parker struggle with one of their attackers, she hadn't seen the second car until it was too late. A man zapped her with a stun gun and pulled her into the vehicle, and then a thick black cloth covered her head. A gun barrel shoved into her neck had silenced her screams.

She couldn't tell how far they drove, but it wasn't long before she'd been pulled from the car, hood still covering her eyes. An unbelievable roaring, which she later realized was the Gulfstream, filled the air, and she was forced up a staircase. Only once her arm was secured to the chair in which she now sat was the hood removed.

Through this entire ordeal, what scared her the most was that none of her captors bothered to conceal their faces. None of the three men were worried that she knew what they looked like. Which only meant one thing.

She wouldn't be around to identify who'd kidnapped her.

"We should be landing in just under one hour. Jessica," the man who'd spoken to Parker said, "will get you anything you require. Within reason, of course."

The stewardess's blank expression never changed. Apparently she didn't find anything about the situation to be strange.

Erika remained silent, unwilling to give him the satisfaction of a response.

Trim and muscular, with close-cropped black hair going slightly gray at the temples, she assumed the man who spoke was the group's leader. He was all business, whether on the phone with Parker or directing his men after they'd grabbed her. He had military written all over him, and there wasn't an ounce of compassion on his hard, weathered face.

Seated across the plane, the presumed leader spoke softly into a bulky phone. She'd never seen one, but Erika had read enough to guess he was using a satellite phone.

"The message was delivered, sir."

Erika leaned toward him, straining to catch every word of the one-sided conversation.

"Chase understands what is required. He knows we have Dr. Carr, and will bring the items you requested. Where is the rendezvous point?"

A pen scratched across the paper in his lap.

"Understood. I'll pass this along immediately."

He severed the connection, fingers flying rapidly over the phone's keyboard.

"Don't worry, Dr. Carr." He turned without warning, his rapid movement making her jump. "You will be seeing Mr. Chase this evening. Once we have the documents and your electronic equipment, you will be free to go. Until then, try to relax."

Erika never responded, afraid that her voice would betray the primal fear coursing through her veins.

Unless Parker and Nick could save her, she knew this man was going to kill her.

Chapter 49

Boston, Massachusetts

Two hours before the appointed deadline, Parker stepped off a Bell 407AH helicopter that had carried him, along with Nick and a five-man team of CIA operatives, from Philadelphia to downtown Boston. Slung across his shoulder was a worn leather bag containing the copies of Revere's letters and Erika's two laptops.

Prior to leaving Philadelphia, the bespectacled CIA tech in Nick's office had installed several combination tracking and listening devices in Parker's clothes. One in each shoe, one in his belt, and one in his wristwatch. Each device, no larger than a pebble, transmitted real-time GPS coordinates to an Agency satellite hovering miles overhead. Nick carried a portable receiver that displayed the location of all four tracking devices, overlaid on a digital map of the area. The devices also contained tiny microphones that would transmit anything Parker heard to Nick's receiver. As long as the trackers worked, Nick could pinpoint Parker's exact location anywhere on the planet while listening to what he was saying.

Strong winds buffeted Parker as he stood atop the Federal Reserve Bank building in Boston's Financial District. From this vantage point, the men were presented with a breathtaking view of a beautiful New England landscape. Boston Harbor stretched to the horizon, sails of every color floating across the inky black water, onboard lights reflecting off the rainbow of canvas.

Parker had little time to appreciate the scenery. "Time to go," Nick said, shouting to be heard. "My team needs to get in position before you arrive."

Through a thick steel door held open by a wide-eyed security guard, their small group filed into a freight elevator that whisked them thirty-two

217

floors down to street level. Outside of a rear entrance, they found two black Suburbans, engines running.

What was it with these guys and Suburbans?

Ensconced within the seemingly ubiquitous metallic beasts, the grim-faced operatives thundered to the Beacon Hill neighborhood of Boston. A full moon lit the way, no clouds barring the golden-white rays of light from splashing across the city.

On the brick-lined downtown sidewalks, Parker spotted groups of people sitting outside of restaurants, laughing and enjoying a beautiful summer evening. Surrounded by five killing machines armed to the teeth, Parker found the normal, carefree diners to be strangely out of place.

The ride passed in silence, and fifteen minutes later their small caravan came to a halt five blocks from Louisburg Square.

Lights off, the rumbling cars nearly disappeared among the gas lit streets, shielded by elegantly landscaped trees.

"Let's hear the plan one more time, Parker."

Nick had laid out the operation for him in excruciating detail before leaving his office, and several more times in the helicopter. Parker knew it inside and out, but the CIA man spoke from experience when he declared that practice made perfect, and the only guarantee you had about a battle plan was that something would go wrong.

"I get out here and wait until nine forty, and then I walk to the address. You and your men will have secured the perimeter and established positions."

Nick nodded, double-checking the Heckler & Koch submachine gun in his grasp.

"After I make contact, I verify Erika is alive. When I physically see her, I use the word *crazy* in a sentence. That's your cue to bring the noise."

The slide racked shut on Nick's sinister gun. "Correct. We infiltrate the target area, secure you and Erika, and exit immediately. Any resistance will be eliminated with lethal force."

Parker focused on his breathing, which was surprisingly calm. He felt the kind of nerves he used to get before a game in college, positive energy he could channel and use to his advantage.

Only now the stakes were much higher. If he failed and this didn't go as planned, Erika wasn't coming home.

"Did the techs find anything in Drake's computer?"

"Not yet. When we landed they said it would take at least another hour to break through the firewall."

Nick glanced down, toward the luminescent dial on his wrist.

"It's time."

Parker glanced at his watch, identical to the ones Nick and his team wore.

Here we go.

His door slid open and a warm breeze filled the air-conditioned vehicle. Tinged with salt, it brought his senses into razor sharp focus. Parker's feet hit the ground, every nerve on edge, but his mind was clear. Erika was counting on him.

Nick nodded once, confidence personified. The door closed, and both vehicles pulled away.

Parker was on his own.

Forcing himself to move slowly, Parker walked over the brick sidewalks, all of which were lit by beautiful gas streetlamps. These homes really were amazing. The CIA computer whiz had done a property search on every property in the area, but unfortunately none of them were owned by Spencer Drake or anyone they could definitively associate with the billionaire businessman.

Twenty-five Louisburg Square was owned by one Jonathan Smith. Mr. Smith listed this as his secondary residence, with a PO Box as the forwarding address. Despite the best efforts of Nick's team, they had been unable to locate Mr. Smith. Apparently, he had purchased the home two decades ago and had since vanished. No other homes were listed in his name, no helpful tax records, no government identifications ever issued other than a passport which had never been used.

The property taxes were paid every year by a corporation based in Switzerland, and even Parker realized the futility in trying to get information from the Swiss.

Four-story red-brick homes surrounded him on every side. Wooden shutters, all painted a uniform black, framed the numerous windows fronting every structure. From within most buildings, light could be seen, electric illumination that lent a warmth to the area, a sense of hominess and tranquility among the opulence.

Except for the house, which he now faced. Every window was dark, ominous.

A shrill screeching filled the air. Parker jumped, searching all around. *What was it?*

Through the thudding heartbeat that filled his ears, he realized it was a cell phone ringing.

But he didn't have one.

On the ground, sitting on the first step that led into his targeted house, a glimmer of light. Leaning in, he realized that a smartphone had been placed on the step, facedown. He hadn't seen it in the darkness. When he saw the touch screen, his lungs froze.

Instead of displaying a phone number across the top, there was a sentence.

Answer the call.

His thumb touched the screen. "Hello?"

"Come inside, Mr. Chase. The door is open."

The line went dead. With no other choice, he walked up the stairs.

White marble framed a sleek black door. The knob turned easily in his grasp.

It was pitch black inside the home, his vision limited to a few feet inside the frame. The yellow gaslight behind him reflected off a polished wooden floor, casting a lone shadow into the gloomy depths. From out of the darkness, an unfamiliar voice spoke in clipped tones.

"Take three steps forward. Keep your hands where I can see them."

Parker obeyed, the door sliding closed on noiseless hinges. He blinked rapidly, desperately trying to adjust to the dark interior.

"Do you have what we requested?" The same voice, now to his left. A soft squeaking sound, like rubber-soled shoes on hardwood floors, came from his right.

"In the bag." Parker tapped the leather satchel for emphasis.

"Are you armed?"

"No."

"Hold your arms straight up in the air. If you make any sudden moves, you die."

Parker obeyed, arms skyward. A pair of gloved hands appeared from the darkness, rapidly patting him down. Suddenly a brilliant white light flashed in his eyes, blinding him.

"Stand still."

The hands flipped open his bag for a moment, while Parker was still seeing stars. Before he could react, the bag was closed.

"So far, so good. Continue this way, and don't worry. Everything will be fine."

He didn't believe them for a second.

"Where's Erika? I want to see her."

"In due time, Mr. Chase. For now, follow us."

Several seconds later, a penlight snapped to life behind him, washing soft luminescence on his surroundings which allowed Parker to make out the home's elegant interior. Polished wood framed every wall, the plaster surfaces painted white. He was immediately struck by the lack of ornamentation. There was not a single picture, rug, or lamp visible. Nothing to indicate that anyone lived here. The word that sprang to mind was *sterile*.

"Follow your guide, Mr. Chase. I don't have to tell you what will happen if you attempt anything foolish." The hard barrel of a gun jabbed into his ribcage, the message clear.

Ahead, a man of about his size appeared. Rather, the rear of a man appeared. Clad in dark clothes, with thick black boots underneath his cargo pants, he never turned to face Parker. He spied night vision goggles draped around the man's neck. To Parker's rear, at least one man held the light, a pistol in his grasp. He was surrounded.

"Move." The leading guide disappeared, and Parker hurried to catch up.

He needed to keep Nick in the loop, and the only way to do that was to talk.

"Where are we going?"

"Shut up. No more questions."

The pistol jammed into his back once more.

In the darkness, Parker's senses took on a heightened state, compensating for his lack of sight. With his shadow being thrown forward by the backlighting, he could see little save the areas immediately around him.

The old wooden floors didn't creak as they walked. Whoever really owned this house had taken care of it. Still, down the hallway, which seemed to lead on forever, he failed to spy a single personal touch. It appeared the home was uninhabited.

Why would they bring him to an empty house? Especially one with neighbors all around. It didn't make sense.

"Stop." The lead guide reached to his left, hand disappearing into the inky black void outside the penlights reach. A soft creaking noise indicated a door had opened.

"Go left. Down the stairs."

Wooden handrails descending into the blackness, uncarpeted steps beneath his feet. As his lead guide descended, Parker spotted what appeared to be a stubby machine gun strapped across the man's chest, not unlike the weapons Nick and his team carried. These guys were definitely not your average thugs. Military-grade assault weapons meant two things, neither of which made Parker feel any better. The men were deadly serious, and money was not an issue.

Once they hit solid ground, he suddenly realized Nick had never said anything about the tracking devices' limitations. These things had better work underground.

Cement floor stretched unbroken on all sides. It was as though the steps descended into the middle of a wide-open area, an expansive underground pasture.

"Get moving." The gun barrel again. Parker hurried to catch up with the leader, who had made a sharp right. Parker ran through a mental image of the ground floor above. This path would take them toward the rear of the property, which he had been told contained a small, fenced-in yard.

A door soon appeared, painted the obligatory black, a sharp contrast with the white concrete walls. Through the doorway, and then a musty smell filled his nose. Amazingly, the passageway into which they stepped was not a storm entrance. Instead, it appeared to stretch to infinity, damp air replete with earthy overtones the only indication they were underground.

Parker continued forward, counting his steps. One hundred thirty later, they arrived at an identical black door, never once passing underneath any type of opening or skylight. At roughly three feet per step, they had traveled almost four hundred feet from the rear edge of the structure he'd entered. Which meant he was no longer on the same property. Nick and his team were now watching an empty house.

He really hoped the tracking devices were working.

Through the door at the end of the tunnel, Parker found himself in a basement identical to the one they'd just left. White walls and a bare concrete floor led to a staircase, at the top of which was an equally empty, unfurnished home. The unbroken march halted abruptly at the front door of the new house, and the flashlight went out.

Once again plunged into darkness, Parker could see little except for the hazy outline of the doorway he faced.

"Hold still, Mr. Chase. I'm going to put a bag over your head." A coarse sack slid over his eyes and settled loosely on his shoulders. With one hand guiding him, Parker heard the front door slide open, and a rush of warm air flooded into the empty home.

"Move forward. There will be one step onto the porch, then five to the street."

The directions were precise, but Parker walked clumsily, stumbling over the top step and buying a few precious seconds. An iron hand steadied his course. While they walked, his ears strained for any sound, any way to identify what was happening.

The rumble of an idling car engine was all that he heard. No voices, no stereos playing music or cars passing by.

What sounded like a car door clicked open, and a hand guided his head down.

"Into the car."

Plush leather greeted his backside, high enough from the ground to tell him this was another sport utility vehicle. Parker would bet his last dollar he could guess the make and color.

He was guided across the smooth leather to the far seat, which he assumed was behind the driver. As soon as the door closed, Parker was thrown into the cushioned backrest, the engine roaring. During the ride, not a word was spoken. On the rare occasion the vehicle would stop, he didn't hear a thing outside. No other traffic, no passing pedestrians or police sirens.

The engine's roar was mind-numbing, and it was a shock when the car jerked to a halt. His door opened, and a monstrous wind assaulted his body. The sound of a helicopter rotor turning was unmistakable.

For the second time that night, Parker boarded one of the flying contraptions. This time, however, he was half shoved and half stumbled on the monstrous bird, which promptly lifted off. Without a headset, all he could hear was the whirring blade that chopped through the air overhead, his senses thrown into disarray.

After an interminable ride, Parker's stomach rose into his throat as the bird descended. Head pushed low, he stumbled from the passenger area, completely disoriented. Unlike earlier, when high winds had buffeted his body atop the Federal Reserve Bank, there was no wind and precious little sound upon his exit.

Several pairs of footsteps joined his on a brief walk, before all sounds of the outside world vanished as they passed through a doorway. How large, or to where it led, he had no idea.

A twisting and turning course took him through whatever structure they'd entered. His only clue about the area lay beneath his feet, and he alternately felt thick carpet or slick, hard floors.

"Stop."

Clasped to his shoulder, the hand that had guided him here now shoved a leather bag against his chest and then whipped the black bag from his head. Bright lights assaulted his eyes, and he clenched them shut to avoid the painful glare, his satchel clutched in both arms.

"Welcome, Mr. Chase. I'm so glad you could join us." A new voice, directly in front of him. One eye cracked open, and he found himself staring at a man he'd never met, but who he knew intimately.

Spencer Drake.

Chapter 50

Weston, Massachusetts

"I do hope your journey was comfortable."

Drake removed his hands from charcoal gray suit pockets, absentmindedly touching his slick hair. Across from him, surrounded by Tom Becker's men, Parker Chase glared at him with undisguised hatred.

"Where is Erika?"

When Parker spoke, Drake saw the surprisingly muscular man's eyes flash with angst. Drake had specifically chosen this meeting place to maximize Parker's discomfort.

Five minutes ago Drake's personal helicopter had landed on his helipad, located on the roof of his home in Weston, a suburb fifteen miles from downtown Boston. They were in the main building of his compound, which sprawled over nearly a hundred acres. Vast rows of hedges and trees lined the estate, offering the privacy he required, free from any prying eyes.

"I trust you have everything we asked for?"

Parker tapped the bag once, but made no move to open it. "I want to see her."

A reasonable request.

"As you wish."

He nodded toward Becker, who disappeared down a hallway. While they waited, Drake watched Parker study his surroundings.

They were standing in one of the home's reception areas. A vaulted ceiling soared thirty feet overhead, tinted glass windows comprising one entire wall, the view of suburban Boston breathtaking. A double stairway behind Spencer led up to the second level of his home, which overlooked the floor on which they now stood. Above that, a third level was visible,

225

partially obscured behind a low wall that lined the top-floor balcony. Various original works of British art graced the walls, the centerpiece of which was an original painting of Sir Winston Churchill, one of the few men whom Drake considered a peer.

Two sets of footsteps echoed from the nearby hallway.

Clad in the same clothes in which she had been abducted, Dr. Erika Carr walked into the room, one of Drake's men following closely behind.

Even after all she'd been through, Drake had to admit she was stunning.

"Are you all right?"

Chase made no move to reach for her, holding his ground. She didn't respond at first, and Spencer found her eyes locked on him, loathing in each.

"Yes, I'm fine."

Chase stood rigidly still, one hand on the leather satchel around his shoulder.

"Satisfied, Mr. Chase?"

The intensity on Parker's face was unlike anything Drake had ever seen. Palpable rage fixed on him like a laser, a scarcely controlled sense of violence emanating from the man.

"Before I give you this bag, you're going to let her go."

Spencer was glad there was a guard on either side of Parker. He was slightly worried that Chase might take a run at him, and he had no inclination to have his teeth knocked out.

"You are not in a position to make any demands."

Even with the three armed men to his rear, Spencer took a step back. No need to give Chase any incentive.

"However, as a show of good faith, I'll agree."

Was Chase really this stupid? Drake and Stirling had discussed their move hours earlier, after finalizing their plans for fleeing the country, personal fortunes intact. Two days ago, after learning that his grandfather's telegram had been accessed by the CIA, Nigel had quietly obtained fifty million dollars' worth of oil futures forecasting a sudden drop in the price of a barrel, the exact opposite of what Spencer had been purchasing. His transaction had barely been processed when Sheik bin Khan dropped a bomb on the market with his announcement that OPEC would double exports beginning today, and within twelve hours his investment had yielded a tenfold return.

Half a billion dollars wealthier, Nigel's plane was going wheels up in the morning, and Spencer Drake would be on board. On paper, the Securities Exchange Commission would be able to pinpoint almost a billion dollar loss in his personal fortune. Drake expected that in the immediate fallout following this financial disaster he would be vilified by the American public, along with every other CEO who used their clients' money to recklessly gamble on the market. The inevitable finger-pointing would ensue, and he doubted that the average American would ever learn that Spencer Drake had orchestrated the increased trading in oil futures. They would paint every participant with a broad stroke, and he would go down in history as only one member of an extensive rogue's gallery of entitled villains.

A small price to pay for ensuring the United States was appropriately humbled.

"Please escort Dr. Carr from the grounds."

One of Becker's men gestured for her to follow him out of the room. The guard had been instructed to take Erika to a nearby room and wait. Parker Chase was in for a surprise later this evening. Drake was going to shoot her while he watched. The thought sent a tingle of anticipation up his spine.

Erika ignored the man. "No. I'm not leaving without Parker."

"It's all right," Parker responded in an even tone. "I'll be fine, and I'll see you soon."

Chase turned to face Spencer, that unsettling fury still lighting his face.

"Whoever the hell you are, if you or any of these bastards hurt her, I will kill you."

"Mr. Chase, I'm a man of my word. I will not harm her."

"How is she going to get home? I came here in a helicopter, in case you forgot. I have no idea where we are."

"You are less than fifteen miles from Boston. After we conclude our business, I promise you will be reunited and will be free to go wherever you please."

"Parker, he's lying. I don't trust—"

"Erika." Chase held up one hand, his eyes never leaving Drake's face. "We don't have a choice. Do what he says."

This was going to be easier than he'd imagined. So much for Parker Chase putting up a fight. Without another word, Erika was led down the hallway, a pistol trained on her back.

"Now that she's cared for, would you be so kind as to hand over your bag?"

Chase handed the brown leather bag to Tom Becker, who inventoried the contents.

"It's all here, sir."

"All three letters and both computers? Excellent. One question, Mr. Chase. How do I know you didn't make any copies for safekeeping?"

"Are you crazy? Do you think I wanted any of this?" His arms spread wide, indicating the four armed men.

"Erika was simply doing her job, and she happened to find that letter from Revere. How was she supposed to know it was there?"

Which raised an interesting question. "I never did learn where she located the document."

"It was in a box of Alexander Hamilton's correspondence that she was studying," Parker explained. "There was a book in there, and apparently this letter was hidden underneath the cover. I guess the binding just came loose over the centuries and when she opened it, this letter fell out."

How amazing. Hamilton had hidden the letter hundreds of years ago, and for some reason, never acted on the intelligence. He would probably never know why this information fell through the cracks. The vagaries of fate could be whimsical indeed.

"Fascinating. I suppose I'll just have to trust that you wouldn't be so foolish as to cross me."

"Who the hell are you, anyway? Why are you so interested in these letters?"

Spencer and Nigel had also discussed this. Stirling, before he'd departed for the airport, had recommended Drake shoot both Chase and Dr. Carr immediately. Spencer, however, saw no harm in telling Parker his plans. After all, it wasn't as though Parker would be able to share them with anyone.

"Mr. Chase, these letters caught my attention because they are the only remaining link to an organization that was founded over two hundred years ago, at the end of your Revolution."

A sharp laugh of disbelief. "You're telling me that the group Revere talked about still exists? That's ridiculous."

"No, Mr. Chase, it is factual. And as of today, we have finally completed a mission that began two centuries ago."

A glimmer of doubt flashed across Parker's face.

"We have destroyed the economy of the United States."

Chapter 51

Keep him talking.

It was the only hope Parker had. If he could get Drake to detail his plan, tell him exactly what was going on, Nick would have all the evidence he needed to storm in here and save the day.

Of course, if Nick wasn't able to hear him, Erika was likely dead, and he would soon follow. A feigned look of confusion added to the ruse. "What are you talking about?"

Drake was a man who obviously loved an audience. "You're in the business, Mr. Chase. Think about what is happening."

"Are you talking about the oil imports? Get real. That was all OPEC. Unless you're cousins with a crown prince, you can't control them."

"Mr. Chase, you have no idea what I am capable of."

The man was so arrogant, so assured of his superiority, he never noticed Parker analyzing his situation, looking for weaknesses. Maybe Drake thought his flitting gaze was a sign of fear. Or maybe his ego was just that big.

"To answer your question, yes. I am responsible for the impending collapse of your country's economy."

His country? This guy was nuts.

"To be honest, I did not accomplish it alone. No, I was aided by some of the very same men who brought America to its knees several years ago. The same men who bankrupted this nation with their wild speculation once again found the chance to enrich themselves with others' money too great to ignore."

"Who are you talking about? Derivatives traders?"

"Not at all. I went straight to the top this time. My colleagues from every other financial firm of note in America. It took surprisingly little encouragement to convince them to join me, and once they began doubling their investments, the work was done."

If Nick didn't show up soon, Parker was going to have to improvise. From what he could see, there were two men to his rear, one on either side, both within arm's reach. Two men flanked Drake, and one was to Parker's right, the apparent leader of the group who'd brought him here.

The two behind him wouldn't be a problem, but he'd be a sitting duck while he was fighting them. Turning your back on three armed men was never a good idea.

"And to think, I have my fellow industry leaders to thank for giving me this idea in the first place."

"What are you talking about?" Parker asked, genuinely curious. "Are all those guys in on it with you?"

Harsh laughter greeted the question.

"Of course not. In 2008, when the mortgage crisis imploded the world economy, I was given the blueprint for how to achieve my goal. The only trait greater than American ingenuity, and I mean this sincerely, is your overwhelming greed. Every day, across the nation, greed is glorified. Think of the lavish lifestyles of celebrities that are chronicled on reality television. Pure mental rubbish, yet millions of people are drawn to these hideous creatures, people willing to sell their soul for money. Models and athletes endorse luxury brands far out of reach for most citizens, yet young people borrow their way into massive debt simply for the privilege of driving the right car or wearing the right shoes." Drake was really on a roll now. "No, Mr. Chase, I did not need help to convince your fellow citizens to abandon their morals. America is starting to resemble ancient Rome more and more with each passing day. A once great civilization whose time has passed, a world power on the decline not through the influence of or due to assault by any other nation, but because of the very people who live within its borders. America is rotting from within, a lethal disease characterized by greed, entitlement and ignorance."

Even though the man was planning to kill him, Parker found his argument compelling. "All right, let's say I believe you. You orchestrated this oil crisis. Why did it take you two hundred years to finally do it? Have you and all your anti-American buddies been twiddling your thumbs all this time?"

"Hardly."

Drake moved toward a beautiful wooden bar to Parker's right, adjacent to the hallway down which Erika had recently disappeared. A crystal tumbler sparkled in his hand, amber liquid flowing from an elegant bottle.

"Care for a drink? No? Suit yourself." Drake swirled the liquid around his mouth. Behind him, Parker could sense the guards growing restless, hear their weight shifting back and forth. If Parker could keep Drake going, his men might be distracted when Nick arrived. Assuming he ever did.

"There have been several attempts to effect this same attack on your nation, some of which you will know. World War II, perhaps?"

Even though he already knew, the look of shock on his face was sincere. "You're telling me you started a global war to destroy America?"

"No, we didn't start it. We merely insured America was involved, with the hopes that years of warfare would bankrupt the economy."

Parker couldn't help himself. "Guess that didn't work out like you'd planned."

Spencer shrugged. "Unfortunately, no. With Europe in ruins, America actually came out in a much stronger position of economic power post-war. However, there have been other, more successful operations in the past."

He was getting worried. If Nick took much longer, it would be too late. "Such as?"

A glance at his watch. Nick had three minutes. If he wasn't here, Parker was taking matters into his own hands.

"Now is not the time or the place for such a discussion."

Drake's shark-like eyes, black as night and devoid of compassion, focused on his own.

"Aren't you curious as to my identity?"

Unbelievable. Here he was, confessing to abetting the most disastrous conflict in world history, and he was worried that Parker didn't know his name. "You're some rich bastard with an inferiority complex. I don't really care what your name is."

As expected, anger lit up Drake's face like a candle. Getting the man to go on a tirade would only buy more time, and emotional people tended to make mistakes.

"What I am is a messenger from the greatest nation on earth," Drake thundered, "sent to bring your miserable country to its knees. As I'm sure you've heard, revenge is a dish best served cold, and right now, I can tell you it is delicious."

He tipped the rocks glass back, draining it. "My name is Spencer Drake. I am the CEO of Aldrich Securities, an organization established by royal decree for the sole purpose of destroying your nation. In the past week, we have eliminated your Treasury secretary as well as the worthless Chancellor of the Exchequer in England. We are single-handedly responsible for the redistribution of world power." His words stopped the breath in Parker's chest. Could he possibly be serious?

"Now," Drake chuckled softly, "I realize my organization will soon be insolvent. However, by that time my colleagues and I will be directing the return of England to her rightful place atop the global hierarchy. There will be no limit as to what we can achieve."

Parker blinked rapidly, a plan forming. He could worry about the rest of the world later. During Drake's enchanting soliloquy, his men's attention had noticeably drifted. Nick had ninety seconds.

"Unfortunately, you won't be around to see it." From the hallway behind Drake, one of his men reappeared, leading a blindfolded Erika. "And neither will your beautiful girlfriend."

Drake whipped the white cloth from her eyes. "Parker? What's going on?"

She only glanced at him, her face turning violent when she realized what had happened. "You bastard. You're never going to get away with this."

"Ah, the old cliché. Sorry, dear, but this isn't a movie. It's already too late."

Drake reached under his jacket, a shimmering silver handgun appearing in his palm.

"Dr. Carr, as a special thank you for locating these letters, I will allow you to choose who dies first. You or Mr. Chase. Hurry, we've not much time."

Her mouth dropped open, but Parker wasn't watching anymore. A rapid series of calculations raced through his mind, just like they did during a football game. Each person became a piece on the board, a potential target or ally that he had to account for.

"You're crazy. You can't do this."

"Actually, I can." Drake turned toward Parker, the gun barrel rising.

"Good-bye, Mr. Chase."

Six of them, two to his rear, two in front, and two on his right. Erika was his only ally. "Just so you know, Spencer Drake, every single word you've said has been recorded by the CIA. The man who was with us when you kidnapped Erika is an agent."

Drake's smirk never wavered.

"I was worried that you may bring some type of recording device to this meeting. As such, my security team took the liberty of using an electronic frequency disruptor from the moment you entered my house. Regardless of what you claim to be carrying, this entire house became a veritable dead zone when it was activated. I'm terribly sorry, but your transmissions, if they ever existed, were not received."

If what he said was true, Parker and Erika were on their own.

"I commend your efforts, Mr. Chase." The gun came up. Time slowed, Erika's piercing scream filling the air. With his eyes locked on Drake's hand, he saw his trigger finger tighten, the gun barrel rise slightly. White fire flashed from the muzzle.

Chapter 52

The sharp whine zipped past his chest, a supersonic symphony of death. Parker twisted, one arm grasping the man behind him. The bullet grazed a searing pain across his ribs, just as he pulled the man around, directly behind his back, and into the bullet's path.

A sickly thud confirmed what he couldn't see. With one arm holding the wounded man, Parker tore the pistol from his grasp and fired, two shots slamming into the second guard behind him, red holes blossoming on the man's chest.

As gunfire erupted from across the room, Parker saw Erika elbow her guard in the mouth, followed by a swift kick to the groin. He was down, and she dove behind the bar, out of sight.

Still holding the wounded man, Parker kept the guy between him and the other guards across the room. Apparently they didn't care too much for their comrade, because as Parker held him with a forearm across the neck, his entire body shook violently.

Bullets slammed into his torso, which fortunately stopped them from hitting Parker. Unfortunately, this killed him instantly, and the human shield became dead weight.

To his left was a thick leather couch. Still covered by the perforated corpse, Parker dove for cover, shooting blindly as he fell. His shoulder thudded off the polished wooden floor and he scrambled behind the couch, momentarily hidden.

"Get him," Drake roared over the gunfire.

Two men were dead, one guarding Erika was down. That left two guards and Drake to deal with. He could only hope Erika was still safe.

Parker raised the dead man's gun and ripped off two shots. It was enough to stop the barrage of bullets, and he poked his head above the couch. Both men to his left had hit the deck. All he could see of Drake was

234

the silver barrel of his gun poking around the corner of the bar. It seemed Spencer was going to leave the dirty work to his minions.

The wooden floor beneath him was slick. When Parker looked down, red liquid was smeared underneath his body, blood dripping from his ribcage where the bullet had grazed him. He ignored the pain, focusing on what he could do against the three remaining assailants. Right now, he needed a distraction.

"I need all security to the main level now." The group leader's voice, now a few octaves higher courtesy of Erika's knee, reached his ears.

Check that. Right now he needed to get the hell out of here.

Gunshots came from behind the bar. A stolen look revealed Erika was at one end, Drake and his revived team leader hunkered down in the hallway, just far enough back that he didn't have a shot. The other two men were still on the ground, without cover. They spotted his head and opened fire.

He was stuck, and running out of time. If those two guys on the ground surrounded him, it was over. What had his football coach said? The best defense was a good offense.

Parker realized that the couch he was cowering behind didn't reach the entire way to the floor. Instead, a thin flap of leather ran the length of the bottom, which actually rested on wooden legs about six inches high. When he lifted the flap, he could see underneath it and across the room. Two sets of elbows crawled over the ground, one to either side.

A humorless grin crossed his lips. Two shots and the first pair stopped moving. Two more and the second pair stopped, slumped to the ground. However, Parker had little time to savor his victory.

Shots that had been coming from Erika's position suddenly stopped, a heartfelt and profane string of curses filling the air. She was out of bullets.

Without thinking, he jumped from behind the couch and started firing in Drake's direction.

"Follow me," Parker shouted at Erika as he raced toward the hallway directly behind her. On the way, he scooped up a second gun from the ground, the handle slick with blood. "Move it."

Her doe-like blue eyes wide with fright, she raced ahead of him, running down the hallway through which he had entered the room while blindfolded. Plaster chips filled the air as they ran, the walls around them disintegrating under a hail of gunfire. Doorways branched off on either side, but he had no idea where any of them led.

"How did you get here?" Parker shouted.

She ran beside him, blonde hair flailing across her face. "Long story. I was blindfolded when I came through this hall, but I think," she said as he struggled to recall which direction he'd turned upon entering the house, "we take a right up here."

A dead end loomed ahead, and Parker darted right. The hallway was massive, easily wide enough to drive one of those ubiquitous Suburbans through. In front of them was a single door, larger than the others they'd seen.

"Through here," Erika said. "I think this leads to a roof." He twisted the handle, and warm night air flowed inside. A star-filled sky was overhead, small dots of light accenting a bright moon shining down on the house.

Except that house wasn't the right word. This place was more than a house. It was a sprawling complex, more akin to a college campus than a private residence. One had to look no further than the massive helicopter parked on a rooftop fifty feet away to realize this was no ordinary dwelling.

Angry voices came from inside, and Parker slammed the door shut behind him. "I flew here on that thing."

The whites of her eyes were brilliant in the moonlight. "So what now? How do we get down?"

"Over there." He pointed toward the top of a ladder that hung off the roof, two curved metal poles leading down.

He let her go first. Once she was clear, he grabbed the rails and turned to descend.

The door behind him slammed open, footsteps scraping across the rooftop. A flurry of shots from his pistol sent their assailants scurrying for cover, but Parker wasn't sticking around for this fight.

Fifteen feet below, his feet found grass. Beside the towering mansion, which easily rose forty feet overhead, there was little light, and Parker pressed himself against the outer wall, chest heaving.

"How did they bring you here?"

Erika glanced around, desperately searching for any familiar sign. "We flew here in a jet, but on the car ride from the plane I was blindfolded."

"Great," Parker said. "We have no idea where to go."

"Hold on, I didn't finish. When I was being held here, before you came, they let me walk around a bit. From inside that room you just shot up I could see a road over there." She pointed into the woodlands that surrounded them. "Several cars came and went, so it's not Drake's private access route. If we can get through these woods, we might be able to flag someone down."

Overhead, he could hear the men chasing them getting closer. Judging from the number of voices, they'd found help.

"I have a better idea. Come on."

Given that there was a helicopter parked overhead, Parker figured that they were standing next to a massive enclosed area of some type, maybe a hangar or garage. He'd seen the moonlight glint off polished metal, barely visible around the structure's edge thirty feet away.

He led Erika around the corner. "Oh, yes. Now this is what I'm talking about." Parker had been right. They'd been leaning against a garage wall, and sitting in front of him on an enormous driveway were several cars. Actually, it would be an insult to refer to these machines as mere cars. He wasn't a gear head, but he knew the distinctive black stallion framed in yellow when he saw it.

The car door opened, and a muted overhead light confirmed it. The keys were inside.

"Get in."

Erika slid into the passenger seat, and when Parker turned the ignition, eight cylinders of Italian engineering whined to life, pure speed emanating with every vibration. He'd never driven a Ferrari. Now was as good a time as any to start.

Molten rubber spread across the ground as he let off the clutch, giving the 458 Spider nine thousand rpm's of thrust to work with. It was unlike anything he'd ever experienced. One moment they were sitting still, the next his head was smashed against the buttery soft leather of a racing seat and it was all he could do to keep the car straight. Xenon headlamps flashed to life, just in time for him to see the ninety-degree turn ahead.

He swerved, and unbelievably, the exotic race car hugged the curve like a mini dress on Hugh Hefner's girlfriend. He didn't even have to tap the brakes. Erika's mouth formed a perfect circle.

"Oh my."

"You still have that gun?" Parker asked.

It took her a moment to speak. "Yes."

"I hope it's loaded, because we have company."

Her head whipped around just in time to see three other pairs of bluish headlights whip around the bend. Orange flashes appeared from two cars, and the rear window on his new racing machine shattered.

"Damn them. You shouldn't shoot at a car this nice."

All thoughts stopped when Erika began to fire. Inside the ridiculously small interior of the vehicle, each gunshot was like a bomb, smashing his brain against the inside of his skull.

"Hold on," Parker shouted, or at least he tried to, but he couldn't hear his own voice with the ringing in each ear. Ahead of them, the road bent sharply to the left, trees whizzing by at a blinding pace on either side.

He accelerated through the curve, half expecting to slide off the paved roadway and smash into a tree. Of course, he was wrong, and the unparalleled manufacturing that went into every one of Enzo Ferrari's beauties kept him on course.

"I'm running out of bullets." She had to shout in his ear to be heard over the roar of wind whipping through the vehicle.

"If we can get on the highway, we'll be fine. There's no way they could catch us in this." As he spoke, the road dipped, and a turn appeared. They had to be getting close.

Parker barely slowed for the curve, the streamlined car firing through the turn like a bullet.

Directly at a closed gate.

"Shit. Hold on."

Traveling at nearly one hundred miles per hour, he mashed the brake and the clutch, one hand twisting the wheel hard left, the other pulling the emergency brake. With all four tires smoking, the carbon fiber vehicle slid across the pavement like it was sheer ice, hurtling toward the massive double gates blocking their exit.

As they careened to a deadly impact with the unforgiving steel gates, the car skidded around so Parker's headlights were facing the oncoming vehicles that were now rounding the corner.

Amazingly, the high performance anti-lock brakes came through, bringing the Italian powerhouse to a tooth-rattling stop inches from the gate. Erika grabbed the gun from his lap and lowered her window, already taking aim.

Tires in danger of melting smoked on the asphalt, the car bolting ahead, hugging the left side of the road. All three cars had slowed for the turn, expecting to see a heap of crushed carbon fiber at the gates.

Instead, Erika unloaded her gun, spraying bullets through the interior of one car.

"I think I got one."

Sure enough, as he whipped around the hard right turn, only two pairs of headlights followed.

"But I'm out of bullets."

They were headed back to Drake's stronghold, unarmed and outnumbered.

"Parker, we're going to run right into them. Whoever's still at Drake's place will mow us down." She was right. They were trapped.

As trees flashed by on either side, perilously close, an idea popped into his head. Born of desperation, it was ludicrous, would never work. He should wait, try to outrun these guys and find a phone to call Nick. But trusting in Nick was what had put them here in the first place. Look how that turned out.

"Put on your seatbelt." They didn't have any more bullets, but he and Erika were far from defenseless.

"What are you going to do?"

In response, he hit the brakes and pulled the emergency lever, executed the same one-eighty he'd perfected moments ago. When they ended up facing the opposite direction without hitting any trees, Parker thought that he may have missed his true calling in life.

"Parker, don't do it. We'll never survive in this little car." She could read him like a book, his stony countenance all the confirmation Erika needed.

"This car is worth a quarter million dollars. I'm sure it has good air bags."

Without waiting for permission, he popped the clutch and hammered the gas, flooding the screaming engine with fuel. Like a missile, they shot toward two pairs of oncoming headlights that had just come into view.

He drove directly down the middle of the paved roadway, aiming to bisect the pair of onrushing vehicles. Mere feet from the road's edge, thick rows of unforgiving lumber flashed past on both sides.

There was no place to go. Erika screamed, terror joining the roar of air whipping through their windowless car, an ideal soundtrack for the evening. Parker's eyes were open for the end.

Except it didn't happen. Right before the three cars would have met in a twisted, shattered mess of broken bones and crushed metal frames, the two oncoming cars veered off to either side, last second losers in this game of chicken.

They should have stayed straight. Their exotic vehicles, designed for maximum speed and luxury, were no match for the solid, unforgiving tree trunks that lined the roadway. Each car's front tire rode up Parker's hood, lifting the cars until they were perpendicular to the ground. Each vehicle sliced through the air like a knife until they slammed into the thick cords of living oak. Ten feet in diameter, the trees barely flinched on impact.

To his right, one vehicle crumpled like a tin can when it hit, the rear bumper joining the doorframe in a race to meet the front tires. Anyone inside was instantly crushed, and for good measure, their corpses roasted to a crisp when the racing fuel inside the car's gas tank ignited.

A tremendous fireball turned night into day.

To his left, the other driver fared slightly better. His car, flipped nearly on the passenger side, slid through the first row of trees, sparks flying as the roof was torn off. It was when he reached the next layer of rock-hard sycamores that things went south.

A nearly identical fireball filled the air, scorched metal jammed against the thick trunk.

"If we live through tonight, I'm going to kill you." All of this, and of course she still had something to say.

Parker's heart hammered wildly against his chest. His skin tingled, a euphoric sensation overtaking his body. He was weightless and rocket-fueled at the same time, a feeling unlike anything he'd ever experienced.

They were alive.

Only after a few moments of heavy breathing did he notice the light. Outside, above the roof of their car, which now had two dark tire treads on the hood, an orange glow pervaded the darkness.

"Parker. You set the forest on fire."

Apparently high octane racing fuel burned quickly. What moments earlier had been an inky black sea of leaves was now a raging inferno.

"Can you climb?" Parker asked.

Calm as could be, she turned to face him, the roaring fire sparkling in her eyes.

"What in the world are you talking about?"

"The gate. If we can't find a doorway, can you climb over? I'm not going back to Drake's house, and if we move now, I bet that blaze will distract him long enough for us to get out of here."

"If it means we escape, then yes, I can climb."

Beleaguered tires left just a little more rubber on the road as he bolted away from the growing fire.

"The whole Boston fire department's going to be here soon. There have to be a hundred acres of woodlands in this place."

"I hope Drake burns with it."

Now that the fire was behind them, the star-studded sky overhead was visible through the windshield, spider web cracks radiating from where the tires had crushed it.

The gate looked taller than he remembered.

"There should be a door around here somewhere." He spotted one ahead, and Parker jumped from the ruined Ferrari, a twinge of guilt in his heart. Drake was an asshole, but his car didn't deserve this.

"It's locked." Erika tugged on a doorknob, but it wouldn't budge. "It's made of steel. We're not getting through it."

Peering upward, he guessed the gate was ten feet high. Tall, but he could jump and grab the top.

"Here, climb on." Parker laced his fingers together to form a step for Erika's foot. "I'll boost you up. Once you're over, I can jump up and haul myself across."

To her credit, Erika didn't complain. She planted her foot in his hands and stretched, Parker pushing her toward the sky.

"I got it." Her weight lifted, and one arm hooked the fence, her body flush against the wall. As she grasped for a hold with her other arm, a strange thing happened.

The wall exploded.

Razor-edged shards of broken concrete stabbed them both. A deep thumping reverberated in Parker's chest, his lungs suddenly unable to draw breath. Erika lost her grip and tumbled into his arms, her body lit like an angel falling from the heavens when he caught her.

Except it wasn't heavenly light shining down. She was in the center of the brightest searchlight beam he'd ever seen. It was painful, so intense that his eyes forced shut without instructions from his brain.

Only when a familiar voice came down from the sky did he realize the searchlight was mounted on a helicopter that churned overhead. "Stay where you are. If you move, the next shot is at your head."

Spencer Drake's magnified voice came through a bullhorn. Parker turned his back to the beam, still unable to see anything. Chilled night air blasted them both, Erika's hair flying like Medusa's snakes as the helicopter hovered overhead.

"Turn around, and keep your hands in the air." Drake was on the ground, shouting at them. Shielding his eyes, Parker could see a ladder

241

dangling from the bird, the rope contraption swaying wildly in the swirling winds. The rotor wash was intense, so loud that he could barely hear Drake from thirty feet away.

"Mr. Chase, you've caused me quite a bit of trouble tonight. Still, I must thank you for bringing the items I requested to my house. I appreciate your cooperation."

"Why are you doing this?" Parker shouted, hands in the air. "We didn't want to get involved with any of this."

Now on the ground, Drake held the same silver handgun he'd carried earlier, and it was leveled at Parker's chest.

"Unfortunately we cannot always choose the path we take. You two have proven to be quite the resourceful pair. I've actually enjoyed this little game of ours, but sadly, it must end."

"You think this is a game?" Erika was incensed, moving toward Drake as she screamed. "You're going to destroy hundreds of millions of lives. People who've never done anything to you, people who trusted greedy scumbags like you with their money. You have no right to do this."

"I have no right?" Drake was ten feet away, his gun waving in the air. "Don't dare talk to me while you stand here on land that was stolen from England, ripped from the rightful owners after all we had done for you. You *peasants* need to be put in your place, reminded that if it weren't for the British Empire you would all be wearing loincloths and riding horses. Britain made this country, and your colonist ancestors stole it. You and every one of your pathetic countrymen will be reminded who is the true superpower."

Parker could see Drake was losing it. He was close enough now that the roaring winds wouldn't be enough to send his bullets astray.

"America is a cesspool of greed and entitlement," Drake continued. "Money is king in this country, glorified above all else. I've seen what wealth can do to a man, have spent enough time amongst the so-called *elite* of your nation to realize that this country is rotting from within, corruption and entitlement eating away at the heart of your republic." Drake leveled the gun at Erika, an evil grin on his face. "America will soon feel the very shame that Britain experienced, know what it is like to fall from the top. Vengeance is now ours, and you will be in your rightful place, under the heel of the greatest nation on earth." His finger tightened on the trigger. "Good-bye, Dr. Carr."

Parker dove into Erika, tackling her to the ground as Drake's pistol spit fire. The bullet ripped into his right shoulder with the force of a cannonball, throwing him against the wall. It was oddly warm, as though hot water had spilled on his shoulder.

When he hit the ground, pain burst through his body like fireworks. Teeth clenched, his breath coming in quick gasps, Parker grabbed the wounded shoulder. His hand came away soaked in warm blood.

"How pathetically valiant of you, Mr. Chase."

Erika's scream filled the air as Drake leveled his gun at Parker's chest. Outlined by the powerful spotlight, the maniac appeared to be a specter, black as night, a demonic outline in human form.

Parker could see Drake's finger curl around the trigger. An inch more that would end his life. With his good arm, Parker pushed Erika, away from the madman with the gun, away from danger.

He heard a soft whistle, a bullet coming to kill him.

The helicopter exploded.

In a fiery ball, larger and louder than any explosion he'd ever seen, the helicopter directly behind Drake's head erupted into a ball of white-hot flame. Twisted metal hung in the air, suspended by the burning rotors.

A moment later, gravity asserted itself, and the flaming inferno fell to the ground, slamming down not twenty feet from them. No one moved, their eyes transfixed on the destruction.

"Put the gun down. I repeat, put the gun down, or we will open fire." Parker realized the deep thumping in his chest hadn't stopped. Lying at the base of the perimeter wall, they looked up into the dark underbelly of a second helicopter, which blasted Spencer Drake with a blinding light of its own.

One hand shielding his eyes, Spencer Drake didn't drop the gun. His mouth moved, but Parker could tell no sound came out. The man was in shock, completely caught off guard.

"This is your last warning. Drop the weapon or we will open fire." Parker didn't need that warning. While Drake was still mesmerized by the thundering helicopter, he bolted from his spot at the base of the wall and flew toward the armed man.

Injured shoulder planted into Drake's chest, Parker laid him out, as hard a hit as he'd ever made, on or off the football field. He *felt* the ribs break, sensed Drake's sternum crack in half as he landed on him, bringing the full weight of his body to bear. The silver gun went flying out of reach. Drake was out cold. Breathing, but not going anywhere.

"Nice hit." Nick Dean's amplified voice came down from the open helicopter door. As the chopper drifted downward, Erika was suddenly in his arms, her face buried in his chest.

"It's over," he said, holding her tightly. "You're safe now."

Epilogue:

Two weeks later
Key West, FL

A warm breeze blew through his hair, the salty air filling Parker's lungs as he looked out over the sparkling blue waters. All around him, people sat in bamboo chairs with their bare feet in the sand. Waiters flitted about in tropical shirts holding trays of seafood fresh from the open-air kitchen.

It was without a doubt one of the most unique establishments he'd ever visited. Situated on a stretch of sparkling white sand that lined the Gulf of Mexico, cloudless blood-red skies overhead, the dining room was unlike any other on earth.

Parker sipped a cold bottle of beer, beads of condensation running down the brown glass. His white linen shirt was partially unbuttoned, sleeves rolled to the elbows. His shoulder still ached, a white bandage where the bullet had gone through. Fortunately it didn't hit anything major, and he was expected to make a full recovery. Erika sat across from him, stunning as always in an aqua blue summer dress that matched her piercing eyes.

"Key West isn't so bad, don't you think?"

She drained the last of her beer before answering. "It's amazing. I can't believe we're still in America. The beaches are so *white*." She kicked some sand his way, the white grains splashing against his tanned leg. He hadn't worn long pants all week, and loved every minute of it. Eyes hidden behind aviator sunglasses, Parker took in the scene, a sense of utter calm descending over his body. Soft chatter floated past on salt-soaked air, the beach a picture of serenity.

Of course, it didn't last, and the cell phone on their table began to vibrate fiercely.

"Must you answer that infernal thing? We're on vacation." She peered over the top of her oversized sunglasses in mock anger. He thought they made her look like a bug.

"It's Nick." He'd been expecting this call all day.

"Hey there, old man. What's up?"

"What's up is I'm wasting my time dealing with your ridiculous requests instead of doing my job." Nick may have sounded angry, but Parker knew it was just an act. After all, the man had just been promoted to Special Agent in Charge of the CIA's Philadelphia office, largely based on his role in uncovering the plot to destroy the US economy. Considering that Parker had handed him the man responsible for the attacks, Nick couldn't be mad at him.

"How did it go?"

"The transaction has been authorized. I can officially inform you that the Internal Revenue Service has no interest in any financial transactions you make in the next ten days. This would include any wire transfers made to or from any German banks. Any money you acquire in this time frame will also be exempt from taxation."

Parker's cheeks threatened to displace his ears. As soon as she saw him grinning like an idiot, Erika knew it had gone through and raised her glass in a salute.

"Consider it a token of appreciation from the federal government. It was signed off on by none other than the new Treasury secretary."

"Thanks, Nick. I owe you one."

"We'll call it even. Are you ever going to tell me where that money came from?"

A sly grin spread across Parker's lips.

"Let's just say you don't want to know."

"Fair enough. While I have you on the line, there's someone who wants to speak with you. Hold on a second."

The line went silent.

Erika gave him a quizzical look, mouthing, *"What's going on?"*

"I'm on hold. Nick said someone wants to talk to me. Oh, and now I'm rich. Order another round of beers."

Two weeks ago, Spencer Drake had been taken into custody for a litany of federal crimes, the centerpiece of which was being charged with conspiracy to overthrow the government. That constituted treason, and he was facing the death penalty.

However, his arrest hadn't been mentioned in a single newscast. The CIA and FBI had worked together to keep the entire ordeal under wraps. After what they'd found on Drake's computer, he would never take a free breath again. Nick told Parker it had been a wake-up call, a stark message that the United States was wholly unprepared for a new kind of threat; one from within its own financial system.

E-mails and phone records had revealed the extent of Drake's treachery. Within days of his capture, Secretary of the Treasury Gerard Webster had resigned, citing personal reasons. Across the Atlantic, recently installed Chancellor of the Exchequer Colin Moore had also resigned unexpectedly, the official explanation that he'd suffered a mental breakdown and simply was not up to the arduous requirements of his position.

What saved the economy, however, was OPEC's abrupt announcement that they had settled on a different course of action and would not be doubling their production of oil. Production had remained constant for the past few weeks, and all indications pointed to a gradual increase in output. After an initial flurry of activity, the markets had calmed, and investors had moved on to other targets, oil futures now in the rearview mirror.

One thing that still bothered Parker was the timing of Drake's plot in regards to OPEC's completely unexpected announcement that oil output would increase twofold. Drake either had access to OPEC's internal communications, or had a big shot from the organization in his back pocket. He was leaning toward the latter, but Nick had refused to discuss the issue, only saying it had "been taken care of."

The sudden and still unexplained death of the president of OPEC, Sheik Khalifa bin Khan, was likely just a coincidence.

As he was considering these possibilities, wondering just how far this conspiracy stretched, the most recognizable voice in the world picked up the phone. "Am I speaking with Parker Chase?"

Parker must be hearing things.

"Yes."

"Mr. Chase, this is Harrison Knox."

"President Knox?"

"That's correct, son." President of the United States Harrison Knox, the leader of the free world, was on the phone.

"Mr. President, sir. What can I do for you?" Behind her gargantuan shades, he could see Erika's eyes roll.

"You've already done your country a great service, Parker. Special Agent

Dean told me about your heroic efforts, and I wanted to personally thank you for helping our nation avert a catastrophe."

Parker's mind was swimming. He was talking to the *president*. "I'm glad I could be of service, sir. It kind of just fell into my lap."

"A man never knows when opportunity will knock. You answered the call, Parker, and your country is grateful."

"It was my pleasure, sir. I'm just glad we stopped Drake before he could do any real damage."

"As am I, Parker. If you ever need anything in the future, give me a call. I won't forget this."

Despite his awe, Parker couldn't help but think of the disastrous effect the crisis would have had on the president's reelection campaign next year. Harrison Knox definitely owed him one.

"Thank you, sir. I appreciate that."

"Any chance Dr. Carr is around? I'd like to thank her as well."

"She's right here, sir. One moment."

Skepticism was all over her face as Erika took the phone. "This is Erika Carr. To whom am I speaking?"

Her jaw nearly touched the sand as the president's smooth voice filled her ear.

Priceless.

As she stuttered through the conversation, Parker sipped his beer and tried to process the past five minutes. Here he was, sitting on the beach in Key West, talking to the President Harrison Knox.

Who now owed him a favor.

And if that wasn't enough, his net worth had just grown by exactly fifty million dollars. That crazy dream of starting his own investment firm suddenly came into focus. If he played his cards right, this could be just the beginning.

"Holy shit."

Erika didn't swear very often. Talking to the president certainly called for it.

"That was Harrison Knox. Parker, the *president* just called you. And he wanted to talk to *me*."

"Yeah, we're buds now."

Erika sat in silence, mouth hanging wide open.

"I think this calls for a toast." He raised his bottle. "Come on, get it up."

Her empty beer went up.

"First of all, to my beautiful girlfriend, for getting me involved with yet another ridiculous lunatic hell-bent on killing us. Thank you for that, I really mean it."

He dodged as the beer bottle whistled past his head. "I'd also like to say I'm excited to see what the future brings. I've been thinking, and since I could now actually afford it, I'm going to look into opening my own investment firm."

Beautiful blue eyes flashed as she took off her awful sunglasses. "Really? That's amazing, Parker. I think you should do it."

"Then it's settled. Chase Investment Services will soon be open for business. I'm thinking I need to be closer to the coast, within an hour or so of New York if I really want to compete with the big boys."

Her face lit up. "Do you mean move to Philadelphia?"

"I don't know." He rubbed his chin, radiating indecision. "Do you think that's a good idea?"

Slowly, taking her time, Erika stood. Her lithe figure floated across the sand and settled into his lap, gaze never leaving his. "I think it's a wonderful idea."

As the sun set, golden rays illuminated her face, alight with a promise of things to come, and he knew she was right.

"Then so do I."

An island band started to play, steel drums mixed with keyboards, a breezy tune filling the air. With a coy smile, Erika grabbed his hand, and they darted through the sand, music filling his soul and the world falling away as they danced amidst the tropical paradise.

GET THE ANDREW CLAWSON STARTER LIBRARY

FOR FREE

Sharing the writing journey with my readers is a special privilege. I love connecting with anyone who reads my stories, and one way I accomplish that is through my mailing list. I only send notices of new releases or the occasional special offer related to the Parker Chase or TURN series.

If you sign up for my mailing list, I'll send you a free copy of the first Parker Chase and TURN novels as a special thank you. You can get these books for free by signing up here:

DL.bookfunnel.com/L4modu3vja

Did you enjoy this book? Let people know

Reviews are the most effective way to get my books noticed. I'm one guy, a small fish in a massive pond. Over time, I hope to change that, and I would love your help. The best thing you could do to help spread the word is leave a review on your platform of choice.

Honest reviews are like gold. If you've enjoyed this book I would be so grateful if you could take a few minutes leaving a review, short or long, on this book's Amazon page.

Thank you very much.

Author's note

Much of the plot for this novel focuses on the intricacies of finance and how, in skillful hands, transactions can be manipulated to suit one's purpose, nefarious or otherwise. It is alluded to that the concept of proprietary trading, central to the successful execution of this theoretical scheme, will soon be declared illegal by the federal government.

The situation is factual, and refers to what is commonly called the Volcker Rule, which was mandated by the Dodd-Frank Act of 2010. The intent of the Volcker Rule is to prevent banks, which hold federally insured deposits and can borrow from the Fed at reduced rates, from putting depositors' money at risk.

In April 2012 the Federal Reserve stated that banks have until July 2014 to fully conform their activities and investments to the Volcker restrictions. However, the Fed has the authority to further extend the period of compliance beyond July 2014 at their discretion.

Aside from the ongoing regulatory initiatives, this book was meant to entertain and enlighten. Informed and inspired debate, whether internal or among individuals, is crucial to furthering an understanding of any industry or enterprise, including America's financial system. As demonstrated by painful, concrete consequences rooted in the 2008 crisis, an uninformed electorate risks much by sitting back in blissful ignorance while a handful of unethical individuals decimate the futures of many. Taking an interest in and understanding a complex and often confusing banking system is the first step in regaining control of a country's financial future.

Acknowledgements

First and foremost, I have to thank my three resident financial gurus, Rob, Steve, and my father. As I fumbled my way through this unfamiliar world, it was only with their kind help and endless patience that I was able to detail this hypothetical crisis without sounding extremely obtuse. I also have to thank my team of volunteer readers, which includes the aforementioned trio, along with my mother and sister. A huge thanks goes out to Alicia for her invaluable proofreading services. Thank you to Kelsey for putting up with endless evenings spent pounding the keyboard, often in frustration. And I cannot forget our new friend Graham, who has grown from a loveable black ball of fur into one of the most entertaining creatures on four legs. To everyone who has joined me along the way with either moral or intellectual support. Friends, family, and fellow authors, I thank you.

As always, any and all mistakes in this text fall squarely on my shoulders.

To you, dear reader, thank you for taking time out of your life to join me on this journey. I hope you enjoyed the experience. If so, I'd love to hear from you. I can be found on my website, andrewclawson.com. I invite you to consider reading my first novel, *A Patriot's Betrayal*, or my latest works, *Dark Tides Rising* and *A Republic of Shadows*.

If you liked this book, please consider leaving a review. If not, let me know why. I'm always looking for ways to improve.

Dedication

For my grandparents

Also by Andrew Clawson

Have you read them all?

In the Parker Chase Series

A Patriot's Betrayal

A dead man's letter draws Parker Chase into
a deadly search for a secret that could rewrite history.
Free to download

The Crowns Vengeance

A Revolutionary era espionage report sends Parker
on a race to save American independence.

Dark Tides Rising

A centuries-old map bearing a cryptic poem sends Parker Chase
racing for his life and after buried treasure.

A Republic of Shadows

A long-lost royal letter sends Parker on a secret trail
with the I.R.A. and British agents close behind.

A Hollow Throne

Shattered after a tragic loss, Parker is thrust into
a race through Scottish history to save a priceless treasure.

In the TURN Series

TURN: The Conflict Lands

Reed Kimble battles a ruthless criminal gang
to save Tanzania and the animals he loves.
Free to download

TURN: A New Dawn

A predator ravages the savanna. To stop it, Reed must be
what he fears most – the man he used to be.

Check my website AndrewClawson.com for more details,
and additional Parker Chase and TURN novels.

Praise for Andrew's Novels

Praise for *A Patriots Betrayal*

"A Patriots Betrayal had me hooked from the first page!"

"The characters were well developed and authentically true to life. The story was incredible, realistic, and historically intriguing."

"The mystery and suspense had me so intrigued that I had to keep reading."

Praise for *The Crown's Vengeance*

"Moments of sheer intensity make it hard to put this book down."

"This one is just as exciting and fast paced as the first, with new adventures flying at the couple in every turn."

"Be sure you set aside enough time to finish this one, you'll not want to put this one down until you read the last page."

Praise for *Dark Tides Rising*

"Yet another gem-filled yarn weaving fact and fiction."

"A story that is so well written it keeps you from putting the book down."

"Very fast and action-packed. Can't wait for the next amazing tale."

About the Author

Andrew Clawson is the author of the Parker Chase and TURN series.

You can find him at his website, AndrewClawson.com, or you can connect with him on Twitter at @clawsonbooks, on Facebook at facebook.com/AndrewClawsonnovels and you can always send him an email at andrew@andrewclawson.com.

Made in the USA
Monee, IL
17 October 2020